Never Underestimate Girls!

Text copyright © Joseph Jethro

All rights reserved. No part of this publication may be reproduced, distributed, or transmitted in any form or by any means, including photocopying, recording, or other electronic or mechanical methods, without the author's prior written permission. Such written permission must also be obtained before any part of this publication is stored in a retrieval system.

All characters of this publication are fictitious, and any resemblance to actual persons, living or dead, is purely coincidental.

First published in Great Britain in 2024

ISBN: 978-1-917452-18-2

josephjethro45@outlook.com

Also, by Joseph Jethro:

- Undercover Gangster: Blood Ties In The Shadows
- Secret Gangster: My Life's All About Violence
- Triple Caste Gangster: He Never Told Her

Chapter 1

The air buzzed with life in the golden embrace of a sun-drenched meadow. The grass, a lush carpet of emerald, swayed in rhythmic response to the playful breeze; each blade cradled dewdrops like precious gems, winking at the sun as it ascended higher in the pale blue sky. The warm breeze carried secrets, whispering forgotten promises and days of happiness as it ruffled the hair of a joyful family who sat beneath an ancient oak, their laughter mingling with the distant song of a lark, a melody that seemed to rise from the very heart of the earth. Butterflies fluttered from blossom to blossom, their delicate wings carrying secrets whispered by wildflowers. And then a russet squirrel darted across the grass, its bushy tail a flash of crimson. It vanished into the gnarled embrace of a hazel tree, leaving behind a trail of curiosity.

Stella, a wide-eyed little girl, pointed excitedly. 'Layla! Look, a squirrel!' Her voice held a mix of wonder and awe.

Layla, the older sister, grabbed Stella's little hand. 'It went up that tree. Let's follow it!' she cried.

Their laughter trailed behind them as they raced across the emerald expanse, the grass bending under their eager feet.

Meanwhile, beneath another sprawling tree, Alexandria, a charming eight-year-old lost in innocent daydreams, sat amidst a scatter of daisies. She plucked each petal with care, her fingers stained yellow and green. The world around her blurred as imagination wove its threads.

Suddenly, Stella and Layla tumbled upon her, a joyful collision of laughter and giggles. Alexandria squealed in surprise, then joined in with her little sisters' laughter. 'You two are so mischievous!' she teased, tossing a handful of grass and daisies at them.

JOSEPH JETHRO

The petals clung to Stella's curly hair, transforming her into a floral explosion of giggles. Layla's laughter bubbled forth. 'Check your hair out, Stella!' she exclaimed, pointing playfully.

'Alex,' Stella whispered, her eyes sparkling. 'Try and catch us!'

And so, the two cheerful sisters dashed away, their laughter echoing through the meadow. Alexandria called after them. 'I'll count to ten!'

Sera, their mother, sat at the edge of the emerald expanse, her eyes tracing the path of her daughters as they disappeared into its heart. The meadow stretched like a forgotten secret, its lush greenery concealing ancient mysteries. The air hummed with happiness, and Sera's heart swelled with love and care for her girls.

But sadness, like a shadow, has a way of seeping into the happiest of hearts. Worry throbbed in her body, a silent ache that tightened her chest. These moments of sibling camaraderie were precious, yet she knew they were ephemeral, like dewdrops evaporating under the morning sun.

Jacob, her husband, sat by her side; his smile held a mix of pride and love. 'They're so happy,' he murmured, his gaze following the girls, whose laughter danced among the wildflowers.

Sera's sea-blue eyes clouded. 'Yes,' she replied, her voice brittle. She tilted her face towards the sky, where a flock of birds glided, their wings catching the golden light. 'But happiness is fleetin'. Our peaceful years are numbered.'

Jacob frowned, puzzled. 'What do you mean?' he asked.

Sera's voice trembled, 'I have only one purpose now: to protect Alex from the demon's desires.'

The weight of her words hung heavy in the air, casting shadows over the sun-drenched meadow. Sera's resolve was unwavering, but fear weighed on her heart like a stone. The tranquil days would fade, replaced by a darker chapter, one she hoped to shield her daughter from at all costs.

NEVER UNDERESTIMATE GIRLS!

Jacob's smile faded, replaced by a solemn expression. 'Don't worry,' he whispered, his voice gentle. 'Everything will be perfectly fine. She'll be safe. The demon's curse won't breach our protection.'

Sera's gaze remained fixed on the happy girls. Stella's ash-brown hair caught the light, Layla's laughter echoed like wind chimes, and Alexandria chased them, her innocence a fragile shield against the encroaching shadows.

'She's a curious lass,' Sera whispered, her voice heavy with concern. 'Soon, she'll be lookin' for answers I'm not ready to give. She's already askin' about her dad, and when I dodge the question, I see the sadness in her eyes.'

Alexandria twirled, her laughter joyful. Layla held her hands, and they spun together. 'She's so unaware,' Sera continued, 'unaware of the danger that's lurkin'.'

Jacob tried to reassure her. 'She'll understand when she's older,' he said. The breeze blew softly through his blond hair, and he smiled at Sera, but she looked away, her face reflecting sorrow.

'But the demon's shadow looms,' she interjected, her voice breaking. 'She's bloodthirsty and has already made Alex's father insane.'

Jacob's bright green eyes locked onto Sera's, questioning and intense. 'Why doesn't Alex's father care for his flesh and blood?' His voice was a mix of anger and sorrow.

Sera's voice wavered, her gaze distant as she recounted the past. 'When Alex was born,' she began, her voice soft. 'I remember him liftin' her delicate body, cradlin' her in his arms. His lips brushed her forehead, and he smiled, promisin' love and protection.' She clenched her fingers, knuckles white. 'In that moment, I felt like the happiest woman alive. But then...' Sera's voice dropped to a whisper, 'he took Merona away from me. The joy shattered, replaced by a gnawin' fear. I knew he'd do the same with Alex.' Her eyes welled with grief. 'Alex, my sweet child, innocent and full of wonder. He seeks to harm her, to taint her soul. But I won't allow it. Even if I die protecting her.'

JOSEPH JETHRO

Her gaze shifted to the lush grass beneath her feet, determination carved into every line of her face. A cloud shadowed the meadow, and rain droplets fell like tears from the sky. Yet, a rainbow arched across the horizon, showering the emerald grass with hope. In this fleeting moment of sunlight and sorrow, Sera vowed to fight for Alexandria's safety, undeterred by the encroaching darkness.

NEVER UNDERESTIMATE GIRLS!

Chapter 2

Ten years later

Raindrops hammered the gleaming bonnets of police cars as they traversed London's bustling and frantic streets. Their pursuit was relentless, fuelled by an unyielding determination. They aimed to catch their elusive enemy, but Kenny, the heartbeat of evil, wasn't an easy target; he owned a web of influence which covered every shadowed crevice of the city. The complex network woven by threads of violence and murder had infiltrated the hearts of corrupt officials, allowing Kenny to outwit justice itself. Nevertheless, the police force remained resolute, their mission clear: apprehend him and shatter his illusions of invincibility.

Officer Leo's voice crackled through Officer Sera's walkie-talkie. 'We believe we've pinpointed his location,' he stated, his words infused with urgency.

Sera's heart pounded with intensity. 'Where is he?' she asked, adrenaline surging through her veins.

'His car is parked on Grimwood Street. You need to get down there immediately,' he replied.

Leo's urgent message lingered in Sera's mind as she swiftly typed Grimwood Street on her navigation system. She hit the sirens and sped off towards the scene. The tarmac blurred beneath her tyres, and determination burned within her heart. Besides her, Officer Michael gripped his seat tightly, knuckles white with tension. As they hurtled towards danger, the weight of responsibility pressed down on him.

Grimwood Street materialised before them, and Sera scanned her surroundings, looking for any signs of their target. The streetlamps flickered, casting dim light upon the cobblestone pavement, and lonely buildings leaned towards each other, their secrets locked within their ageing walls; ivy clung to them like a worn shroud, concealing windows with black silk. A gust of wind howled, letting out a terrifying noise that chilled the bones but revealed no hint of suspense. 'Are we on the correct street?' Sera asked.

'Yes,' Leo responded confidently.

Sera's eyes darted around the deserted street, which offered no solace. 'Only two cars parked,' she murmured, 'and there's no one in 'em.'

'But you're in a cul-de-sac,' Leo insisted, 'Kenny has to be there.'

Sera and her brother, Michael, emerged from the police car. Their faces bore the unmistakable look of determination. 'We'll investigate,' Sera declared.

'Take care,' Leo cautioned. 'Remember who you're dealing with.'

'I don't think we'll forget that,' Michael replied. He switched on his flashlight and started to examine the area. A cat darted into a narrow alley, vanishing like a shadow.

Then, from a nearby building, two figures emerged.

'Get back!' Sera hissed, yanking Michael behind a nearby car.

'Who are they?' he whispered. His trembling hand reached into his pocket and found the cold steel of his gun; he wrenched it out, fear striking his heart.

'I don't know,' Sera replied, peering over the car's bonnet, gun drawn. 'Blimey, they've seen us!' She flung herself to the ground as bullets suddenly whizzed past.

'Is everything going fine?' Leo asked, his voice crackling through their walkie-talkies.

'We need backup,' Michael's voice was filled with urgency, 'We're under attack!'

'I'm on it,' Leo assured.

'Come on, Michael, we gotta get out of here!' Sera urged, fingers tightening around her weapon.

Michael fired, but the assailants wore bulletproof vests. 'Oh God, they're well protected!' he exclaimed.

'Keep firin'!' Sera shouted.

Both sides exchanged brutal volleys of bullets. Sera and Michael took cover behind the car as bullets hammered against it. 'Stay low!' Michael shouted as a bullet crashed through the car's window; a glass fragment hit his face, slicing its way through his lip.

A wave of fear and tension surged through Sera as she watched blood trickle from Michael's split lip, pooling onto his trembling hand. Despair clawed at her heart, threatening to overwhelm her, until the distant wails of sirens pierced the night, igniting a fragile spark of hope within her.

'Thank goodness, here comes the backup,' Michael breathed a sigh of relief as two police cars appeared at the end of the street, their blue and red lights cutting through the heavy rain.

'Oh, bother, we've got more trouble!' Sera cried as more men emerged from the darkness, raining bullets on the police cars.

The street transformed into a battlefield, where every life hung in the balance. Amid the chaos, a solitary figure stood, a shadow clad in black. Rain battered his dark hair, causing it to spill upon his forehead.

Sera strained her eyes and stared at him. He stood with his back towards her, the wind weaving through his long hair. Secrets of death and pain seemed to spill from his very being, enveloping him in an aura of evil.

Abandoning cover, Sera acted without regard for any consequences. 'There's Kenny!' she yelled, her voice slicing through the downpour.

'What the hell are you doin'?' Michael's voice trembled with a mix of fear and urgency. His eyes widened as he saw a man aiming a gun at Sera, his finger hovering dangerously over the trigger. Without a moment's hesitation, Michael raised his own weapon, his heart pounding in his chest. The sound of the gunshot echoed through the air as Michael pulled the trigger, the bullet finding its mark with deadly precision. The man crumpled to the ground, lifeless.

NEVER UNDERESTIMATE GIRLS!

Michael's desperate shouts were left unanswered as Sera darted forward. Raindrops blurred her vision, turning the world into a hazy, shimmering landscape. Yet, through the downpour, she knew it was him, Kenny, the mastermind of racketeering, the destroyer of lives, standing just a few meters away.

Four meters separated them, a moment of vengeance and survival. Sera pulled the cold trigger of her gun, but Kenny sidestepped, elusive as smoke. He turned around, eyes widening in surprise, but then his malicious face turned into a twisted grin.

Sera cocked her gun, and so did Kenny. The air crackled with tension as bullets screamed through the air. One grazed Sera's arm, causing blood to stain her clothes. Another tore through her forearm, sending her crashing to her knees, a shrill cry escaping her lips. Her weapon slipped out of her hand, clattering to the ground. Hot tears blurred her vision, mixing with the rain. The pain radiating from her wounded arm threatened to consume her, but the sound of approaching footsteps jolted her back to reality; giving up wasn't an option.

Through the haze of pain and tears, she glimpsed a figure clad in black, brandishing a metal bar; it struck her head, disorienting her. Stars burst before her eyes, and she fought to stay conscious. Then, the unmistakable click of a gun being cocked shattered the silence. Desperation fuelled her, and she tried to stand on her feet, but the bullet found her leg, and she stumbled. Her shoulder slammed against the cobblestone pavement, and dark red blood seeped from her leg, staining the rain-slicked road.

Kenny walked towards her, his footsteps barely audible against the rain-soaked pavement. His presence was like a shadow, insidious and elusive.

Wounded and vulnerable, Sera felt the weight of his malevolence closing in. 'You thought you could ruin my plans,' he whispered, his voice a chilling murmur. 'You'll learn never to cross me ever again.'

'You're the one who ruins lives,' Sera stammered, clutching her wounded leg.

'It's nice to see you wounded like this,' Kenny sneered, kneeling beside her. 'You were dumb to think you could stop me from getting what I want! You can't even save yourself,' he smirked, raising his gun, its cold muzzle inches away from her temple.

'You caused it upon yourself, dumb idiot!' Sera's retort struck Kenny's heart like a jagged blade.

He harshly pressed the gun against her head. 'If it weren't for your spellbinding eyes, none of this would have happened,' he spat.

Sera met his eyes, her mind a whirlwind of fear, but with confidence, she spoke. What was the worst that could happen when her life was already at stake? 'I can't save Alex or myself,' she declared. 'But, Kenny, never underestimate that girl!' she shouted, then, with a desperate surge of adrenaline, she lunged for her gun, fingers closing around the cold metal. Kenny, caught off guard by the sudden movement, stood frozen, eyes wide. The air reverberated with the sharp staccato of gunfire as she fired five bullets in rapid succession. Two found their mark, tearing through Kenny's leg. He staggered, the pain in his leg causing him to shout out a filthy swear.

Anger flared within him. 'You won't stop me,' he hissed.

The gun clicked.

Pain exploded in Sera's chest, an unbearable ache that stole her breath away. Darkness encroached, but not before she glimpsed Kenny's vanishing shadow.

Michael witnessed it all. Tears blurred his vision as he ran through the rain. Bullets sliced through the air, one hitting his leg. 'Sera!' he screamed as he stumbled forward. The strong taste of blood covered his tongue as the side of his face slammed against the pavement's edge.

Sera lay on the ground, blood pooling around her fragile body. Her breaths came in ragged bursts as her life slowly started to slip away. Desperation clawed at Micheal's heart like a wild beast as he heard

NEVER UNDERESTIMATE GIRLS!

her gasp for breath. He slowly stood up, his wounded leg causing him to scream with agonising pain; he clenched his fists, trying his best to ignore the unbearable ache that shot through his body. Limping towards Sera, he knelt beside her and grabbed her hand. 'Sera, Sera,' he stammered.

Her voice, a fragile whisper, reached him. 'Brother...I know...it won't be easy...but...please...keep my daughters...out of danger...' she gasped, breathing her last.

'I promise, I'll do anythin' to protect 'em,' he choked out, tightening his grip on her hand. He hoped she heard his oath, but he couldn't be sure; tears burst out of his eyes, and the rain shared his sorrow.

Chapter 3

Alexandria stood before the mirror, her reflection a portrait of lethal allure. Her blue eyes were rimmed with an inky black eyeliner that accentuated their intensity. Mascara-coated lashes framed those eyes, casting delicate shadows on her cheeks, whispering secrets of danger and vengeance, and her sharp cheekbones lent her an air of elegance and mystery. But it was her lips that held the true power; she painted them blood-red, a crimson so deep it seemed to pulse with life. As she pressed her lips together, the colour intensified, leaving no doubt: she was a predator, her beauty a weapon.

A year had slipped away since her mother's tragic murder while on duty. Alexandria, her petite frame encased in a bulletproof vest, felt the weight of grief as she pushed back a lock of brown hair behind her ear. The memories of her mother's smile were raw and unyielding, leaving her torn between anger and sorrow. Each day, the bulletproof vest reminded her of the void left by her mother's absence, a constant ache that fuelled her resolve to find answers.

She sighed as she remembered how she had obtained this unconventional garment.

She recalled how her heart had skipped beats as she stood in her mother's room a month after her death, surrounded by the memories of a life dedicated to law enforcement. The polished badge, the neatly folded uniform, and the framed commendations were all reminders of her mother's commitment to justice. But it was the gun and the bulletproof jacket that had drawn Alexandria's attention.

She had hesitated, torn between grief and determination. Her mother had always taught her to respect the law and uphold justice. Yet, in this moment, Alexandria felt the weight of her loss, the void left by her mother's absence. She had reached for the gun, its cold metal unfamiliar against her palm.

NEVER UNDERESTIMATE GIRLS!

'I'll make things right,' she had whispered, slipping the weapon into her bag. The bulletproof jacket followed. Its weight reminded her of the dangerous path she was about to tread. Alexandria knew she wasn't a police officer, but she had her mother's spirit and unwavering resolve to protect others. And if that meant bending the rules, so be it. As she left the room, Alexandria glanced back one last time. Her mother's legacy now rested on her shoulders. She would wear the jacket, carry the gun, and fight for justice, even if it meant breaking a few rules.

The memory remained in Alexandria's mind like a distant dream, and she gently tapped her fingers against the desk. 'Mother, I miss you,' she whispered to the quiet room.

Her gaze shifted abruptly from the mirror, drawn to the gentle breeze that flowed through the open window. The curtains danced, their rich fabric brushing against the polished marble floor. Crossing the room, she leaned against the windowsill, her eyes tracing the contours of London's cityscape. The sprawling city lay before her, a tapestry of lights and life. The gentle afternoon light painted delicate shadows across her face as memories flooded her mind. She recalled the laughter of childhood, the tender warmth of her mother's hand in hers. Those precious moments had slipped away too quickly, leaving Alexandria to ponder whether she had truly savoured them. She knew she couldn't change the past, couldn't bring her mother back, but she could take revenge on the man who had claimed her mother's life.

Glancing at her leather jacket, which lay sprawled on the bed, she picked it up, her fingers tracing the seams. With a determined look, she slipped her arms into the sleeves. The cool leather hugged her skin, familiar and comforting. Pulling the jacket close, she felt its weight settle on her shoulders. The scent of aged leather enveloped her, a heady mix of memories and anticipation. She pulled the zipper halfway up, the metal teeth engaging with a satisfying click.

She retrieved a gleaming weapon from her drawer, the same gun which she had taken from her mother's room. She slid it into her hidden waist holster, its weight a constant reminder of her role in the world's dark side.

As she stood there, memories and sunlight intermingling, she vowed to honour her mother's legacy. The polished weapon concealed close to her waist was a reminder, a promise to protect, to fight for justice in a city that thrived on evil shadows. Alexandria's gaze shifted from the view outside to the mirror once more. Her reflection stared back, eyes holding secrets, lips painted in defiance. Her allure was a double-edged sword, but beneath it all, she carried the memory of a mother's love, a beacon in the darkness. And with that thought, she stepped out of her room, black stilettos clicking softly against the marble floor, ready to face the city that had seized her mother.

Alexandria moved with purpose down the vast hallway. Her posture was unyielding, her chin tilted upwards. Her eyes held secrets, challenging the shadows, and her arms swung naturally, her fingertips brushing against the furnished wallpaper. Her confident stride was suddenly interrupted by a familiar call. 'Yo sis, ya lookin' great!'

Alexandria swung her head around, her gaze locking onto her younger sister. She leaned casually against the wall, her hands pushed deep into the pockets of her blue jeans. Her blue eyes, adorned with a delicate sweep of baby pink eyeshadow, sparkled mischievously. Loose waves of blonde hair cascaded over her shoulders, and her glossy pink lips moved effortlessly. 'What's the vibe today?' she asked, moving away from the wall.

'As usual,' Alexandria replied, gently smiling. 'What ya doin' anyhow?'

'I was lookin' for ya 'cause I got some good news up ma sleeve,' Layla grinned.

'And the good news is?' Alexandria asked, raising an eyebrow.

'Uncle Micheal's gonna be out today,' Layla beamed. 'That gives us a better chance. We'll have no one to put a stop to our mission.'

NEVER UNDERESTIMATE GIRLS!

'Remember, sis, we can only go on a mission if somethin' turns up,' Alexandria replied smoothly. 'Where's Stella?' she suddenly asked, eyes darting from left to right as if expecting her to emerge from the shadows.

'She must be in her room,' said Layla. 'Let's take a peep.'

Together, Alexandria and Layla walked down the hallway, their anticipation palpable as they reached Stella's bedroom door. Layla knocked softly, waiting for a response.

'Come in!' Stella's voice emerged from the room.

'Sounds like she's got somethin' botherin' her,' Layla whispered as she pushed the door open, revealing Stella's bedroom.

Layla's gaze swept through the room, finally settling on Stella. There she was, sitting cross-legged on the soft carpet, a screwdriver in her right hand and something metallic in her left. Her eyes, a shade of soft hazel, revealed her character; she was a girl who preferred the quiet corner of life, finding solace in the pages of old books. But beneath that timid exterior lay an adventurous spirit. She would slip away from her mundane routine whenever the opportunity arose, seeking justice and treading her way through dark alleyways, and her fiery temper, when provoked, had earned the nickname 'Hushfire'. Push the wrong button, question her principles, or threaten her loved ones, and you'll witness a transformation. Her eyes narrow, her lips tighten, and suddenly, she becomes a force to be reckoned with.

Layla stepped further into the room, Alexandria following close behind. 'What ya doin'?' Layla asked in a hushed voice.

Stella looked up, a small, nervous smile curving her lips. 'Look,' she said, holding up the metal object in her hand. It was a drone camera, its sleek design repaired and calibrated to perfection.

'Oh, I see you've fixed your drone camera,' Alexandria said, settling beside Stella and wrapping her arm around her shoulders. 'You're a right clever lass,' she complimented, admiration sparkling in her eyes.

'Yes, I've meticulously fine-tuned the lens, significantly enhancin' its power. Now, when we need to snap a pic of even the slipperiest criminal, we won't be stopped,' Stella replied.

'Only if I were like ya, brain box,' Layla grinned.

Stella blushed, pushing a loose ringlet of ash-brown hair behind her ear. 'Well, actually, I hope I were brave and strong-hearted like you two. You're the ones that do all the action. I just sit at home and give you two the live updates.'

The atmosphere in the room suddenly shifted as Alexandria removed her arm from Stella's shoulders, wrapping it around her own knees. The air thickened, the tension palpable. 'It's been a year,' she sighed, her gaze distant. 'And we still can't get our hands on our mother's murderer.'

'That guy,' Layla grumbled, clenching her fists. 'He's like a slippery fish, evadin' capture even by the police.'

'Yeah,' Stella agreed with a mournful sigh.

Alexandria's resolve hardened. 'Don't lose hope,' she said firmly. 'We'll catch him, even if it costs us the world or even the universe.' She glanced at both Layla and Stella, determination burning in her eyes. 'Are you with me or not?'

Layla and Stella exchanged a glance, their bond unbreakable. 'Why wouldn't we be?' they replied in unison, ready to chase justice through shadows and secrets, their determination fuelled by love and sisterhood.

Chapter 4

Officer Scoot sat nervously in his unmarked police car, the dim glow of the dashboard casting shadows across his tense face. His finger moved anxiously across the screen of his smartphone, the weight of horrifying news pressing down on him like a leaden cloak. The city hummed outside, oblivious to the gravity of the revelation he was about to share with his fellow companion, who sat absentmindedly in the passenger seat. 'You know,' he began, his voice low and strained, 'in this past month alone, seven teenage girls have met their tragic end in London.'

Officer Luca swivelled in his seat, eyes wide with shock. 'Seven?' he exclaimed, struggling to comprehend the magnitude of the loss. 'Has the murderer been apprehended?'

Scoot's gaze met Luca's, his frustration evident. 'The detectives haven't yet pinned down a suspect,' he replied in a taut voice. 'But they suspect a common link, a shadowy gang lurking in the background of each murder.'

Luca clenched his fists, the weight of responsibility settling heavily on his shoulders. 'These murderers,' he muttered, 'they're like stubborn weeds, pulled out one day, and they sprout back the next.'

Scoot's expression darkened. 'What I can't fathom,' he confessed, 'is how someone can extinguish so many lives without a shred of remorse.' He paused, his gaze fixed on the glowing screen of his phone. 'Hang on,' he said, squinting. The words on the BBC's website seemed to pulse with a life of their own, each letter throbbing as if imbued with secrets. Scoot continued to stare at his phone, his eyes wide, as though he'd suddenly gone blind and couldn't decipher the words.

Luca studied his face. 'Are you alright, mate?' he asked.

'It says here,' Scoot stammered, finger tracing the screen, 'that they believe Kenny's the background puppeteer. And that he himself was present in four of the murders!'

JOSEPH JETHRO

Kenny, the name sent a shiver down Luca's spine. 'He's the guy who killed Michael's sister,' he recalled.

'Yeah, that bloody dog,' Scoot spat, bitterness tainting his words. 'Michael was a good mate of mine when he worked as an officer. But as you know, he quit after his sister's murder.' He clenched his fists. 'I can't count how many innocent souls, maybe not all of them were innocent,' he corrected himself, 'but either way, Kenny's killed too many people. My mind can't wrap around it.'

Luca leaned against the cold leather seat, staring out at the bustling city beyond. 'London,' he whispered, 'is morphing into a hellish landscape. If we don't close in on these malevolent forces...'

Before he could complete his sentence, Scoot's earpiece emitted a sharp, urgent beep. Reacting swiftly, he pressed it and began speaking in a crisp tone, 'Officer Scoot speaking.'

Luca watched, heart pounding, as Scoot's expression shifted from concern to urgency. 'What's the situation?' he asked as Scoot activated the sirens.

'Eagle's Park,' Scoot replied, jaw set with resolve. 'There's a gun battle. Backup is urgently needed.'

Thoughts sped through Luca's mind at a dizzying pace. 'Who's the suspect?'

Scoot stared at the road in front of him. 'Kenny,' he replied bluntly. 'He's trying to kill a teenage girl. We're going in to rescue her while some other officers will try to grab him.'

The police car hurtled through the streets, sirens wailing, towards Eagle's Park. The city blurred past, the buildings gleamed, their windows reflecting red and blue flashes, and the heartbeat of the metropolis pulsed with danger.

The scene unfolded before them as they screeched through the park's gates and into the car park. Police cars were scattered like abandoned toys, their flashing lights casting an eerie glow in the warm sunlight. The air reeked of gunpowder, and the ground trembled with the faltering rhythm of gunfire.

A gang of ruthless men fought the police force, their faces concealed by masks, their determination deadly. Bullets whizzed through the air, leaving trails of destruction. The park, once a haven for families and picnics, now resembled a battlefield. Trees quivered, their leaves torn apart by stray bullets.

Breathing heavily, Scoot and Luca leapt from their car, guns at the ready; the ground was covered in shell casings, and fear hung thick in the air.

'Where's the girl?' Scoot shouted, his voice filled with worry. His eyes darted through the chaos, desperate for a glimpse of her.

Then, a frantic voice answered. 'Behind that car, but reaching her will risk lives!'

Scoot sought cover behind a nearby vehicle, and Luca remained by his side. Their faces mirrored the same fear-stricken expression.

'Watch out!' Luca's warning cut through the air as a black SUV skidded past. Its heavily tinted windows revealed nothing; it was Kenny's car, the gangster who had orchestrated this deadly event.

'That's the gang's boss,' an officer yelled, his voice filled with determination. He sprinted towards a police car, flung the door open, and jumped inside. The engine growled to life, and the chase began. The tense air crackled with urgency, a desperate pursuit it was, weaving through narrow, labyrinthine streets. The piercing sirens echoed off the walls, filling the air with their urgent cries; each twist and turn intensified the stakes, shadows dancing across the tarmac as police and criminal raced towards an unknown destination.

Meanwhile, within Eagle's Park, the gang's brutality intensified as they witnessed their boss attempting to escape. Guns blazed, and the city held its breath, a tragic collision of desperation and spite. The relentless noise of bullets echoed through the air, each shot a sharp, piercing sound that reverberated in the officers' ears. Amidst the chaos, the overwhelming intensity of fear gripped them, tightening its hold until their senses blurred into a disorienting haze. Every nerve in their bodies screamed for clarity, but the violence that surrounded them and the dread of death made it impossible to focus.

Suddenly, pain exploded in Scoot's arm, an unbearable pain that stole his breath away. 'Oh gosh!' he screamed, clutching the wound. 'I've been shot!'

Luca's eyes widened, fear etching every line on his face. They huddled behind the shelter of a police car, breaths laboured, trapped in a nightmare from which there was no awakening.

'I don't know how we're going to get the girl!' shouted Scoot, clenching his teeth.

'We can't even save ourselves,' Luca whispered. 'These men aren't going to give up.'

As Luca's cold words sank in, despair threatened to swallow Scoot. But then, a sudden noise pierced the thick air like a sweet but determined breeze. Scoot spun around, heart pounding. 'Not her,' he stammered.

The air bubbled with tension as a diamond-white Merc glided to a stop, its engine growling like a caged beast. The windows were rolled down, revealing a young girl; her bright blue eyes resembled the sea on a summer's day, and currents of soft brown hair spilt down her back like a waterfall. Her red lips spoke with elegance. 'I reckon you'll be needin' some help,' she stated with a warm smile that contrasted with the danger around them.

'What are you doing here? This isn't some joke, young lady!' Scoot's anger flared. 'You know the rules!'

The girl smirked, her gaze unwavering. 'My name's Alexandria,' she said, her voice as cool as ice. 'I don't deal with jokes. I deal with reality.'

Without hesitation, she rolled up the car windows and floored the accelerator. The Merc shot forward, a blur of determination. She set her sights directly on Emma, the stranded girl who was taking cover behind a distant vehicle.

'That girl's going to get herself killed!' Luca's cry rang out.

Bullets tore through the air, their malevolence leaving nothing but a trail of destruction. The Merc's side window exploded into shards, glass raining down like deadly confetti. Alexandria's foot slammed on the brake, her breath hitching, but she wouldn't give up that easily. She pulled her bulletproof vest over her head, ensuring no maximum damage would be possible. With renewed determination, she hit the gas again.

As the Merc surged forward, Alexandria scanned her surroundings. Abandoned cars lined the carpark, their exteriors dented by stray bullets.

Suddenly, a red car reversed out of a side bay. Alexandria's fingers tightened around the steering wheel. She swerved left, trying to avoid a collision, but the red car veered towards her. Her front bumper collided with the red car's side, metal screeching in protest.

The infuriating driver rolled down his window, a smirk playing on his lips. 'Girl, you think you're some superhero,' he sneered, pulling a gun out of his waist holster. 'Say bye-bye.'

Just as he was about to take action, Alexandria retrieved her own gun in a swift motion and pulled the trigger. The bullet ripped through the air, hitting the man square in the chest. His eyes widened in shock as he breathed his last.

Alexandria's foot pressed the accelerator, but the red car blocked her path. There was no way she could manoeuvre around it. Her instincts surged, a primal force urging her forward. She glanced at the stranded girl, desperate and vulnerable. There was only one way to reach her.

With adrenaline coursing through her veins, Alexandria flung open the car door. Fuelled by hope and sheer willpower, she leapt into the fray.

JOSEPH JETHRO

Propelled by malevolent intent, bullets sliced through the air, their trajectories bending as if drawn by invisible strings. She anticipated their paths, her reflexes honed to perfection. With fluid grace, she sidestepped, ducked, and spun, avoiding each lethal projectile.

Alexandria's hair flowed like a river of burnished copper, cascading in lustrous waves that fanned out behind her, forming a radiant silk screen that shimmered in the sun's harsh glare. The wind, playful and insistent, toyed with the edges of her leather jacket as she executed a flawless front flip. In that moment of airborne grace, a bullet sliced through the air, its deadly intent thwarted by her outstanding agility. It left only a whisper of its passage, puncturing the loose fabric of her jacket with silent precision. In Alexandria's dangerous dance, there was an otherworldly elegance, her every move a mesmerising blend of lethal intent and breathtaking beauty.

The gun in her hand spat fire, each bullet finding its mark. Four men collapsed in a tangle of limbs. Their menace was extinguished; they were no longer a threat. But Alexandria had no time for triumph. The frightened girl, eyes wide with terror, still awaited salvation.

She leapt behind abandoned cars, using them as shields. Bullets ricocheted off metal, leaving dents and scars, but Alexandria remained unscathed amidst the chaos. Her movements composed an exquisite ballet of survival, each motion resonating with fluid grace. The world blurred around her, colours bleeding into one another, and fear was but a faint whisper against the thunderous roar of her unwavering resolve, propelling her onwards.

With a final burst of speed, Alexandria closed the distance. She stood next to Emma, her expression unwavering. Her smile cut through fear, a beacon of reassurance. 'You're safe now,' she whispered as Emma's tears flowed freely.

The air pulsed with tension as Alexandria's voice sliced through the ear throbbing noise. 'Are you hurt?' she asked, her sharp blue eyes scanning for any threats.

NEVER UNDERESTIMATE GIRLS!

'No, just get me out of here,' Emma sobbed, vulnerability and confusion infused in her voice.

Without hesitation, Alexandria removed her bulletproof vest and draped it over Emma's trembling shoulders. 'Come,' she commanded, her tone gentle. 'Stick to my heels, and you'll be safe.'

Emma watched, her eyes wide with a mix of fear and admiration, as Alexandria rose with the grace of a panther, her spirit unyielding in the face of danger. With a burst of speed that blurred her movements, she sprinted towards cover, her footsteps reverberating with the echo of courage. Sliding behind a nearby car, she crouched low; her breaths were slow and deliberate, each one a silent testament to her unwavering resolve.

Emma, caught in the grip of uncertainty, hesitated but soon followed, her heart pounding, a frantic rhythm against her ribs. Then, in a moment of terror, she let out an ear-splitting scream.

Alexandria whirled around, but it was too late. A man with eyes as cold as steel lunged at her. He slammed her against the car with brutal force, causing her gun to clatter to the ground, sliding just out of reach.

He loomed over her, retrieving a knife that gleamed ominously in the sun's light. His sly grin was a grotesque mask of evil. 'You'll wish you never got involved,' he sneered, his voice dripping with malice.

'Let me go!' Emma's voice was a shrill shriek of panic as another figure emerged from the shadows. He seized her arms, wrenching them cruelly behind her back, his grip unyielding. One hand secured her wrists with brutal efficiency while the other nonchalantly plucked the smouldering cigarette from his lips. His laughter was a harsh, grating sound that dripped with contempt. 'Girls are such easy prey,' he mocked.

'Daxton, enough with the insolence and silence her,' the knife-wielder commanded, his gaze never leaving Alexandria.

'With pleasure, Kato,' Daxton replied with a cruel chuckle. He slapped his hand over Emma's mouth; she responded with instinctive ferocity, biting down hard on his finger. 'You little bitch!' Daxton cursed loudly.

Kato shook his head in disdain and raised his knife, its blade poised to plunge into Alexandria's heart. But she met his gaze, determination stamped across her face. 'You're gonna regret choosin' this path,' she declared.

She delivered two precise knee strikes to Kato's ribs in a fast motion that was too quick to follow. The impact sent shockwaves through his body, forcing him to stagger back in surprise. Seizing the moment, Alexandria's leg arched through the air in a powerful crescent kick that connected with Kato's jaw. He stumbled back further, pain contorting his features.

With agility born from desperation and skill, Alexandria rolled forward and snatched her gun from the ground. She aimed and fired in one fluid motion; the bullet found its mark in Kato's head.

Turning to Daxton, who had managed to shove his cigarette back between his lips and was fumbling for his own weapon, Alexandria executed an aerial manoeuvre that defied gravity. Her tornado kick was a whirlwind of force that sent Daxton reeling back; his finger squeezed the trigger of his gun reflexively. The bullet struck him in the leg instead of its intended target, which was supposed to be Alexandria. He collapsed to the ground, screaming with agony.

'Now you can die the death you deserve,' Alexandria spat venomously as she delivered one final kick to Daxton's face. Blood erupted from his nose as he lay on the ground in disbelief and excruciating pain. 'I bet you didn't expect that from a girl,' she taunted with a cold laugh. 'Didn't your father ever teach you that girls can bring empires to their knees?' She flicked her hair over her shoulder and turned to Emma, who looked like she was about to collapse.

'Let's get out of here,' Alexandria said softly, offering Emma a warm smile. Together, they ran towards Alexandria's waiting Mercedes-Benz, their hearts pounding fiercely with adrenaline and survival.

NEVER UNDERESTIMATE GIRLS!

'Get in the car, NOW!' Alexandria's voice sliced through the gunfire as she swung the back door open. 'Stay low!' she yelled as she and Emma jumped into the sanctuary of the Merc.

Alexandria's foot slammed on the gas pedal, propelling them forward. Yet peril was far from over. Bullets hammered against the car's body. One bullet pierced the windshield, sending shards of glass dancing through the air, slashing Alexandia's face. She grimaced with the pain, and then a bullet whizzed past her arm, its lethal intent narrowly missing her; the air seemed to ripple with the noise of danger as it ripped through one of the back seats.

Another bullet whistled perilously close, a whisper of death grazing her shoulder; it tore through fabric and flesh, painting her clothes in a stark crimson. 'That really...hurt!' she roared, fury and pain intertwining in her outcry.

With one hand on the steering wheel, she reached for her gun. The man who'd fired that shot was in her sight. She pulled the trigger with a bitter vengeance and watched as her bullet found its mark.

The tarmac blurred beneath Alexandria's wheels as she sped out of the park, insistence surging through her veins like an electric current.

Upon reaching the main road, she parked beside a bright pink Kawasaki and swung her door open. 'Layla,' she called, her voice urgent. 'Take this girl to the safety of the police station. I'm goin' after Kenny.'

Layla stood beside her motorbike. The wind blew through her blonde hair, each strand reflecting the sun's harsh glare. Her blue eyes locked with Alexandria's in a silent vow. 'Stay safe, sis,' she replied with a reassuring smile, securing her pink helmet firmly in place.

Still quivering from fear's cold embrace, Emma unclasped Alexandria's bulletproof vest and handed it over. 'You'll need this,' she said in a shaky voice.

Alexandria clenched her jaws; she had a score to settle.

Chapter 5

Back in her car, Alexandria pressed her earpiece. 'Stella, this is Alexandria. Have you located Kenny yet?' Her words were sharp, infused with the desperation of a predator closing in on its prey.

Stella's reply was swift. 'Yes, I've got him on my drone's camera. He's slipped past the police, headin' up Sunset Road.'

A torrent of rage flowed through Alexandria's veins. How could the police lose him? Her fingers wrapped around the steering wheel as she activated the engine. The car's growl resonated with her steely determination, a sign of power and purpose as she tore down the road, shattering the silence with her defiance of speed constraints.

'He's dartin' off Sunset Road now,' Stella's voice pierced the air, laden with urgency and persistence. 'Headin' for the motorway. You need to hurry!'

Sunset Road blurred past in a streak of tarmac and fury. Alexandria recklessly manoeuvred past other vehicles; their horns blared, and curses flew out of their windows.

But Alexandria's focus was laser-sharp: apprehend the felon. Her foot hammered down on the accelerator, and the tyres let out a piercing wail as she executed a perilous left turn, leaving rubber imprints on the road.

'You're right behind him!' Stella's urgency cut through the racket.

Through her shattered windscreen, Alexandria's gaze narrowed; a menacing black SUV loomed ahead, its sleek form mocking her. 'Is he in that damn SUV?' she spat out, her tone as sharp as a dagger's edge.

'Affirmative,' Stella's confirmation came crisp and clear.

Merging onto the motorway, Alexandria's foot was unyielding on the pedal, pushing the speedometer needle beyond seventy; the wind howled through her window, ruffling her hair. The SUV was her prey, and it was excitingly close; its glossy paint seemed to sneer at her. 'I'm catchin' up with him!' she cried, turning sharply onto the second lane.

NEVER UNDERESTIMATE GIRLS!

Aligning her vehicle with the black beast, she rolled down her left window and drew her firearm with a steady hand.

But the driver was no ordinary man. Bullets spat from the SUV, shattering glass. Alexandria's grip tightened on the steering wheel, but she lost control. Metal met metal, and both cars skidded into the third lane, smashing against the centre reservation.

As her world spun out of control, her head slammed against the door. Airbags inflated, suffocating her, and then her breathing increased as she felt her car coming to a sudden stop; her mind felt unstable, but determination burned hotter than the searing pain.

She flung the door open and stumbled out, knees hitting the unforgivable tarmac. Fresh air brushed against her face, and then she heard the unmistakable thump of rotor blades slicing the air. A helicopter hovered, a rope dangling beneath it - an escape for none other than the murderer himself.

She gritted her teeth and slowly stood up, her body battered and bruised. The chopper, a metallic eagle, circled above, its pilot a secret ally. The SUV's door, which was now twisted and mangled after the crash, swung open, revealing the man who had dodged justice for far too long. Highlighted by the retreating daylight, he stepped out, a menacing shadow against the fading light. The biting wind whipped through his ebony hair, each strand a dark ribbon that danced with the whispers of forgotten secrets. His eyes, glacial blue, held the weight of unseen storms, their depths mirroring the frozen skies above the poles.

Indigo irises, sharp as icy daggers, bore into the sky. He kept his back facing Alexandria, his gaze fixed on the hovering chopper. She, in turn, studied him; he was a puzzle wrapped in shadows waiting to be unravelled. The setting sun bathed him in misleading warmth, concealing the venom that lay beneath. He was no stranger to death. The memories of her mother's murder reverberated within her, driving her relentlessly to pursue him. Twelve lunar cycles had passed since she had embarked on this blood-soaked quest, tracking him through the underworld maze. The police, too, sought him, but their efforts were useless; he was a phantom that could easily slip through their grasp.

The helicopter's blades sliced through the air, their metallic song resounding with Alexandria's unwavering resolve. She couldn't allow him to escape, not after the killings he had committed. Her legs, lacking adrenaline, felt heavy and stiff, but she forced herself forward.

The gun, an instrument of revenge, weighed heavily in her hand, a symbol of justice and a reminder of her mother's blood. Determination, strong and unyielding, bubbled within her veins. With the hammer cocked, she sprinted towards him, her breaths ragged, her pulse a battle drum.

The man stood before her, a shadow in the twilight. As Alexandria squeezed the trigger, the bullet leapt from the barrel, its trajectory a promise of reckoning. But on the last and most vital moment, he swivelled, a dance of fate, and the bullet missed its mark, vanishing into the open expanse.

Less than a meter separated them, Alexandria stumbled back, her finger froze on the trigger, and time hung suspended.

The man's jet-black hair danced in the wind, encircling a face barren of regret. His cold eyes bore into hers, and she knew this was the man, the murderer, the one who had baffled the police, slipping through the cracks of the law.

With no remorse, he aimed a glimmering gun straight at her and pulled the trigger; the noise of the bullet being released echoed. Alexandria stood frozen even though she could see danger hurtling towards her; she couldn't tear her eyes away from the man's face. His eyes held her captive, and then an agonising pain shot through her body as the bullet hit her leg; she fell, her grip on her gun slipping. Her vision went hazy, and blood stained her face as it met the tarmac.

The man walked towards her, his lips twisting mockingly. Alexandria raised her head, hair flowing around her face like a river of sweet water. Her gaze, both helpless and defiant, locked onto him. In his hand, a gun gleamed, its cold metal swallowing the warmth of the setting sun.

Her body trembled, weakened by fear and adrenaline. 'You've taken so many lives,' she muttered, her voice barely audible, as if afraid the very air would betray her.

Tears welled in her eyes, and she stared down at the ground, unable to comprehend the brutality before her. 'How could you?' she whispered, her words trailing off as the man's gun struck her face with brutal force, splitting her lip. Blood seeped out of the cut, staining her white shirt, and pain shot throughout her body. Death hovered as she waited for the slightest movement of the man's finger on the trigger.

His smirk widened, and then he mysteriously smiled instead of delivering the final blow. 'Alexandria,' he whispered, his voice like a velvet blade. Her name hung in the air like a curse.

'How do you know my name?' she stammered, her mind spinning. Had he been watching her? Studying her every move? The chopper's relentless blades drowned her thoughts, their rhythm a noise of urgency.

The helicopter loitered above, a mechanical dragonfly in the sky. Below it, a rope dangled that promised escape, swaying gently within the man's grasp. He looked down at Alexandria and then grabbed the rope, his hand stretched towards her, an offer that didn't sound like reality. 'Andria, come with me,' he urged, his voice low and insistent.

Alexandria's gaze lifted to meet his, her eyes reflecting a mix of determination and uncertainty. The name 'Andria' resonated within her, a nickname that felt surprisingly suitable. More distinguished than the universal 'Alex' she was usually called by. For a fleeting moment, she savoured its uniqueness, but then she quickly shook the thought from her mind. There was no time for distractions; she had to stop him.

A surge of stubbornness propelled her upwards in an attempt to reach him, yet her gun lay just beyond her fingertips, its presence taunting her efforts. Agony and pain ran through her body like searing bolts of lightning, and then she collapsed; there was nothing she could do.

As the man ascended, he locked his cold eyes onto hers. 'This isn't over,' he whispered. 'I'll be back for you.' The helicopter lifted him, and he soared above, his eyes still holding untold stories, dark and ancient. Then, he vanished, swallowed by the horizon.

Sirens wailed; help was on its way, but Alexandria's gaze remained fixed on the empty sky. How had he known her name? The question lingered in the air, unanswered, as the world blurred around her.

Chapter 6

In the quiet headquarters of the police station, Officer Zackery stood like a sentinel beside the moonlit window. His sharp green eyes, keen and vigilant, pierced through the glass, surveying the city's heartbeat below. The room was a testament to law and order, with walls adorned with commendations and a map dotted with coloured pins marking cases old and new. His desk, a sturdy oak fortress, bore the weight of countless files and reports, each a story of justice in progress.

Zackery's fingers raked through his salt-and-pepper hair, a habitual gesture that eliminated his frustration. The soft knock at the door was a familiar interruption, yet it resonated differently within these four walls, where every decision weighed heavy with consequences.

He strode across the room, his steps deliberate on the cold tile floor. The door opened to reveal his assistant, a figure of unwavering loyalty. 'Sir, Officer Luca has information that he believes is very beneficial,' the assistant reported.

Zackery's response was curt, his tone leaving no room for ambiguity. 'If Luca's got valuable information, then send him in. Otherwise, he can save his breath,' he declared, his gaze as incisive as his words.

Acknowledging the order with a quick nod, the assistant retreated, leaving Zackery to return to his solitary vigil over the paperwork that lay sprawled on the desk like a puzzle begging to be solved. He sank into his chair, the leather creaking under his weight, and exhaled deeply. 'Time to dig through this mess and make some sense of it,' he muttered with a mix of determination and disdain.

The air was thick with tension as another soft knock punctuated the silence. 'Enter,' Zackery commanded, his voice a blend of authority and weariness.

The door creaked open, and Zackery's assistant entered the room. Officer Luca trailed behind him; his presence seemed to fill the room with an air of despondency. Zackery's gaze, sharp as a blade, cut through the distance between them. 'Luca, my old comrade, I trust you to bring tidings that will lift the gloom over this dreary day,' he said, a hint of bravado infusing his words.

Luca's response was heavy with concern. 'Chief, it appears the day's burdens weigh heavily upon you,' he began, only to be cut off as Zackery surged forward in a sudden storm of fury. Seizing Luca by the collar, Zackery's eyes blazed with an intensity that could melt steel.

'Save your comments for another day,' he hissed, his grip tightening like a vice. And then, after a tense moment, he released Luca, stepping back as if to regain his composure. 'Out with it then. What news do you bring?' he demanded.

Luca straightened his uniform, his voice regaining strength. 'I bring a glimmer of hope in our pursuit of Alexandria. I believe we may be able to give her a prison sentence or at least drag her into court,' he declared.

Zackery's impatience was palpable. 'Speak plainly, Luca. How do we ensnare her in the web of law?'

Luca leaned towards Zackery. 'She was at the scene during Kenny's assault on the girl. There are witnesses, myself included, who saw her armed with a gun,' he revealed.

A laugh erupted from Zackery, sharp and sudden as lightning. 'I admire your positive outlook, but it might be a bit too hopeful. Luca, you're naïve,' he scoffed.

Undeterred, Luca pressed on. 'Send me with Detective Jakie. If I'm with him, we can convert this lead into a solid conviction.'

Zackery paused, leaning against the cold wall as he considered the proposition. 'It's a chance,' he mused aloud. 'But Jakie and you are like hot oil and cold water. Together, you are like an exploding volcano.'

'I'm aware,' Luca conceded. 'But it's a risk worth taking.'

Zackery returned to his chair with a heavy sigh. 'So, you witnessed Kenny's men trying to kidnap Emma? I wonder why they didn't want to kill her because they could have if they wanted to. What purpose does she serve in his twisted game?'

'They never intended to kill her. She was meant to be taken alive,' Luca responded.

'Why her? What makes her the target of such madness?' Zackery pondered, the question hanging in the air like thick smoke.

Luca shook his head solemnly. 'Sir, Kenny's mind has been a labyrinth of madness since he escaped from prison. He has mercilessly slain seven innocent young women in cold blood,' he remarked in a grave tone.

Zackery's laughter was dark and hollow, a stark contrast to the gravity of their conversation. 'Indeed, his mental instability has been the root of his heinous actions, beginning with the atrocious harm he inflicted upon his own daughter and spouse,' he responded, his voice filled with disdain.

Luca observed Zackery's reaction closely. 'You appear to be quite entertained by this grim narrative,' he noted, the corners of his mouth lifting in an optimistic smile.

Engulfed in a wave of sardonic laughter, Zackery's eyes snapped towards Luca with startling intensity. 'You are dismissed,' he declared. 'I will arrange your departure with Jakie. And let me be clear: I expect this operation to proceed without any unnecessary complications.'

'Understood, Sir,' Luca acknowledged with a nod, his expression unreadable as Zackery's assistant escorted him from the premises.

Chapter 7

The sterile hospital room enveloped Alexandria like a shroud, its walls aseptic and unforgiving. Her body, battered and stitched, lay horizontally on the bed, each stitch a testament to what she had gone through. Layla, her steadfast sister, maintained a vigilant presence by her side. Her hand, steady and warm, rested on Alexandria's trembling arm.

Alexandria's lips curved, a fragile attempt to smile, but the scars engraved across her face twisted the expression into something almost grotesque. She squeezed her eyes shut, seeking refuge from the pain that gnawed at her insides like a ravenous beast. Tears slipped free, tracing wet paths down her cheeks and onto Layla's comforting hand.

'You'll be sound, sis,' Layla whispered, her voice as gentle as a breeze rustling through leaves. She wiped Alexandria's tears away, a futile gesture against the torrent of emotions.

Beyond the sterile confines, the sun tiptoed above the horizon, casting streaks of light upon the aseptic walls. Rain tapped rhythmically against the windowpane, a mournful sound that mirrored the turmoil within Alexandria.

The enigmatic man's mysterious words resonated in her mind, haunting her thoughts: *This isn't over.* His words clawed at her mind like a wild grizzly bear.

She had tried to stop and halt his reign of evil, but her efforts had been useless. Now, fear coiled around her heart like a blood python, squeezing tighter with each passing second.

Across the room, Alexandria's uncle, Michael, sat, his soft gaze unmoving. His phone buzzed softly, causing him to shift his attention and retrieve it from his pocket. His hushed conversation hung in the air. 'Yes, I know it's quite unbelievable,' he stated. 'Well, I guess it's happened now. So…you're comin' in a few minutes?' he fell silent, then sighed. 'Bye, see ya.' He hung up and combed his brown hair with his fingers.

'Uncle Michael,' Stella whispered, her voice trembling.

'What's up, kiddo,' Michael inquired, his attention shifting towards Stella, who was resting her head against his arm.

'Do you think Alex will get better?' The words spilt from Stella's lips, her voice a fragile whisper. A solitary tear escaped her eye, carving a glistening trail down her cheek before resting softly on the sleeve of her red jumper.

A nurse engrossed in her typing overheard. 'Of course, she's going to get better, sweetheart,' she reassured with a warm smile. 'Rest, healing, and time, that's all she needs. Her wounded leg will mend, and soon, she'll be up and running.'

Comforted by the nurse's words, a weight lifted off Stella's heart. She glanced at Alexandria, whose eyes were sealed shut, perhaps wandering through a maze of thoughts and dreams.

'She's gonna be fine,' Michael whispered, his voice a soothing balm, as he noticed a shadow of doubt flicker across Stella's face. Gently wiping away her tears with his thumb, he kissed her forehead tenderly.

'I hope so,' Stella whispered back, her gaze lingering on Alexandria, who bore scars both seen and unseen.

The room settled into an uneasy silence, punctured only by the nurse's keyboard, a soft, rhythmic typing.

Alexandria's mind flickered like a dying bulb, surrendering to the pull of sleep. Suddenly, her eyes shot open to the noise of the door swinging open. An officer walked into the room, his presence disliked by the three sisters.

His dark eyes scanned the scene, his gaze settling on Alexandria, who resembled a battle-worn soldier emerging from the fray of war. Her paleness matched the moon's ghostly glow on a dark night, and bandages cocooned her left arm and leg. 'I can't believe your niece has taken it this far, mate,' he scolded, side-eyeing Michael.

'I know, can't believe it either,' responded Michael.

Alexandria, silent but furious, felt a surge of energy ignite within her. 'Officer Luca,' she hissed, her voice dripping with mockery and weariness. 'Your presence is hardly a pleasure.'

He straightened, adjusting his uniform. 'Manners, Alex. You'd do well to remember them.'

Her anger flared like a wildfire, ready to consume everything in its path. 'You need to brush up on your job! I was closer to catchin' that guy than you were!' she proclaimed confidently.

Layla tightened her grip on Alexandria's hand. 'Easy now,' she urged. 'Yer gonna mess things up big time.'

'Perhaps if the police had done their job properly, we wouldn't be in this mess in the first place,' Alexandria blurted, anger etching her features.

Luca's gaze slid to the nurse, who stood to one side observing the commotion. 'She's acting like she isn't even injured,' he muttered.

'Remarkable recovery,' the nurse replied in a bewildered voice. 'She was in a dire state not long ago.'

Luca leaned against a wall, his eyes fixed on Michael.

'So, how's your trainin' been going, mate?' Michael asked in a casual tone.

'Well, quite good, but it's bloody stressful when you have to trail behind that young b...' Luca swore under his breath. The nurse turned towards him in shock, and he casually continued speaking to Michael. 'You should know him. His name's Detective Jakie Theodore,' he said, a hint of frustration in his voice.

Michael grinned, 'When I used to work as a police officer, I never liked him either. He's got a lot of pride.'

Luca raised an eyebrow. 'Why did you quit? Was it because of him?' he joked.

NEVER UNDERESTIMATE GIRLS!

'Oh, no,' Michael replied, shaking his head. 'It's just that...you should know.' He stopped speaking and glanced at Alexandria, then sighed, 'I've got a lot of responsibilities, ya see.'

Luca's curiosity finally got the better of him. 'So, what's your job now?' he asked, leaning forward with interest.

Michael sighed and gave a small smile. 'At the present time, I haven't got a job, ya see. But in the near future, I'm plannin' to become an author,' he replied, his eyes lighting up with a hint of excitement.

'An author?' Luca exclaimed, his eyebrows shooting up in surprise. 'What got you interested in that type of job?'

Michael shrugged his shoulders, a thoughtful expression crossing his face. 'Since ma youth, I've always loved writin' stories,' he said. 'And, well, the main reason is that I wanna stay close to my nieces. I really can't bear the thought of them slippin' out of my grasp again and gettin' themselves into trouble.'

'I don't know why you're usin' the word 'trouble' because I think *what we do* is quite fun,' Alexandria said in a sassy tone.

Michael and Luca side-eyed one another but didn't react to Alexandria's comment.

Luca pulled his phone out of his pocket and began flicking through it absentmindedly.

Layla, who had been listening intently, finally spoke up. 'So, officer, what's the score? What ya crackalackin'?' Her voice cut through the air, sharp and direct.

Luca glanced up, meeting Layla's gaze. 'I've come to question your big sister,' he said, his expression serious. 'But first, I need Detective Jakie to join us.' He rolled his eyes.

At that very moment, there was a gentle knock on the door, and the nurse, her manner both professional and cautious, swung the door open, revealing a young man.

He wore a black trench coat that hung just below his knees, its fabric whispering secrets of midnight escapades. His complexion told stories of accomplishment and failure. His deep charcoal grey trousers flowed elegantly, brushing against polished leather shoes. His golden hair, meticulously styled, seemed to defy gravity. Each strand was over-gelled, the tips curling around his neck like tendrils of power.

His impression was both professional and classic, as if he had stepped out of a film. He stood in a straight posture and stated, 'Is Alexandria here?'

'Yes,' the nurse affirmed quietly. 'Please come in.'

He stepped into the room like a shadow cast by the dim light filtering through the window. His golden amber eyes, glossy as marbles, held secrets engraved in their depths, and his smile, a sly crescent, spread across his face, revealing teeth that gleamed like polished ivory.

Stella, whose cheeks naturally bloomed with the soft hue of shyness in the company of strangers, found herself nervously drumming her trainers against the polished tiles as the man cast her a small smile.

Alexandria had never encountered this man before, yet her instincts flared like a match struck in the dark. The air around her seemed to thicken, and her pulse quickened. She didn't like the look of him, the way his gaze lingered, as if he could unravel her secrets with a mere glance.

'Ah, so you must be the famous Alex?' he inquired, stepping forward with a notebook at the ready.

'No, I'm not,' she muttered, cheekiness simmering beneath her breath.

'I beg your pardon?' he frowned, taken aback by her audacity.

'Oh, she's just bein' herself,' Layla interjected with a strained smile, quickly attempting to diffuse the tension.

The man ignored her and focused on Alexandria. 'I'm Detective Jakie Theodore. I have a few simple questions for you, if you don't mind.'

NEVER UNDERESTIMATE GIRLS!

'Ask away. But you know what? Trivial questions bore me to bits,' Alexandria retorted, her attention seemingly more captivated by the patterns on the ceiling than the conversation at hand.

'Alex!' Michael chided, his voice filled with concern. 'What's gotten into you?'

'She's just full of surprises these days,' Luca murmured with a smirk.

Jakie shot him a sharp glance before turning back to Alexandria, his voice slicing through the thick air. 'Let's get down to business then. What's your address?'

Luca leaned back, his smirk widening. 'I've asked her that so many times. It's practically imprinted in my memory,' he chuckled.

'Do not speak, Luca,' Jakie said sharply.

As Alexandria mumbled her address, her gaze never leaving the ceiling, Jakie jotted down the details, his pen dancing across the notepad. 'And what age are you?'

'Eighteen,' she stated plainly.

'Eighteen,' Jakie repeated thoughtfully. 'Such a tender age for such...complexities!'

'Tender age,' Alexandria sneered. 'How many people have to tell me that?'

Jakie's eyes narrowed as he peered into hers, searching for something beneath the surface. 'Why were you at Eagle's Park?' he pressed with a hint of suspicion in his voice.

'What kind of question is that?' Alexandria scoffed dismissively. 'Why do you think I was there?'

'I need a simple answer,' Jakie insisted firmly.

'I was there enjoyin' a serene stroll,' she smoothly lied.

'The witnesses claim you arrived after the chaos had already erupted,' Jakie countered.

'Fine! I went to confront that murderer, but as you can see, it didn't go as planned!' Alexandria's frustration spilled forth.

'Weren't you explicitly instructed by local authorities to steer clear of criminal activities?' Jakie probed further.

'If I hadn't been there, that girl might have been killed or worse,' Alexandria shot back defiantly.

'And there were no police officers present?' Jakie asked, acting confused.

Alexandria let out an exasperated sigh. 'Of course, there were police, but they were about as useful as a chocolate teapot. I had no choice but to step in.'

'No, you did not have to intervene,' Jakie retorted sternly.

'Yeah, I did!' Alexandria fired back.

'Enough,' Jakie commanded calmly yet authoritatively, raising his hand to silence her.

Alexandria huffed and crossed her arms over her chest, wincing slightly at the dull throb in her arm, a painful reminder of the bullet that had grazed past her.

'Now, take these documents and read them thoroughly,' Jakie instructed as he handed her a stack of papers. 'Should you have any questions, call this number,' he added, pointing to a scribbled series of digits in the corner of the top sheet.

Alexandria glanced down at the papers with disdain. 'What is this nonsense?' she asked.

'Read it, and all will become clear,' Jakie replied with a knowing smirk. 'But remember, none of this applies if you can refrain from meddling in matters best left to the police.'

'And if the police are incapable of handlin' it? Am I then permitted to step in?' Alexandria asked with a mischievous tilt of her head.

'No, you are not,' Jakie stated emphatically. 'Now, please, read those papers.'

With an exaggerated roll of her eyes, Alexandria shifted her gaze down to the stack of papers cradled in her hands.

NEVER UNDERESTIMATE GIRLS!

Jakie sighed, a hint of weariness in his gesture as he closed his notebook. 'Well, that's all for now.'

'What do you mean 'that's all'? You haven't even asked her the crucial questions,' Luca interjected, his voice heavy with disbelief.

Jakie brushed him off with a dismissive wave. 'I'm the detective. I know what's essential, and I've covered it. There's no need to delve into every little detail.'

Luca's expression contorted with frustration. 'But you've skipped the details regarding the *gun*...'

Jakie cut him off with a decisive raise of his hand, his tone brooking no argument. 'I know what I'm doing. Years of experience guide my instincts, Luca. And you? You're just a trainee,' he stated flatly.

As Jakie turned to leave, his eyes lingered on Alexandria for a little longer. 'I have a feeling we'll be seeing each other again soon,' he said, almost to himself, before striding out of the room's door, his golden hair catching the light as he went.

Luca glared at Alexandria, his emotions a turbulent mix of embarrassment and anger. 'Bye, mate,' he grumbled to Michael, who stared at him with a sarcastic *'wow, that was amazing'* expression.

Luca stormed out of the room, his footsteps resonating like distant thunder. He left behind a palpable silence, a testament to the clash of words and unspoken truths that had transpired out of the conversation.

The nurse's voice cut through the quietude of the hospital room like a scalpel scraping against marble floor. 'Some officers!' she said with a shake of her head. She then turned to Michael, who was standing by the door, gazing out at the empty corridor.

'Ain't got a clue what got into them officers,' Michael replied, turning to face the nurse, his shoulders lifting in an unconcerned shrug. His voice held a hint of weariness as if he'd seen too many of these scenes play out before.

A sudden, authoritative voice cut through the air, ricocheting off the hospital walls and startling Michael, causing him to suddenly turn around. He was met by the imposing figure of a man clad in the unmistakable navy blue of a police officer's uniform, adorned with a gleaming badge and a duty belt that held the promise of law and order. The officer's eyes scrutinised Michael with a piercing gaze that seemed to strike his very soul. 'Michael? Might you be the one I'm seeking,' he asked, a faint smile playing upon his lips.

Michael's brow furrowed in suspicion, his mind racing with possibilities. What could this officer possibly want with him? 'Yes, the name's Michael,' he confirmed, his tone filled with curiosity.

The officer extended a firm hand, the gesture exuding professionalism. 'Officer Ezekiel,' he declared, his voice filled with a jovial tone that belied the seriousness of his attire. Michael accepted the handshake. 'I need to speak with you privately,' Ezekiel stated, his steady tone leaving no room for argument yet somehow managing to sound reassuring.

Micheal glanced back at Alexandria, who was scrolling through the papers that Jakie had given her. She had a disapproving expression on her face.

'We'll step aside,' Officer Ezekiel suggested. 'I fully understand if you're hesitant to leave your nieces unattended.'

Michael gave a slow, reluctant nod, and they moved towards a secluded corner within the hospital's corridor.

With his hands buried in his trouser pockets, Officer Ezekiel let out a weary sigh. 'The incident involving your niece has come to my attention. It's always disheartening to hear such news,' he confessed.

'Yeah,' Michael muttered, his mind overflowing with unspoken retorts.

Ezekiel's voice was measured as he spoke. 'I believe it's time for some honesty, *Micheal*.'

'Honesty?' Michael repeated, his confusion mounting. 'What exactly are you implyin'?'

NEVER UNDERESTIMATE GIRLS!

'I'm referring to the tragic murder of Alexandria's mother,' Ezekiel clarified, his gaze unwavering.

Michael's heart skipped a beat. 'My sister's murder?' he questioned, a chill running down his spine.

'You were present that fateful night, Michael. You witnessed her last moments,' Ezekiel pressed on.

Feeling cornered, Micheal hesitated momentarily before saying, 'What ya tryna say? Your questions sound bare accusin'.'

'On the contrary, I'm merely seeking confirmation. You did see her pass away, correct?' Ezekiel countered, his composure unshaken.

'Yes, I was there,' Michael admitted, his frustration evident. 'To be straight, this line of questionin' is distressful. You speak of my sister's death as if it holds no significance.'

'Listen, I understand your pain,' Ezekiel sympathised. 'And that's exactly my point. I understand your niece's distress, too. As an officer of the law, I'm simply asking you to share the truth with her.'

Michael's bewilderment was palpable. 'I'm not understandin' what you want from me,' he said.

'Reveal to Alexandria the details of her mother's demise, who, how, and why. It may prevent her from taking drastic measures to uncover the perpetrator herself,' Ezekiel explained calmly.

Micheal's eyes narrowed as he studied Ezekiel. 'You clearly don't grasp how young minds work,' he retorted. 'If I disclose everythin' as you suggest, she'll spiral out of control. And if she unravels, it could spell disaster for us all. So let me be very clear: I will not disclose any such information.'

'If that is your decision, then so be it,' Ezekiel responded smoothly. 'And please take my words as guidance, not as a command.' With that, he offered a polite nod and departed.

Michael stood in the sterile hospital corridor, his gaze following Ezekiel's retreating figure until it disappeared around a corner. A heavy sigh escaped his lips as he massaged his temples, the tension from their heated conversation pounding through his head like a relentless drumbeat.

Meanwhile, Alexandria was in a surge of fury. 'Just watch what I'll do to that stupid Detective Jakie once I'm out of here,' she shouted, flinging the papers he'd left behind.

'Alex, please don't act like this,' Stella implored gently.

'It's all nonsense, Stella. These papers are just…garbage,' Alexandria yelled.

Layla leaned towards her, concerned. 'What do they say?'

Alexandria's explanation was filled with anger. 'To put it bluntly, they're bloody threatenin' to haul me into court if I interfere with any criminal activity again! Can you believe that? All I want is justice,' she lamented, her body sinking deeper into the hospital bed's embrace.

Layla and Stella exchanged shocked glances. 'They wanna take ya to court?' Layla repeated.

'Yeah, tragic, isn't it?' Alexandria's voice was heavy with sarcasm as she lay back, exhaustion creeping into her bones.

'Isn't it odd that the police only suspect ya? Why not me or Stella?' Layla pondered aloud.

'You should be thankful for that,' Alexandria murmured, her eyelids slowly closing.

The room door creaked open, and Michael stepped inside, his presence heavy with weariness and worry.

Layla looked up at him with concern. 'What happened out there?' she inquired.

'It's nothin' for you to worry over,' Michael assured her, settling beside Stella. 'Some folks just can't see past their own egos.'

Alexandria shifted uncomfortably, a soft groan escaping her lips. 'When can I leave this place?' she whispered faintly, the weight of yesterday's chaos pressing down on her: failed mission, blood-soaked tarmac, and the haunting memory of the murderer's eyes.

NEVER UNDERESTIMATE GIRLS!

The nurse approached with a compassionate look. 'The officers didn't leave any instructions. So, I suppose you can depart once you're feeling better,' she sighed, her fingers tracing the edge of a clipboard. 'However, I sincerely hope you're not contemplating an early departure. Your condition remains precarious, and you must rest for a few hours before I can authorise your discharge.'

'I just wanna go home,' Alexandria pleaded softly.

'If your doctor agrees, you may be able to go home this evening,' the nurse replied softly. 'For now, rest is crucial.'

Those words settled over Alexandria like a heavy blanket as she sank into the bed, the sheets cool against her skin. Yet she didn't feel safe. Her mind was tormented by confusion and lingering questions. The enigma of Detective Jakie's actions, or rather, his inactions, was especially troubling. Why had he ignored the gun? His silence on the subject was mind-boggling. Was he secretly on her side, or was there a more extensive scheme at play? These haunting thoughts ushered her into a sleep that was everything but peaceful, filled with ominous dreams.

Alexandria's eyes flickered open to the sound of a subdued conversation. Stretching languidly, she scanned the room until her eyes settled on Michael, who was engaged in discussion with a doctor near the window.

'Sis, yer finely awake. You've been kippin' for yonks,' Layla whispered.

'Are we gonna be goin' home yet?' Alexandria whispered.

Michael turned away from the doctor, his expression weary and ashen. 'I've just spoken with your doctor. She's given us the green light to leave,' he said in a grateful tone.

Chapter 8

Michael's tired body sank into the plush embrace of the sofa, the fabric yielding to the weight of his exhaustion. The day had been a relentless marathon, and now, finally, back home, he exhaled a sigh that carried the weight of a thousand responsibilities. 'I gotta call your dad and inform him about yesterday,' he confessed, glancing at Alexandria.

'You haven't told him yet?' asked Stella

Micheal looked at her, eyes tired and weary. 'Nah, I didn't wanna freak him out while he was airborne. He was on his way to Scotland, as you all know.'

Layla pulled her phone out from the depths of her pocket, her eyes dull and tired from all the hours that had slipped by. 'Today was probably the deadest day,' she complained, her voice heavy with boredom.

Michael's gaze sharpened, his stern expression cutting through the room. 'Well, you girls should all be glad I've kept ma cool today,' he stated.

Stella, usually the quiet one, stammered an apology, her face contorting as if she'd swallowed something bitter. 'Uncle,' she began, 'we're really sorry.'

But Alexandria, sitting across the room, dared to scoff. Her eyes sparkled with defiance, and her lips curved into an arrogant smile. 'Why should we be sorry, Stella?' she remarked. 'We didn't do anythin' wrong.'

Michael's patience wavered. 'Alex,' he said calmly. 'I've had enough of your cheek!'

Alexandria leaned back, her posture nonchalant. 'Uncle,' she replied steadily. 'I'm not givin' you cheek. I'm just statin' facts.'

Michael's frustration spilled over. 'I try my best to keep you girls out of danger,' he confessed, 'and look what you do when I turn my back for less than half a day.'

NEVER UNDERESTIMATE GIRLS!

Layla seized the opportunity to prod. 'Uncle, yer always talkin' about keepin' us out of danger. Is there somethin' yer hidin' from us?' she asked.

Michael remained silent, his gaze fixed on the world beyond the window. Then, abruptly, he turned to face the girls. 'There's a lot of things you girls don't know,' he declared.

Before Layla could press further, Michael's phone buzzed, and he swiftly picked it up. 'Hi, what's up?' he answered. 'What?' he asked, abruptly standing up. He paced up and down the room with a frowned brow. 'What does that mean?' he snapped into the phone. 'You actually need me now? I've just had one hell of a day because of those girls...what! Why do you want me at the head office? I don't even work there anymore.' There was another long silence as he listened to the person on the other side. 'Alright, I'll be there, although I don't fancy leavin' the girls alone...Ok, Ok, catch you in a few minutes.'

He slipped the phone into his pocket and looked towards the girls. 'Mate wants a word, so I'll be off for a few hours. AND,' he added, emphasising each letter. 'I do not want you girls to get yourselves into any type of trouble, and let me repeat myself, *I do not want you girls to get yourselves into any type of trouble.*'

'No worries, Uncle, ya can trust us,' smiled Layla, her assurance unwavering.

'Trust,' Michael scoffed, 'is the only thing I can't swing!' he said, leaving the room.

The three girls heard the front door slowly open, then shut with a loud bang, and the mansion fell silent.

Stella collapsed onto the sofa, breathing heavily. The excitement from their adventure still pulsed through her veins, but now reality settled in. 'Dad's not gonna like what we did,' she muttered, glancing at Layla, who was filing her nails and staring at Alexandria's bandaged leg.

'At least yer wounds weren't that bad, sis,' Layla said, her voice calm despite the chaos that had unfolded the day before.

Stella nodded, acknowledging Layla's statement. She was also relieved that Alexandria's injuries were not that bad.

However, Alexandria was lost in her own thoughts, her gaze fixed on the white bandage wrapped around her calf.

'Sis, is there somethin' up?' Layla asked. 'Yer usually the first one to boast about what we've done.'

Alexandria shifted slightly, running her fingers through her hair. 'I just can't shake off what that man said to me.'

Layla raised an eyebrow. 'Which man?' she asked.

'Kenny, the murderer who we were trying to stop,' Alexandria replied, her voice distant as if replaying the encounter in her mind. 'He knew my name.'

Layla's filing halted mid-stroke. 'He clocked yer name?' Her eyes bore into Alexandria's, searching for any signs of deception.

'Yeah,' Alexandria confirmed. 'It's weird, isn't it?'

'Weird?' Stella repeated, walking towards the window and pulling back the curtain; she peered outside as if expecting shadows to leap from the darkness. 'That's not weird, that's downright alarmin',' she declared.

Stella's heart raced, her pulse throbbing in her ears as she stood by the window, her gaze flickering on the street beyond. The room felt scorching hot, and the atmosphere was charged with anticipation. But then suddenly, her phone shattered the silence, the shrill noise making her jump. She fumbled in her pocket, retrieving the phone. As she glanced down at the screen, her face turned pale. The caller ID displayed a single word: 'DAD.'

She hesitated, her thumb hovering over the answer button. Taking a deep breath, she answered the call. What news awaited her on the other end?

Jacob's urgent and disapproving voice crackled through the line. 'Stella, is that you?' he asked.

NEVER UNDERESTIMATE GIRLS!

'Yeah, Dad,' she replied in a low voice. 'How's it goin' down Scotland?'

'Don't try to change the subject,' he snapped. 'I found out what you and your sisters did. Alexandria was all over the news!'

Stella's heart sank. 'I know, Dad. Isn't that cool?' she asked, trying to cheer up the situation.

'No, it's bloody not,' he responded. 'She could have been killed. Where is she? I want to talk to her right now!'

Stella handed the phone to Alexandria, who took it with a mix of defiance and nervousness. 'Hi, Dad. What's up?'

'Why haven't you been picking up my calls?' His voice crackled with frustration.

'I lost my phone while on my mission,' Alexandria admitted.

'You're saying 'my mission' with such calmness as if I approve of it. How many times do I have to tell you?' Jacob's anger flared. 'Stuff like that is damn right dangerous. I've only been away for two days on my business trip, and I've got another two weeks left, and look what you girls have gotten yourselves into again!'

'Dad,' Alexandria's voice wavered. 'You couldn't even think about askin' me somethin' else before you started shoutin',' she stammered, not knowing how to respond to him.

'You couldn't even act upon my advice,' he shot back, 'and not get involved with the police for once! So, now you better listen to me. I want you to stay in the house until I return from Scotland,' his voice trailed off, and then he suddenly asked, 'Why didn't Micheal inform me about all of this when it happened? Where is he?'

'He's gone out, someone called him,' Alexandria replied.

Jacob paused, his concern palpable. 'Oh, my goodness, did the house's address get given away?'

'Yeah, Dad,' Alexandria replied. 'I don't understand why you sound so worried.'

'Just listen to me,' he insisted. 'Until Michael gets back, I don't want any of you to leave the house unless it's urgent. Have you got that?'

'No, Dad, I haven't!' Alexandria's anger flared. 'I'm eighteen years old, and I don't need to be told what to do!'

His response was annoyingly calm. 'Alex,' he said, his tone measured. 'You just wait till I get home. I'm going to give you a long lesson on how to talk to your dad!'

The words 'your dad' hung in the air, a phrase that sent shivers of anger down her spine. She couldn't hold back; the true reason behind her attitude spilt out, raw and sharp. 'You're not even my real dad!' she shouted, her voice trembling with suppressed rage. 'Why should I listen to you? And by the way, no one will stop me from findin' Kenny and gettin' revenge!' The name tasted bitter on her tongue - Kenny, the one who had shattered her world, leaving her heart fractured and bleeding.

The room buzzed with tension, each word a spark igniting the air. Alexandria's outburst reverberated off the walls. Her knuckles were white as she clenched the phone, and then, with anger, she hung up. She turned to face her two little sisters, Layla and Stella, whose eyes were wide like startled goldfish. Innocent and unknowing, they were caught in the crossfire.

Alexandria's emotions were a tempest raging within her. She longed to shield Layla and Stella, her half-sisters, from her anger, but Jacob's stern voice still hung in the room, a terrible presence.

'He doesn't even care about what I've gone through,' she burst out, her words a desperate plea. But they fell on deaf ears. Layla and Stella remained quiet, their gaze flickering between her and the cold marble floor. They were bound by blood ties she could never fully embrace. They were Jacob's true daughters.

Yet, in that delicate moment, they were more than that; they were allies in pain, united by the shared memories of their mother - the need for justice burned within them all, a fire that transcended lineage. So, beneath the surface, their loyalty was robust and together, their hearts stood ready to confront the man who had destroyed their lives, even as despair clawed at Alexandria's soul.

She ran out of the room, intending to seek solace in her bedroom, but the pain in her leg caused her to stumble on the stairs. Clinging to the handrail, hot tears streamed down her cheeks. Stella's soft voice followed her, a lifeline for these miserable moments. 'Alex!' she whispered.

'Go away,' Alexandria sobbed, forcing herself upright; she limped to her bedroom and slammed the door shut. In despair, she flung herself onto the bed and closed her tear-filled eyes. The bed sagged under her weight as she sank into it. Her trembling fingers traced the delicate silver necklace around her neck, a precious gift from her mother. 'Only if Mother was here,' she whispered, tears slipping down her cheeks and onto her shaking hand.

Chapter 9

Alexandria concealed her face with quivering hands as she sank into the plush embrace of her cushion. The room enveloped her as she surrendered to the torrent of grief; memories crashed against her heart like relentless waves. 'Where's my dad?' she whispered. The unanswered question drifted through the dimly lit room. Anger surged within her, and she threw her frustration at the walls. 'I hate Mother for keepin' him a secret!' she cried out.

Suddenly, the door creaked open; Layla stood there, her eyes swollen from crying. Her voice, filled with empathy, cut through the room. 'Listen, sis,' she whispered. 'If that was the case, why would ya tirelessly seek answers about her murderer?'she said, entering the room, her footsteps deliberate against the soft carpet. She settled at the edge of Alexandria's bed, her presence both comforting and unsettling. 'What's with all the yellin'?' she inquired gently.

'Leave me alone!' Alexandria shouted.

'Listen up, I'll never leave ya,' Layla whispered. 'Tell me what's tearin' ya apart.'

Alexandria's sobs intensified. 'I hate my family!' she confessed. 'Why did my dad abandon me? Why am I kept in the dark?'

Layla's next question pierced her soul. 'Ya don't hate me, do ya?'

Alexandria's response was swift, fuelled by years of suppressed emotions. 'I will always love my family, but I despise your dad!'

Layla recoiled, disbelief dripping off her face. 'Ya don't even know what yer bangin' on about. One minute, yer sayin' ya hate yer family, and now, yer sayin' ya like them, and ya don't like ma dad, who's done so much for ya,' she stammered.

'Don't stick up for him!' Alexandria's anger flared. 'He's never shown me genuine care or love. Mother would have been different if he hadn't come and disrupted our lives.' Her sea blue eyes bore into Layla's,

NEVER UNDERESTIMATE GIRLS!

a silent challenge. 'Why's he stoppin' us from findin' her killer? He was probably behind it!'

Layla's eyes whelmed up with tears; she stood up and ran out of Alexandria's room, leaving her all alone.

Alexandria flopped on her bed and held her head in distress. Had she just shattered the delicate bond that held her and her sisters together by exposing her true feelings about their dad? The love she had with her sisters, was it now irreparably broken?

Guilt gnawed at her insides, a hungry beast feasting on remorse. She flung her legs off the side of the bed, determination propelling her forwards. She needed to mend what she had broken, even if she wasn't entirely sure how.

The pain in her leg was a distant ache, drowned out by the urgency of her motive. She moved down the hallway, the walls whispering secrets of their own. Layla's bedroom loomed ahead, its door a portal to uncertainty. As she neared it, dread filled her heart like ink spilling across paper. She stopped outside, holding her breath.

What would she find? Layla sobbing, perhaps, or pouring her heart out to Stella? Alexandria strained to listen, but there was no sound, only a sinister and suffocating silence. She hesitated, then pushed the cold door handle. The room revealed itself, its secrets laid bare.

And there they were: her sisters, sitting side by side on Layla's bed. Their eyes were fixed on Stella's laptop, a luminous canvas screen. They stared at it as if they'd glimpsed a ghost, their expressions frozen in shock. Alexandria's guilt suddenly intensified, and she shut the door, the click echoing in the stillness.

An urgent hiss reached her ears, a plea, a warning. She opened the door again, and there stood Layla, fear etched across her face. 'Sis,' Layla's voice trembled. 'Someone's broken in.'

These words pulled Alexandria back to reality, and her natural character kicked in. She sprang into action, adrenaline flooding her veins. She sprinted back to her room as fast as her wounded leg would take her, snatched her gun off her desk, and slipped it into her pocket. Its cold metal giving her confidence. She quickly returned to her sisters, feeling confident and excited.

Stella's laptop revealed the intruders, men in black, lurking in the mansion's moonlit back garden. 'We've got to get out of here,' Alexandria declared, her voice urgent and commanding.

Stella's eyes widened, fear spreading across her snow-white face. 'They've broken into the house!' she cried, her voice shrill with panic.

'Where are you goin'?' Alexandria asked as Layla ran out of the room.

'One sec,' Layla called back, her voice urgent, as she bolted down the hallway.

'Layla, get back here!' Alexandria shouted.

But Layla was already descending the staircase, Alexandria's shout following her. As she reached the last step, she hesitated. 'Which room did I leave my gun in?' she wondered aloud. Panic surged through her veins as she sprinted down the hallway and into the living room. She opened a drawer and sighed with relief. 'There you are,' she said, retrieving a pink handgun from the drawer and shoving it into her jeans pocket.

Suddenly, the room door burst open, revealing two armed men. As Layla took three steps backwards, her eyes wide with fear, one of the intruders smirked and exchanged glances with his companion. 'Hey, look, it's a girl,' he taunted, locking eyes with Layla. 'Let's see what she's got?'

In a swift motion, Layla pulled out the pink gun - Alexandria had gifted her this small handgun a few months ago, emphasising its importance for emergencies. When Layla inquired about its origin, Alexandria had evaded the truth, cryptically suggesting that the gun might serve a purpose someday - now that day had come, leaving Layla trembling, her finger hovering near the trigger. However, the adversaries dismissed her threat and laughed, mocking her femininity.

NEVER UNDERESTIMATE GIRLS!

The once-playful pink gun, which Layla had kept as an amusing accessory, now felt deadly in her grasp. She had never fired a shot in her life and had never wanted to, but desperate times demanded desperate measures. The intruders continued to jeer, ridiculing her. 'She's trying to intimidate us with a toy gun!' they scoffed.

Layla's trembling finger tightened on the trigger, the cold metal sending shivers down her spine; her eyes squeezed shut, shutting out the world. This was no game; it was a matter of survival. The deafening roar of the bullet being released echoed around her, and out of sheer fear, she dropped the gun on her foot. Pain exploded through her body, jolting her back to reality.

Her eyes snapped open, and she saw both of the men staring at her with evil grins spread across their faces. The bullet she had fired had made a hole in the wall but had left the men unscathed. Fate had spared them, mocking her desperate act of survival.

One of the men locked eyes with Layla, his gun pointed directly at her. 'I'll teach you a lesson before you die,' he sneered. 'Never shoot with your eyes closed!'

'Wait, Cal!' The other man intervened, his voice urgent. 'Don't shoot the girl. She might be the one we need.'

Layla's heart pounded as she stepped further backwards, her ears still ringing from the gunfire. Cal, undeterred, advanced towards her. 'What's your name, girl?' he demanded.

Layla stared blankly at him, her mind racing. He grabbed her arm, amusement dancing in his eyes. 'You're acting like you haven't got a name, babe,' he taunted.

'Bloody, get off ma arm, ya muppet!' Layla shouted, struggling to break free.

'Tell me your name,' Cal repeated, tightening his grip. 'I'll let you go then,' he let out a sharp laugh. 'Or maybe not. All depends on my mood, girl.'

Layla sighed, her defiance unwavering. 'All right, mate,' she said, her London accent thick as a brick. 'Ma name's: Not Gonna Bloody Listen To Ya!'

Cal's gun hovered menacingly; its cold metal pressed against Layla's temple. His voice, a low growl, sliced through the air. 'Don't get cheeky, or I'll...'

But before he could finish his threat, the room erupted in chaos. The loud crack of gunfire reverberated, filling the space with its echo. Cal spun around, his eyes widening as he took in the scene before him.

The sight of his companion sprawled lifeless on the floor stunned him, his mind struggling to process the shock. And then, like lightning, Alexandria, who had killed his companion, was upon him. She moved gracefully, striking him in the nose with her palm. Blood sprayed, and he staggered backwards in surprise. His gun slipped from his grasp, clattering to the floor.

With unyielding determination, Alexandria twisted his arm behind his back. Pain shot through his shoulder, forcing him to his knees, but his grip on Layla still remained firm, taking her down with him.

The room seemed to shrink around him as Alexandria slammed him against the cold wall; in a swift motion, her arm whipped through the air, her hand rigid and angled like the blade of a sharp knife. In one fluid, practised movement, she targeted Cal's neck, where the pulse of life hummed just beneath the skin. Her strike landed with precision on the soft hollow beside his Adam's apple, the impact reverberating through flesh and bone, a silent promise of her lethal power. He gasped, desperate for air. Then her knee found its mark, driving into his ribs. Stars danced before his eyes, and he involuntarily released Layla.

Cal's pulse raced as Alexandria pointed her gun towards his head. Her smirk was both mocking and lethal. 'Who do you work for?' she demanded.

NEVER UNDERESTIMATE GIRLS!

Cal's defiance flared. 'Why should I tell you?' he gobbed, his knuckles suddenly connecting with her nose. She staggered back, blood splattering across her face.

But she was relentless, fuelled by something deadlier than rage. She pulled the trigger; the bullet tore through Cal's arm, pain searing through his nerves. He gritted his teeth, refusing to cry out. The room spun, and he fought to stay upright. He lunged for his fallen gun, desperation giving him strength. But Alexandria was faster. Her foot connected with his face, a lightning-quick kick that sent him sprawling. The room tilted, and he tasted blood.

'Tell me who you work for!' she demanded, reloading her gun, her eyes unyielding.

'I'll never tell you!' Cal shouted, struggling to rise. 'I'll never listen to a girl's command!'

Her sneer was chilling. Another bullet materialised, and this time, it found his leg. Agony exploded, and he collapsed, blood pooling around him. Fear dripped from his every pore. 'I work for Killer!' he stammered, his voice trembling.

Alexandria's eyes narrowed. 'Killer,' she muttered. 'Don't give me code names. I wanna know his real name!'

'His name's Aron Avellino Issaba,' Cal gasped.

Stella suddenly interrupted their deadly standoff. 'Alex! We need to get out of here!' she called from the hallway.

Without hesitation, Alexandria seized Layla's trembling hand. They fled, leaving Cal sprawled on the floor, bewildered and bleeding.

In the heart of the grandiose mansion, where opulence dripped from every corner, the three girls ran for their lives, their breaths harsh and uneven as they navigated through the maze of luxury.

'We've nearly reached the garage,' Layla sighed with relief as they reached the west wing.

A hallway stretched before them like a runway, lined with intricate tapestries and plush carpets that muffled their hurried steps. As they neared the garage's grand double sliding doors, Stella glanced at Alexandria worriedly.

Despite Alexandria's valiant efforts to mask her pain, the grimace etched upon her face betrayed the agony shooting through her leg. Each stride sent a jolt of pain that radiated from the excruciating wound, yet her determination was as unyielding as the stone walls that loomed around them.

As they arrived at the garage doors, Layla grasped the handles and pushed them open. With a calm sigh as smooth as silk, the doors parted, revealing the girls' escape route. The garage was a gallery of speed and splendour, where sleek machines rested like slumbering beasts, ready to whisk them away to freedom.

Here in the heart of Jacob's estate stood seven meticulously selected automobiles, each a testament to wealth and taste. Jacob, the wealthy owner, had an affinity for the extraordinary. His collection was more than a mere assortment of vehicles; it was a work of mechanical artistry.

The LED lights on the garage's ceiling flickered to life, casting a celestial glow upon the polished surfaces of the slumbering beasts. The air hummed with anticipation.

As Alexandria reached the end of the garage, she opened a lacquered drawer, revealing seven car keys. Her fingers brushed against the cool metal, and she selected one, the key to a posh silver Audi. Stella joined her, and together they leapt into the sleek Audi. Meanwhile, Layla jumped onto her Kawasaki superbike; the engine's deep rumble echoed like the thunderous roar of a lion.

Stella's concern cut sharply through the adrenaline-fueled chaos. 'Have you ever driven this car before?'

Alexandria's smirk held a hint of mischief. 'Not this one, but how hard can it be?' her voice cut through the tension, her fingers gripping the leather-clad steering wheel of the Audi. The engine growled to life, a beast ready to devour the tarmac.

NEVER UNDERESTIMATE GIRLS!

The three girls were bound by more than friendship. They were sisters that destiny had brought together, ready to face dark secrets and danger, but their bond would be tested tonight.

As the automatic garage doors swung open, the tyres screeched in protest. The concrete floor blurred beneath the three girls, and adrenaline surged through their veins.

But danger clung to their tail like a relentless shadow. A man materialised behind them, face obscured by the darkness. His intent was clear; the bullets he fired sliced through the air, a deadly rain of steel seeking flesh. Yet, fate favoured the girls; the projectiles whizzed past, leaving only the echo of their passage.

Layla, astride her Kawasaki, matched her speed with Alexandria's Audi. Her eyes were wide, pupils dilated with fear. She shouted above the wind's roar. 'What's the next move?'

'Let's get on to Dad,' Stella said.

'Don't you dare!' Alexandria's voice held both fury and pity. 'He doesn't need to know what we're doin.' She glanced at Stella, who had tears glistening in her soft hazel-grey eyes, and her gaze softened. 'You don't need to worry. I'll be here for you, I promise.'

'What if we call the police?' Stella proposed in a low voice.

'No way,' Alexandria smirked. 'They can't even solve simple things, let alone handle this.'

The road stretched before them, an endless ribbon woven with uncertainty. Stella's voice trembled as she asked the question that haunted them all. 'What's the plan, then?'

Alexandria's gaze remained fixed on the tarmac, the night swallowing them whole. Her mind raced, cobwebs of possibilities entangling her thoughts, but she had no answers. In the darkness, they hurtled forward, their sisterhood their only compass, fleeing towards an unknown horizon. The city lights blurred, and the wind whispered secrets they dared not hear. Alexandria's resolve hardened, and she vowed silently that she'd find a way to escape this ordeal. For Stella, for Layla, and for the bond that held them together, a bond that was stronger than bullets.

But the question was how?

Chapter 10

'So, sis, where are you takin' us?' Stella asked, hoping for an answer.

Alexandria's grip on the steering wheel tightened, her knuckles white as she navigated the winding road. Her foot pressed hard on the gas pedal. 'Will you stop askin' me that?' she sighed, her voice edged with frustration. 'I'm working on it.'

Stella squinted through the Audi's side mirror. The black car driving behind them seemed relentless, a silent predator lurking in the darkness. 'Is it just me,' she wondered aloud. 'Or has that black vehicle been followin' us for some time?'

'I've been watchin' it too,' Layla shouted over the howling wind.

'Layla, will you put on your earpiece, so you don't need to keep shoutin' at us?' Stella shouted back.

Layla fumbled in her pockets, finally securing her earpiece. 'That car looks really suspicious to me,' she whispered into her earpiece.

Suddenly, the black car surged forward like a predator, closing in on its prey. Its tyres clawed at the asphalt, leaving behind a trail of burnt rubber. Alexandria's Audi, once a symbol of elegance and precision, now became a target. The black car's bumper slammed into the back of the Audi, crumpling the sleek panels and shattering the back window's glass. The impact was brutal, a collision that reverberated through metal and bone alike.

Alexandria's body jerked violently, her head colliding with the unforgiving steering wheel. Pain exploded behind her eyes, and for a moment, the world spun in disarray.

But the chaos didn't end there. The Audi's tyres lost traction, and the vehicle skidded sideways. The road became an adversary, its surface unforgiving as it fought against the Audi's momentum. Sparks flew as the broken back bumper scraped against asphalt, leaving scars that would forever mark this moment.

The Audi, its trajectory altered, hurtled towards a tree, an ancient sentinel standing tall at the roadside. The impact was inevitable. The front of the car crumpled, folding like origami, and the windshield shattered. The airbags shot out, protecting Alexandria and Stella in a cushioned embrace.

But fate hadn't fully completed its mission yet. Flames erupted from the engine compartment. Smoke billowed, thick and acrid, filling the cabin. Alexandria's senses swirled, a mix of pain, fear, and confusion. Darkness encroached, and she lost consciousness.

The menacing black car screeched to a halt, positioning itself just behind the mangled Audi.

In a frantic surge of panic, Stella flung the car door open, adrenaline coursing through her veins. The acrid scent of burning metal assaulted her senses as she scrambled out. She distanced herself from the smouldering wreck, her heart racing.

But Alexandria remained motionless, a fragile figure, and Stella hadn't yet realised that her sister had slipped into unconsciousness.

Layla's motorbike skidded to a halt, gravel crunching under the tyres. She jumped off and ran towards Stella. 'Where's Alex?' she shouted.

'Oh no!' Stella gasped, her chest tightening. 'She's still in the car.' Without hesitation, she sprinted back to the burning wreck. The intense heat from the flames burned her skin as she yanked the door open. 'Alex, get up, get up,' she pleaded, coughing on the thick smoke that curled up from the car's bonnet.

Slowly, Alexandria's eyes fluttered open. 'I wanna find my dad,' she murmured, her voice drowsy.

'Sis, come on!' Layla's urgent voice cut through the air.

'I'm not goin' anywhere,' Alexandria whispered, closing her eyes. 'Where's my dad?' she asked.

Stella's hand closed around Alexandria's. 'Alex,' she whispered. 'Get up.'

NEVER UNDERESTIMATE GIRLS!

A man suddenly emerged from the black car. His eyes gleamed with malice as he lunged at Stella, flinging her to the pavement.

Pain erupted in her mouth, blood staining her teeth. Fury ignited within her as she staggered up, combat instincts kicking in. With precision, she delivered two axe kicks to the man's shoulder, each blow reverberating through bone and flesh. He staggered, wincing in pain.

Stella attempted an uppercut, but he seized her arm, fingers like iron. Using her free hand, she punched him in the stomach, causing him to release his grip. Seizing the opportunity, she unleashed a powerful roundhouse kick to his face, her heel making direct contact with his jaw. Momentum carried him backwards, and he crashed onto the unforgiving pavement.

Alexandria emerged from the Audi, senses intact, gun drawn. She fired a single shot, and the man crumpled, breathing his last.

'I didn't know ya were so good at martial arts, *Hushfire*,' Layla marvelled as Stella pushed a lock of hair behind her ear.

'That's why they say don't mess with the quiet chick,' Stella remarked, adrenaline still flowing through her veins.

'You two get out of here,' Alexandria shouted, bullets rebounding off the pavement as she fired at another man who was emerging from the black car. 'I'll be right behind you.'

Layla and Stella hesitated, torn between loyalty and survival. 'I said get out of here,' Alexandria repeated, her voice as firm as iron shackles.

Layla quickly jumped onto her motorbike, and Stella followed suit. Layla's heart pounded as she glanced at Alexandria, but then she twisted the throttle and raced down the road. Stella's fingers dug into her shoulders, urgency etched on her face. 'Where does she expect us to go?' she wondered aloud, the wind whipping her hair.

'I haven't got a clue,' Layla replied, increasing her speed.

Six minutes flew past, the roundabout blurring as they continuously circled it, but Alexandria remained absent.

'I think we need to go back,' Stella's voice trembled. And then, there it was, the black car, slicing through the night on the other side of the roundabout. 'After that car!' Stella's yell cut through the icy air.

Layla urged her motorbike forward, adrenaline running through her body. She caught up to the car within a few seconds, her eyes widening as she saw Alexandria banging on the back window. 'Oh God, how are we gonna get her out?' Layla's panic surged. 'I've got a plan,' she suddenly cried, passing Stella her gun. 'Shoot the window!'

'Are you dumb?' fear ran through Stella's body as she passed the gun back to Layla. 'Imagine, I shoot Alex, or I shoot you. I've never held a gun.'

'Oh bother,' Layla muttered. 'Take ma phone out of ma bag.'

'Layla, this is no time to snap photos!' Stella protested.

'Don't be daft and just listen,' Layla insisted. Stella retrieved the phone. 'Now throw it at the car's windshield!' Layla commanded, swerving in front of the car.

Stella hesitated for a split second, then flung the phone, finding Layla's plan quite ridiculous. The phone sailed through the air and shattered as it hit the car's windshield. 'What the hell?' the driver shouted in surprise.

'Oops, bad idea,' Layla shrieked as the man retaliated, bullets whizzing past her. She pushed the throttle to its limit, evading the gunfire. The car abruptly veered into a side street, vanishing from sight.

'Get followin' that car, you dope!' Stella's anger fuelled her demand.

Layla turned her motorbike around and entered the small street the black car had sped into moments ago. However, to the girls' dismay, the street led to many more streets, and there was no sign of the black car!

'What are we supposed to do?' Stella's voice quivered with desperation.

'There's only one thing left,' Layla replied, her throat dry from all the tension. 'We're gonna have to call...the police!'

NEVER UNDERESTIMATE GIRLS!

'No,' Stella said. 'Let's search these streets first. I don't want the police to get involved.'

As they searched the dimly lit streets, they eventually found the black car parked beside an old building, but no one was in it.

Then, suddenly, a loud scream erupted from a nearby alley. The raw, desperate cry pierced the dark night. Layla parked her motorbike, and the two girls dismounted. They crept towards the alley, hearts pounding.

'Alex!' Stella gasped as she glanced down the alley. Layla quickly put her hand over Stella's mouth, silencing her.

Before them, just a short distance away, Alexandria struggled aggressively, her hands encircled by a thick rope. The man who held her captive was relentless, his smirk mocking her defiance.

'Let me go!' Alexandria's voice echoed off the stone walls.

'I'm really gonna listen to a girl's command,' the man taunted.

'You better let me go, or else...' Alexandria threatened.

'Or else what?' His laughter grated on her nerves.

'I'm gonna kick the livin' daylights out of you, you bloody pisshead!' Alexandria's rage surged.

The man scoffed. 'My name's Levi. It ain't 'pisshead', girl,' he jeered, shoving her deeper into the alley.

Stella and Layla quietly followed them. 'What's the plan, now?' Stella whispered.

'You think of one this time,' Layla retorted.

'We'll bash that guy up,' Stella suggested, her fists clenched. 'Then we'll escape with Alex.'

'Wow, perfect plan,' Layla's sarcasm was evident. 'What if he has a gun?'

'Don't you have a gun?' Stella shot back.

'Shush,' Layla whispered. 'Where's he takin' Alex?'

'He's leading her to another car,' Stella's eyes widened. 'Oh no, we're gonna have to go back and grab your motorbike.'

The two girls sprinted back to their starting point; their breaths were uneven and laboured. Their motorbike, parked on the curb, awaited them like a loyal steed. Layla's fingers trembled as she fumbled with the ignition. She started the motorbike, and they sped down the alleyway; her mind raced faster than the wheels beneath them.

She followed the car, her eyes focused on its every move. She was a shadow, a whisper in the darkness, determined not to let the man behind the wheel catch sight of her. 'I hope I choose a different colour for ma Kawasaki,' she muttered, her voice barely audible over the wind.

Stella, perched behind Layla, rolled her eyes. 'Well, I told you to go for something more natural,' she scolded. 'But no, you had to be a Barbie doll.'

Layla shot her a defiant look. 'Don't be ridiculous. I didn't wanna be a Barbie doll.'

Stella suddenly pinched Layla on the arm, making her scream.

'Why did ya do that?' Layla protested.

'Look, sis, the car's come to a stop!' Stella pointed out, her gaze fixed on the vehicle ahead. 'You're hurtlin' towards it at full speed. We're gonna crash!'

Layla slammed on the brakes, skidding to a halt behind a grimy garbage bin.

The man emerged from the car, his face twisted in anger. His eyes were dark and mysterious, bearing the weight of countless secrets and danger. His lips curled into a snarl that chilled Alexandria to the core as he swung her door open. 'Get out right now!' he bellowed, the words dripping with venom.

Stubborn and unyielding, Alexandria remained rooted to her spot. 'I'm not goin' anywhere,' she declared, her defiance unwavering.

The man's patience wore thin. 'My boss told me to deal with ya nicely,' he sneered, his fingers brushing against the cold steel of a gun concealed beneath his bomber jacket. 'But if yer not gonna listen, then

NEVER UNDERESTIMATE GIRLS!

I'll have to handle this the hard way,' he declared, retrieving the gun and pointing it towards her.

Alexandria's fear surged as the man continued to threaten her to exit the car. She finally obeyed and stepped out onto the cracked pavement; the pain of her wounded leg shot through her body, but ignoring the pain, she concentrated on the mysterious man. What did he want from her?

He gripped her arm, pulling her towards a nearby rundown building. Its walls bore the scars of time, crumbling plaster, shattered windows, and graffiti that told stories of forgotten lives. Each spray-painted word displayed a sense of despair and desperation.

'Where are you takin' me?' Alexandria demanded, her voice trembling.

The man's grin widened. 'Wait and see,' he said, his tone dripping with sadistic delight. 'But I'll tell ya, yer gonna like it,' he smirked. He shoved the gun back into his hidden waist holster and took out a set of keys, their tarnished metal clinking together. With deliberate steps, he led her to an oddly positioned door among the ruins, unlocked it, and gestured for her to enter.

As she walked through the door, the transformation was astonishing. The tumbledown building's interior had been transformed into a luxurious masterpiece. They stepped into a grand lobby adorned with black marble, its polished surface reflecting the dim light like a mirror. Sparkling crystal chandeliers hung from the ceiling, casting fractured rainbows across the opulent space. Grand velvet sofas lined the walls; their fabric was so rich it seemed to absorb the very essence of lost dreams.

Alexandria's eyes widened as she took in the stark contrast between the decayed outer structure and the newfound splendour within. Once crumbling and weathered, the walls now bore intricate patterns in vibrant hues. Whoever had created these colours had a hunting taste, as if they had glimpsed another world and brought its essence back with them.

Her gaze shifted back to the man leading her deeper into the building. He walked ahead, seemingly unaware of her presence. The thought of escape ran within her veins, a desperate choice. Her hands were tied in front of her, but perhaps her legs could still carry her to safety. She lunged at him, delivering a swift front snap kick to his shoulder. Yet her wounded leg betrayed her; the kick lacked power. He spun around, clearly unharmed.

Before she could react, his fist struck her face. Pain exploded in her head, and she staggered backwards. He closed the distance, gripping her shoulders, and slammed her against a wall. Her mind raced, but her bound hands rendered her powerless. All she could do was stare into his eyes, searching for any sign of mercy or weakness.

'Lower yer gaze, girl,' he growled, his voice a low rumble that echoed through the dimly lit corridor. He glared at her, a predator assessing its prey. 'Before ya regret ya ever came to this world!'

Alexandria's defiance flared. She squared her shoulders, refusing to bow to this stranger's intimidation. 'I'll never listen to you,' she hissed, her eyes piercing his. 'Now listen to me. You better let me go!'

The man's laughter erupted unexpectedly, a chilling contrast to the tension in the air. 'Ya get yer arrogance from yer father, don't ya?' he murmured; his touch was oddly gentle as his finger traced the curve of her hairline.

Alexandria's bewilderment deepened. 'You know my father?' she gasped in surprise.

His face softened, and he leaned towards her, his lips brushing her forehead. 'I'm sorry for the pain I've given ya,' he whispered, and for a moment, Alexandria glimpsed vulnerability in his eyes as his fingers clasped around her face.

Her gaze locked onto his face, and something shifted. The man's features blurred, and suddenly, she saw her mother's reflection overlaid upon his. The same eyes, the same curve of the jaw. Her heart started beating heavily. 'Your hair,' she murmured, reaching up to touch the strands of his brown locks. 'It's like my mother's. And your eyes...they remind me of her.'

The man's expression turned into a scowl. Letting go of her face, he wrenched her hands out of his hair and shouted, 'Don't bloody talk about your mother in front of me!' He grabbed her arms and, without another word, led her down the corridor, avoiding her gaze until they reached an elevator. 'Get inside,' he ordered, pushing her forward.

Alexandria complied, stepping into the elevator. The man pressed a button, and the lift ascended smoothly. He leaned against the polished metal wall, still gripping her wrists tightly. 'Speak,' she demanded. 'You know my father, don't you?' He sighed, avoiding her eyes. 'Why won't you speak to me, you piece of shit?' she shouted, frustration boiling over.

In a fluid and violent motion, his hand struck her cheek; the force of the slap sent shockwaves through her. The sting continued to linger, a painful reminder of vulnerability. 'Don't talk to me like that,' he smirked. 'Ya don't know who I am.'

'Then tell me?' Alexandria pleaded, tears glistening as they rolled down her cheeks.

His breath brushed her ear as he leaned closer. 'I'll let ma boss answer ya.'

'Who's your boss?' she pressed, desperation clawing at her.

'You'll be delighted once ya know who he is,' he laughed. 'But once ya do, I won't have the pleasure of slappin' ya anymore.' His voice dropped to a menacing whisper. 'And if ya tell him what I've done to ya, little princess, you'll suffer the same fate as your mother, this time, at ma hands.'

Fear and confusion battled within Alexandria. How did this man know about her mother's murder?

JOSEPH JETHRO

The lift halted abruptly, and the doors slid open, revealing another massive hallway; they walked down the hallway, which was lined with mahogany doors, each concealing secrets and whispered promises. The air grew heavier, laden with anticipation. The man paused before one of the doors and turned the key in the lock. The hinges groaned in protest as he forcefully pushed it open. He swiftly untied the rope binding Alexandria's hands and shoved her inside. The door slammed shut with an echoing click, the clatter reverberating throughout the room, sending a chill through her soul.

Alone in the room, Alexandria surveyed her surroundings. Jet-black silk drapes framed a window, through which she could see a view of the city skyline, and a royal red sofa stood in the middle of the room. She ran her fingers over the intricate patterns of the wallpaper, feeling a chill run down her spine.

The room itself pulsed with strange energy as if it existed on the borders of fiction, a place where nightmares took root and dreams withered. The air smelled of ancient secrets, and the walls seemed to whisper, their voices a mix of regret and longing.

Where had the man taken her? The question baffled her, leaving her feeling vulnerable and weak.

As the room enveloped her, Alexandria wondered if she'd stumbled into a dream or a nightmare. The man's words echoed: 'You're gonna like it.' But what lay beyond that locked door remained a haunting mystery.

Chapter 11

Alexandria darted across the room, desperate to escape. Her heart pounded in her chest as she scrambled onto the windowpane. She tugged at the window, but to her dismay, it was locked. Frustrated, she jumped back down and scanned the room desperately until her eyes landed on a glass vase standing proudly on a desk.

She sprinted towards the desk and snatched up the vase. 'This better work,' she whispered to herself. Holding the vase high above her head, she charged towards the window and hurled it with all her might.

The vase flew through the air and collided with the window, producing a deafening sound. Alexandria instinctively closed her eyes and shielded her face with her hands as shards of glass seemed to explode around her. When she dared to open her eyes again, she was met with a disheartening sight: the window remained intact, while the vase lay shattered on the floor, its remnants scattered beneath the window and all over the floor.

Panic surged through her as she looked around the room, desperate for any possible escape route. But her surroundings offered no solace. She was trapped. She marched up to the locked door and hammered her fist against it. 'You better let me out!' she screamed, but her plea was met with nothing but an infuriating silence.

Exhausted and defeated, Alexandria sank into the plush sofa, breathing heavily from the adrenaline-fueled escape attempt. Tears flowed down her cheeks like small streams. The dimly lit room seemed to close in on her, its walls whispering secrets of past horrors.

And then, the unmistakable noise of the door being unlocked filled the room. The door groaned open, revealing a middle-aged man clad in a black jumper. A hood concealed his features, casting ominous shadows across his face. Alexandria's heart raced; his presence sent shivers down her spine.

JOSEPH JETHRO

As he advanced towards her, he pushed the hood back, revealing a face both familiar and chilling: he was the same man from the helicopter scene. 'Didn't I tell you we'd meet again?' he laughed, looking straight at her; his eyes were cold and calculating. 'I bet you're confused and scared,' he said, his voice a low murmur. 'But there's no need to be,' a sly grin spread across his face.

'What do you want from me?' Alexandria demanded in a low tone.

His smile was unsettling. 'What do you think I want?' he said calmly.

'You wanna kill me,' she shouted, her anger flaring. 'That's what you wanna do!'

He leaned towards her, his eyes studying her. 'How sad. Why would I want to kill you?' he lifted her face, forcing her to meet his stormy gaze.

His words sent shivers down Alexandria's spine. 'Because you're an evil villain who enjoys bloodshed!'

His fingers traced her jawline, causing her to move her face out of his grasp; he laughed loudly and sat beside her. 'I do enjoy bloodshed,' he admitted, grabbing her hand and pulling her close to him. 'But why would I want to kill my own dear daughter?'

'What the hell are you talkin' about? I'm not your daughter,' she protested, yanking her hand out of his; she stumbled backwards, fear and anxiety overcoming her. 'You're not my dad!'

'Of course, I'm your dad,' he laughed, revealing a set of well-polished teeth, each one gleaming like a dagger in the moonlight. Wrapping his arms around her shoulders, he smiled. 'I've been waiting for this day for years.'

'You liar!' she shouted. She tried to break free from his firm hug, but he held her tightly as if she were an expensive jewel that he dared not let go of. 'Let me go!' she screamed. 'Or you're gonna regret it.' Her threat hung heavy in the air, but he merely chuckled and released her with a grin.

NEVER UNDERESTIMATE GIRLS!

Alexandria leapt from the sofa, and the man watched in gratification as she ran to the room's door and tried the handle. Her effort was useless; the door was locked. Fear clawed at her heart as the man's chilling laughter drifted through the room.

He rose, closing the gap between them. 'Andria,' he murmured. 'How do I know your name?'

'Get away from me!' she cried, her voice a desperate plea. 'And let me tell you, my name's not Andria!'

'You don't know your history then,' he laughed, his voice menacing. 'I, as your father, named you Andria Celeste the first night I saw your pretty little face. Then your mother, being the typical woman she was, named you Alex. That's how your name came to be Alexandria Celeste.'

Alexandria stared at the man, her mind spinning from his revelation. 'Nobody ever told me that,' she stuttered, her voice barely a whisper.

'Had your mother shown you your birth certificate, you would've known,' he sighed, threading his fingers through her hair. 'You remind me of her.'

Alexandria placed her hands softly on his shoulders. 'How can you be my dad?' she whispered, tears glistening in her eyes.

'Because I am,' he replied, kissing her forehead.

Alexandira blinked her tears away, moving her hands away from his shoulders and stepping back. She gazed into his icy blue eyes, and memories rushed back. He was the one whom the helicopter had lifted into the sky. He was the one she'd been hunting. How could he be her father? Nothing made any sense. 'No, you're not my dad,' she exhaled, shaking her head.

'I am, Andria,' he insisted, amusement dancing in his eyes. 'And I can prove it.'

Cobwebs of confusion entangled her thoughts. 'Prove it to me, then.'

'You like to kill,' he began, circling her like a predator. 'And so do I.'

'I don't like to kill,' she shot back, her defiance a fragile shield. 'I like to protect.'

'Ah, Andria,' he whispered, his voice dripping with mockery. 'That's what we both say. I kill to protect my father's legacy. But what do you kill for?'

Alexandria stood at the crossroads of her existence in the softly illuminated room. The air clung to her skin, heavy with the weight of her past. Confusion wrapped around her like a tattered shroud, her only companion in this desolate moment.

The man's words reverberated, sharp and unyielding. His voice, a jagged blade, seemed to slice through her brain, leaving her thoughts frayed and scattered. Why had she been killing? Was it simply amusement, or was there something more profound? The man's question lingered in the air, causing her to blurt out. 'To prove I'm worth more than just a girl, that's why I've been killing.' Hot tears blurred her vision, each drop a testament to the battles fought, the lives extinguished. But was that the real reason? Or was she forgetting something, a buried memory, a hidden motive?

The man who claimed to be her father watched, eyes like storm clouds as if he held the answers within their depths. 'There's no need to cry,' he murmured, his tone almost tender. His eyes, stormy indigo pools, gazed into hers. 'All the killings you've done, they don't matter. Even if half the men you've killed were my men.'

'Why doesn't it matter?' her voice trembled, her heart pounding furiously against her ribcage.

'Because you're my daughter,' he replied in a low voice. 'Both our hearts crave for more blood.' His statement lingered in the air.

Fury surged within Alexandria, a storm of emotions she could no longer contain. The revelation that this mysterious man might be her father was too much to bear. She refused to accept it, and her anger boiled over. She walked towards him, her footsteps deliberate.

NEVER UNDERESTIMATE GIRLS!

She grabbed his hair and then suddenly yanked his head forward and gripped him into a headlock. Without hesitation, she delivered three rapid punches to his face, each blow fuelled by her seething anger. The man seemed stunned by the ferocity of her attack, and his body froze in shock.

Alexandria's nails dug into his skin, her fingers curling like claws. She dragged her hands slowly across his face, leaving angry red welts in their wake. He swore loudly, the pain unbearable.

But he was no ordinary man. With a swift, skilful movement and immense power, he moved her arms from his neck and twisted them behind her back, forcing her to the floor with ease. 'Believe me, I'm your dad because if I weren't, then I would have broken every bone in your body for bloody punching me!' he shouted.

'Get off me, you jerk!' screeched Alexandria.

'Is that what you call your dad?' he asked, his grip on her arms tightening with each passing second.

'If you were my dad, then why did you kill my mum!' she shouted, tears streaming down her face, leaving glistering trails on her cheeks.

He let go of her abruptly, and she fell onto the soft carpet. 'Answer me,' she sobbed, her voice breaking.

He slowly walked towards the window and gazed out, his silhouette framed by the moon's light. 'You're a clever girl but not clever enough. Your research was all wrong,' he sighed, turning to face her. A fresh cut on his lip was bleeding, the crimson liquid trickling down his chin and dripping onto his neck, and the scratch marks Alexandria had left on his pale face stood out like bright pink blusher.

'My research was not wrong,' she spat, her eyes blazing with anger and defiance. 'You're the murderer, and I know it!'

'Andria, your mother's murderer is too cunning for your young brain. He leads people to dead ends,' he replied, walking towards her and extending his hand. She declined his offer and slowly stood up from the floor. 'Listen. I'm your dad, and nobody can change that, sweetheart,' he said, his voice softening.

'Sweetheart,' she scoffed. 'Why are you callin' me that?'

'Because you're my daughter,' he replied slowly, each word clinging to the air.

'How can you be my dad?' she murmured; the word 'dad' felt like another language on her tongue. A slight hope flickered in her heart, but she questioned herself whether this was what she truly wanted: a father who had shed blood.

He sighed, requesting her to sit. They shared the sofa, a strange sense of affection settling between them. His hand disappeared into his pocket, emerging with a polished handgun. The metallic metal gleamed, catching the dim light. 'Andria,' he whispered. 'Look at this.'

She glanced down at the gun, her reflection staring back at her. As she gazed at the weapon, it seemed to reflect not just her physical form but also the inner struggles and emotions she grappled with.

'What can you see?' he asked, his voice as soft as a feather.

'I can see myself,' she replied, her gaze unwavering.

'Now look at me,' his command was gentle. She raised her eyes to meet his. Their features aligned, sharp angles, haunting eyes. 'Compare our faces,' he urged. 'Our eyes. There's no difference.' He smiled, revealing teeth that were disturbingly sharp, almost vampiric, a chilling reminder of their shared lineage. Blood ties that were twisted and knotted bound them together.

Alexandria's gaze shifted to his jet-black hair, which fell over his forehead like a dark waterfall carrying untold stories. The strands seemed to hold secrets, memories, and perhaps regrets. She couldn't help but compare it to her own hair, a different shade, a different texture. 'Our hair's not the same,' she protested.

The man's voice softened as he acknowledged the difference. 'You get your hair from your mother,' he said. His tone held a mixture of nostalgia and warmth. 'Your mother was a lovely woman,' he continued. 'She could put a smile on my face, no matter what the situation.'

Leaning against the sofa, Alexandria crossed her hands behind her head and sighed deeply. The weight of her thoughts pressed upon her, and she closed her eyes, considering the possibilities. A cold yet comforting hand rested on her shoulder. 'You seem lost in thought,' the man murmured.

Alexandria opened her eyes and met his gaze. His smile was both familiar and enigmatic. He put his arm around her shoulders, drawing her closer. 'I love you, daughter,' he whispered.

'It doesn't make sense,' Alexandria confessed, her voice trembling.

'What doesn't make sense?' he asked, his expression unreadable.

'I saw you that day,' she said, tears welling up. 'You were tryna kill that girl in Eagle's Park. *You're Kenny.* I know it.'

The man sighed, leaning against her arm. 'I've done bad things in the past,' he admitted. 'But it's not too late. I can change that past and become a better man.'

'No one can change the past,' Alexandria replied, her tears slipping down her cheeks. 'Not even me.'

'You're a clever girl,' he said, his smile wistful. 'But not clever enough.'

'Tell me who you really are,' Alexandria insisted, her voice firm, determined to crack the case.

'Why shouldn't I tell you? You're my daughter,' he confessed. 'Well, I work for Kenny.'

'You what!' Alexandria gasped, her world tilting on its axis.

'I work for Kenny,' he repeated.

Alexandria stood up sharply and stared straight into his eyes. 'Why would you?'

'Andria,' the man said, smiling. 'I'm as tricky as he is. I only work for him for one reason.'

Alexandria's eyes narrowed. 'And what's the reason?' she demanded.

He stood up, his movements fluid. 'When I get the chance, I'm going to backstab the asswipe,' he whispered.

A small smile curved Alexandria's lips. 'You're so sly and cunning,' she murmured.

His laughter echoed like a dark melody. 'I knew you'd say that. Now listen,' he said, his gaze intense. 'Do you want to get revenge and finish off Kenny?'

'Of course, why wouldn't I?' she said, her voice filled with hope. 'Daddy, that's why I've been killing these murderers. To find him and get revenge.' Kenny was the reason for the blood she had shed.

His eyes held hers. 'So, you're finally calling me daddy,' he smiled. 'You're a good girl,' he said with a hint of pride. 'I know where Kenny is. And I'll be happy to help you kill him.' His words clung to Alexandria, a promise wrapped in shadows.

In that room, blood and secrets intertwined. Alexandria wondered if salvation could emerge from the depths of their shared secrets. Perhaps, just perhaps, their twisted hearts could find solace in the pursuit of justice. She joyfully threw her arms around him, resting her head on his shoulder. Finally, her wish had come true; she'd found her true father, and he'd vowed to aid her in her quest for vengeance.

But then, a question pierced her thoughts. 'Is your name Aron Avellino Issaba?' she asked.

He stared at her wide-eyed as if she'd just sworn at him, and then he abruptly laughed. 'No, no,' he said. 'My name's Wound Trystan Calon.'

'Wound Trystan Calon!' Alexandria exclaimed. 'Who named you that?'

'Well,' he smirked. 'My men call me that.'

'What's your actual name, then?' she pressed on.

NEVER UNDERESTIMATE GIRLS!

'That's a past I've long forgotten,' he replied, placing his silver pistol in her hand. 'Here, keep this. It'll remind you of our shared blood and dangerous secrets.'

The weight of the weapon settled into her palm, a symbol of their twisted alliance.

Chapter 12

The world lay fractured, like glass shards, slicing through Layla's and Stella's hearts. Before them, the dilapidated building stood, quiet and formidable, an enigma wrapped in broken bricks and fractured dreams. The jagged edges of reality cut through their flesh, leaving scars that pulsed with uncertainty.

Stella's gaze lingered on the structure, her mind racing. 'What are we supposed to do?' she wondered aloud.

'I ain't got a clue,' Layla confessed.

But then, suddenly, a spark of hope ignited in Stella's eyes. 'Wait a sec,' she said, narrowing her eyes as she thought over a plan. 'Alex had her earpiece on,' she said thoughtfully. 'We might be able to connect with her, right?'

'There's only one way to find out,' Layla beamed. She reached up and pressed the small earpiece nestled in her ear, feeling the slight click as it activated.

A soft beep confirmed the connection.

Within the building, Alexandria sat beside Wound. His arm was wrapped securely around her waist, pulling her close. His lips curved into a bittersweet smile, and his piercing blue eyes studied her intently as she leaned against his shoulder, lost in thought. The warmth of his embrace contrasted with the cold, pristine surroundings. 'You bear a remarkable resemblance to your mother,' he whispered gently, his voice filled with a mix of nostalgia and sorrow.

Alexandria twisted a lock of brown hair between her fingers and sighed. 'Who was that man that brought me here?' she asked. 'He told me his name was Levi, and honestly, he was really peculiar.'

Wound rested his hand on hers, his touch reassuring. 'He's my lackey. He's a bit of an odd one, but he's my best,' he smiled, intertwining his fingers with Alexandria's. 'You can point a cocked gun to his head, but he'll never betray me.'

NEVER UNDERESTIMATE GIRLS!

Alexandria glanced up at Wound's face. 'Is that so?' she murmured. Her earpiece abruptly let out a low beep. She paused, recognising the signal. 'Layla,' she breathed, her eyes widening. She'd forgotten all about her two little sisters; she had no idea where they were, she didn't even know if they were safe or not.

Wound gazed at her tense face, his eyebrows shooting up in confusion. 'Sweetheart, what's wrong?' he asked.

Ignoring his question, Alexandria moved away from him. *How could I have forgotten about them?* She thought to herself.

'Layla, can you hear me?' she asked, pressing her earpiece, her voice steady and clear.

'Loud and clear, sis,' Layla responded, a hint of relief in her voice. 'Where ya at?'

Wound stared at Alexandria in confusion as she stood up from the sofa, a smile creeping on her face. His gaze shifted to her ear, and he noticed for the first time the small, almost invisible device nestled in her ear. 'An earpiece,' he murmured to himself, now understanding why she seemed to be talking to thin air. 'Just like her mother,' he sighed.

'Listen, Layla, I don't know how to explain this to you,' Alexandria grinned, her excitement bubbling over. 'You won't believe what's happened,' she paused dramatically, savouring the moment. 'I've found my dad!'

'What?' Layla exclaimed, her eyes widening in shock. 'Did ya say what I think ya just said?'

'Yeah, I did!' Alexandria cried out, her voice filled with joy.

'I don't understand,' Layla stammered, her confusion evident.

Alexandria was about to say something when a sharp hiss caught her attention. She glanced up at Wound, whose eyes held an unnatural intensity. He gestured for her to sit by his side with a flick of his hand.

'Sis, explain to me what's goin' on,' Layla pressed on, her voice filled with urgency.

'Wait a sec,' Alexandria replied, removing her finger from her earpiece and sitting by her father's side. 'Daddy,' she whispered, her voice filled with concern as she realised the dramatic shift in his mood.

'Andria,' Wound murmured, his voice low and strained.

'Yes,' Alexandria replied softly.

'Who were you talking to?' he asked.

'I was speakin' to my stepsister, Layla,' Alexandria replied.

Wound combed his hair back with his fingers, a hint of amusement dancing in his eyes. 'Layla Joelime,' he mused, the name rolling off his tongue. Alexandria nodded her head. 'Do you know who her father is?' he asked.

'Of course, I know who her father is,' Alexandria replied, suddenly recalling the heated argument she and Jacob had earlier.

'Name him then,' Wound's order was sharp as a blade.

'Jacob,' Alexandria stammered, caught off guard.

'Full name,' Wound exhaled deeply, his patience running out.

'Jacob Joelime,' Alexandria said, the words barely leaving her lips before Wound let out a high-pitched laugh.

'Jacob Joelime,' he scoffed. 'He's the biggest fool in London. He thinks he can hide behind that name.'

'What are you tryna say?' Alexandria asked.

'Listen,' Wound whispered, leaning towards her.

'I'm listening,' Alexandria sighed, her heart pounding.

'That guy named Jacob Joelime,' Wound began, the name rolling around in his mouth before he spat it out. 'He's the one that snatched you away from me, so I will not permit you to intermingle with this so-called Joelime family.'

'But my stepsisters?' Alexandria stammered. 'They never did anything wrong, so can I...'

'No, I will not allow you to talk to or be with them,' Wound said, his voice firm yet gentle.

NEVER UNDERESTIMATE GIRLS!

Alexandria stared into Wound's eyes, her gaze questioning and stubborn. 'Listen, I won't break ties with them just because you want me to.'

'Then leave me, Andria,' Wound shouted sternly as he stood up.

Alexandria stared at him in bewilderment. 'I can't leave you,' she said, her voice breaking as tears welled up in her eyes.

Wound leaned against the wall, his posture casual yet commanding. 'Choose wisely, Andria. You've got two choices,' he said. 'Either you stay with me, or you go back and live with the...' he exhaled deeply, '...with the Joelime family.'

Meanwhile, after waiting for Alexandria to get back on to her for a few minutes, Layla leaned against her motorbike and sighed deeply, her eyes scanning the horizon.

'What's going on?' Stella asked curiously.

Layla shrugged her shoulders. 'I don't know. Alex was talkin' to me just a second ago. And ya know what, she sounded pretty happy.'

'She sounded happy?' Stella repeated, her curiosity overwhelming her.

'Yeah,' Layla confirmed. 'Oh, she's getting' back in touch,' she said as her earpiece released a low beep. She pressed the earpiece, and Alexandria's voice reached her ears, low and gentle.

'I'm sorry, Layla, but...' her voice trailed off.

'Alex, what's up?' Layla asked, concern creeping into her voice.

'I won't be able to talk to you anymore,' Alexandria replied, her voice barely above a whisper.

'Why not, sis? What's goin' on?' Layla's curiosity was evident as she pleaded for answers.

'My dad won't allow it,' Alexandria's response ignited a spark of fury within Layla, and she couldn't hold her anger back.

'Yer dad won't allow it,' she shouted. 'He's got nothin' to do with our sisterhood! First day ya meet him, and is this the kind of advice he gives ya? I mean, how do ya even know he's yer dad? I thought I was the naïve one!'

'Layla, I know he's my dad, and you don't need to worry about that,' Alexandria sighed, trying to stay calm.

'Well, if he's tellin' ya to break up with us, then go tell him to piss off!' shouted Layla, her voice trembling with rage.

'Don't talk like that, Layla. Do you understand me?' Alexandria retorted sharply. 'Would you like it if I said that about your dad?'

'No, I wouldn't, but don't compare ma dad with yer so-called dad. There's a big difference!' Layla replied.

'No, there isn't,' Alexandria shouted, her frustration spilling forth. 'I mean, yes, there is. My dad's reasonable, and your dad,' she scoffed. 'He's a piece of rotten manure!' Her words were like blunt daggers, stabbing Layla in the heart.

'You're such a...' Layla's words trailed off. 'If you weren't ma big sister, I would have sworn at ya really badly!' she shouted.

Stella, who had been assessing the situation, decided to speak up. 'Layla, explain to me what's...' Layla raised a hand, silencing her.

'Layla, you're a jerk!' Alexandria shouted, her voice filled with anger.

'And so are ya,' Layla replied in a sharp tone.

'Then get lost, and don't ever show your face to me again!' Alexandria shouted.

'Sure!' Layla shouted back. 'Ya won't be seein' ma face again!'

Stella watched as Layla ripped the earpiece off and flung it in the air, frustration and desperation running through her veins.

'Layla,' Stella demanded. 'What was that about?'

Tears welled in Layla's eyes as she met Stella's gaze. 'Sis, hop on the motorbike,' she insisted. 'We've got to dash. Right now!'

'But Alex...' Stella protested.

NEVER UNDERESTIMATE GIRLS!

'Forget the idiot!' Layla's anger surged. 'She claimed she'd found her real dad. She's disowned us for him!' She leapt onto the waiting motorbike. 'Come on, get on! We need to get out of here.'

Still grappling with the sudden change of events, Stella jumped onto the motorbike and clung to Layla's shoulders as they sped out of the alley and through the bustling city, wind whipping their faces.

'Layla,' she implored. 'What are you talkin' about? Alex would never say such a thing. Besides, she doesn't even know who her real dad is.'

'Just don't talk about that jerk,' Layla snapped. 'I don't wanna know her anymore.'

And so, they rode further away from Alexandria, a sisterhood fractured, secrets tearing them apart. The thunderous roar of the motorbike swallowed Layla's sorrow, and Stella wondered if they were hurtling towards salvation or deeper into the dark abyss. 'So, what are we gonna do?' she whispered.

Layla's eyes remained fixed on the road ahead. 'Get yer phone out and ring Uncle Michael,' she replied.

Stella fumbled in her pockets, panic rising. Her fingers brushed against fabric, but her phone was nowhere to be found. 'I don't know where my phone's gone!' she gasped.

'What does that mean? A phone can't just run off, ya know!' Layla exclaimed.

'Seriously, I don't know where it's gone,' Stella stammered. 'Why don't you ring Uncle from your phone?'

'If I had ma phone, then maybe I would have, ya dope!' Layla shouted.

'Hey, don't take your temper out on me. It wasn't my fault you thought it was a good idea to send your phone crashin' into that guy's car window,' Stella shot back.

'Shut up!' Layla's retort was sharp, punctuated by the sudden roar of an engine.

JOSEPH JETHRO

A Maybach S-Class swerved out of a side street, speeding towards them. Layla's reflexes kicked in; she veered her Kawasaki out of the way just in time, the wind tugging at her jean jacket. 'Ya've got such a posh car, and ya can't even drive, ya idiot!' she yelled.

The car's window rolled down, revealing a young man with a cocky smirk playing on his lips. 'Take your anger out on somebody else, you arrogant girl!' he shot back, revving the car's engine before tearing down the road.

Layla clenched her jaw. 'Oh, he's had it now.' She revved her motorbike's engine, determination flashing in her eyes. Without hesitation, she chased the fleeing car, adrenaline pumping through her veins.

'Layla, what are you doin'!' Stella's scream was lost in the wind as she clung to Layla's shoulders.

'Havin' some fun, that's what I'm doin',' Layla's smile was both reckless and defiant.

'You're havin' fun whilst Alex's in danger,' Stella yelled, her voice breaking.

Layla sighed, increasing her speed. 'I said, don't talk about that backstabber. I bloody hate her!'

'Come on, Layla. Pull yourself together,' Stella's tears flowed freely. 'We've got to find Uncle and inform him about everythin' that's happened. Then he can help us get Alex back. God knows what's happenin' to her!'

'Stop bein' a big baby,' Layla's voice turned stern and unyielding. 'She said she'd found her real dad and didn't wanna know us anymore.'

'How do you know someone might have just forced her to say that,' Stella sobbed, desperation in her eyes.

'Just stop bein' weird,' Layla said, turning the motorbike sharply. A deserted street stretched out before her. The car she had been following had vanished, leaving only the faint hum of its engine in the air. 'Hey, where did that car go?' she asked, slowing her speed down.

NEVER UNDERESTIMATE GIRLS!

Stella's sobs intensified, 'Forget about that car, please. Just think about Alex!'

'Oh, yeah, I'll forget about that car,' Layla laughed, her tone sharp, bitterness evident in every word. 'And I'll think about speed!' She twisted the throttle, and the bike surged forward with a burst of sudden speed. The wind whipped through her blonde hair, cooling her mind, but Stella's panic wouldn't be silenced.

'Layla, do you wanna die? What are you doin'? Why are you actin' so horrid? Don't you care?' she shouted, her words a desperate plea.

And then, unexpectedly, Layla burst into tears. 'I know I'm actin' horrible,' she whispered, wiping her eyes. 'But listen, Stella, I really do care. It's just...I can't get over what Alex said to me.'

Stella leaned her head against Layla's shoulder, tears streaming down her face. 'Then come on,' she said in a determined voice. 'Let's crack the case.'

The empty street stretched out before them, silent and eerie. Its cracked asphalt was bathed in the moon's light. Abandoned buildings lined both sides, their windows boarded up, and the graffiti-covered walls told stories of a forgotten past. The air hung heavy with silence, broken only by the distant hum of traffic from a nearby highway. Weeds pushed through the gaps in the pavement, their green tendrils reaching for the sky as if seeking escape from this desolate place. A lone streetlamp stood at the edge of the pavement, its flickering bulb casting eerie shadows on the ground. The wind whispered secrets, carrying dust and memories along the empty road. 'I'm with ya,' Layla whispered. 'We'll bring Alex back.'

Chapter 13

As they sped down the empty street, a polished Aston Martin DB11 raced past them, its sleek silver body shining in the moonlight. The car moved with a predator's grace, its powerful engine growling as it sliced through the wind. Layla watched in awe as the luxury sports car swerved in front of her motorbike, leaving a trail of dust in its wake.

The thunderous song pouring out of the DB11's highly tinted windows vibrated the air around them. It was as if the car itself had a heartbeat, pulsing with energy. Layla's eyes widened, and she couldn't help but admire the machine's sheer elegance. 'Wow,' she breathed, her voice barely audible. 'Now that's one bad boy car!'

Stella, more cautious, leaned closer to Layla. 'We should slow down, Layla,' she whispered. 'This car looks a bit erratic.' She watched as the DB11 swerved right and then left, its movements unpredictable. 'I think the driver must be stoned or somethin'.'

Suddenly, the posh car abruptly came to a stop. Layla shrieked, slamming the brakes on, but it was too late. The motorbike crashed straight into the DB11's bumper. Layla was flung forward, landing painfully on the asphalt. Her knees and elbows scraped against the rough surface, and her breath got caught in her chest.

Stella, too, was jolted. Her ankle twisted painfully as she was thrown from the motorbike. She hit the asphalt with a thud. The world blurred; she saw bits of sky, asphalt, and shining paint.

Layla couldn't understand what had just happened; she was baffled for a while. She took three deep breaths to steady herself, then staggered to her feet, adrenaline surging. Her concern was for Stella. She rushed to her sister's side, ignoring the ache in her own body. 'Stella!' she called. 'Are ya alright?'

Stella winced, clutching her throbbing ankle. 'I think I've twisted it,' she stammered, her face turning pale. 'But besides that, I think I'm ok.'

NEVER UNDERESTIMATE GIRLS!

As Layla helped Stella sit up, the polished silver door of the DB11 swung open, revealing a teenage boy. He appeared well below the legal age for holding a driver's license. His urgency was palpable as he ran towards the girls. His ash brown hair danced in the wind, strands clinging to his forehead. His eyes, a cool shade of grey, reflected the moon's glow, a hint of mystery and sympathy in their depths.

'Blimey, mates!' he exclaimed, breathless. 'Ma apologies. Ya alright?' His gaze locked onto Stella's soft hazel-grey eyes, and a shy smile spread across his face. He extended his hand, offering assistance. 'Ya need any help?'

Stella hesitated, caught off guard by his unexpected kindness. Her shyness surfaced as she stood up. 'No thanks,' she replied, her voice barely audible. Her ankle throbbed, but she didn't want to trouble this stranger.

Layla, however, was less forgiving. She stared at the teenager, her eyes narrowing. 'What type of maniac are ya?' she blurted out, her frustration evident.

Stella interjected, her voice gentle but firm. 'Layla, no need to be rude. I think he just hit the brake accidentally.'

Layla turned towards Stella, shock etching her features. 'Are ya takin' his side?' she snapped, her voice edged with irritation.

Stella's face flushed, embarrassment mingling with pain. 'No,' she stammered. 'I'm just sayin' that you don't need to call him names.'

'Yer actin' like he's yer brother or somethin',' Layla yelled.

The teenager shifted uncomfortably, his eyes flickering between Stella and Layla. 'Well, ya don't know what dark secrets linger out here in these twisted, dirty streets,' he sighed. He stood opposite Stella, and the moon bathed them in another worldly glow, casting shadows that seemed to dance around their intertwined destinies. Stella's hazel-grey eyes held a hint of timidity, while the boy's cool grey gaze reflected a past long forgotten.

Layla's gaze darted between them, and then she froze. Her eyes widened as she noticed the uncanny resemblance; they both wore the same shy smile - the kind that hid more than it revealed. Layla stared at them, her bewilderment growing as the wind blew through their tight ringlets of ash-grey hair. They were like mirror images, separated only by the colour of their eyes.

And then it happened, the moment that shifted everything. The teenager's face turned pale as he locked eyes with Stella. His smile faded, and his lips tightened. Stella felt his uneasiness and stepped towards him, her curiosity overcoming her. 'Is there somethin' wrong?' she asked, her smile fading.

His eyes were filled with worry and urgency. 'Go, go right now,' he pleaded.

But she didn't retreat. Instead, she grabbed his hand, seeking answers. The connection felt electric, like a shared secret waiting to be unveiled. 'What's wrong?' she asked again.

'Stella, ya need to get out of here!' his eyes dashed around as if expecting danger to suddenly leap out of the darkness.

'What! How the heck do ya know her name?' Layla exclaimed, pulling Stella away from him, her protective instincts kicking in.

However, before he could explain further, a sharp voice sliced through the tension. 'Oi, Lucky, what's all the chattin' about?'

Layla and Stella turned around to see a black motorbike gliding to a stop nearby, its engine purring like a happy cat. Two men were perched on top of it, their features mirroring Lucky's, indicating they were his relatives.

'Yer name's Lucky,' Layla scoffed, her anger still simmering. 'Such a fascinating name,' she said sarcastically.

The man who had been riding the motorbike jumped off and did a challenging walk towards Layla.

'Listen, Cas,' Lucky, the teenage boy, stuttered, standing in front of Stella and pulling Layla back. 'I think we've got the wrong girls.'

NEVER UNDERESTIMATE GIRLS!

Cas smirked and grabbed the collar of Layla's jean jacket. 'Tell me yer name, girl,' he smirked, his grey eyes piercing hers.

Layla tried to push him away, but his grip remained firm. 'Why do ya wanna know ma name?' she screamed.

'Tell me right now,' Cas demanded, banging her into the lamppost and spitting on her face. 'Are ya deaf? Answer me!'

Stella couldn't stand it any longer. Pushing past Lucky, she ran towards Cas and delivered a fast roundhouse kick to his back. 'Let my sister go, you beast!' she yelled. But then someone grabbed her by the arm.

Lucky's heart pounded, and he lunged forward, but fear held him back. He could feel Stella's pain running through him as he saw her get flung to the ground.

'Good job, Sash,' Cas complemented, referring to the man who had attacked Stella. 'You deal with her while I try to get this one to talk.'

Sash's weight bore down on Stella, his legs hooking around hers. Lucky felt the pressure, the constriction around his own chest as if he were the one pinned to the ground. 'What's yer bloody name?' Sash's voice dripped with malice.

'I don't think you wanna know,' Stella replied defiantly.

Sash brought his fist close to her face. 'Tell me yer name right now,' he growled.

'My name's *Hushfire*!' Stella shouted. She elbowed him in the ribs, and he yelped loudly out of surprise. Bridging her back, she rolled to the side and kneed him in the face, causing him to let go of her.

'Ya know yer really stubborn,' Cas hissed, tightening his grip on Layla's trembling shoulders. 'And ya know what I do with stubborn girls?' he smirked, his hand vanishing into his coat pocket.

Stella staggered to her feet and ran behind Cas, grabbing his shoulders and putting pressure on his collarbone; she kneed him in the back, causing his grip on Layla to loosen.

Layla took this as an opportunity and kicked him straight in the stomach.

Sash got off the ground and charged at Stella, a malevolent force hurtling towards her. Lucky's instincts kicked in; he couldn't let Stella suffer alone. Lunging at Sash, he grabbed his arm and yanked him backwards. 'What the hell do ya think yer doin', Lucky?' Sash scolded.

'Look, I think we've got the wrong girls, Sash,' Lucky replied calmly, but the truth hung heavy on his heart.

'Well, ya bloody idiot, if we've got the wrong girls, then that gives us permission to do what we feel like,' Sash smirked. 'And the first thing I'm goin' to do is break that girl's bones.'

Lucky felt the threat like a blade against his skin. Sash yanked his arm out of Lucky's grasp and ran behind Stella, who managed to give him a back-kick in the chest. He staggered backwards, minimising the force of the impact.

And then the world tilted; Sash's fist collided with Stella's face, followed by a powerful spinning hook kick that connected with her head.

Stars exploded in front of Stella's eyes, and she collapsed onto the pavement, blood trickling down the side of her face.

Lucky gasped and ran towards her. He grabbed her hand and whispered urgently, 'Get up!'

Layla was still in the fight; her fist sliced through the air, aiming for Cas. But he was no easy opponent. Swiftly, he sidestepped, crossing his forearms vertically across his forehead and chin. Layla's punch connected with his arm, but before she could react, he seized her arm, throwing her off balance. With a firm grip, he pivoted, pulling her towards himself. With surprising strength, he lifted her and threw her onto the ground. The impact reverberated through the air, leaving Layla momentarily stunned.

NEVER UNDERESTIMATE GIRLS!

Lucky's anger surged, a storm of emotions churning within him. 'Boss told us to bring the girl in one piece to him, not get into a fight,' he shouted, fists clenched.

'Well, it wasn't us who started the fight, and besides, our dad - yer boss - never told us that we had to deal with her kindly,' Sash smirked; his father had never taught him kindness. Instead, he'd taught him to survive the streets by using extreme violence.

Cas knelt next to Layla, his voice a venomous whisper. 'So, yer name's Alexandria, ain't it?' he taunted.

Layla choked up blood, tears filling her eyes. 'Why the heck do ya want her!' she shouted.

Cas's response was swift and brutal. He punched her in the nose. 'Don't bloody talk to me like that.' He pulled a knife out of his pocket and placed its cold blade on her arm.

But then Lucky intervened. His grip on Cas's shoulders was iron-strong. 'That's enough!' he roared, desperation etching lines on his face. But Cas was unyielding. He spun around, slashing Lucky across the cheek with the knife. Blood welled up, staining Lucky's skin crimson. He staggered backwards, dazed and disoriented.

'I hope yer not feelin' pity for these lasses,' Cas spat, punching Lucky in the lip; he fell on the road, blood dripping from his face.

Stella, still recovering from the kick, watched in horror. Her gaze locked onto Lucky's face, blood dripping from the deep wound on his cheek. Instinctively, she reached out, fingers trembling, desperate to bridge the gap between them. But he was too far away, and the world blurred as darkness threatened to swallow her whole. At that moment, Stella felt Lucky's pain as if it were her own, a raw ache that mirrored the violence around them.

Sash's laughter echoed, a cruel sound of betrayal. He kicked Lucky's side, the impact jolting his ribs. 'I always knew ya would turn yer back on us, Lucanus,' he sneered, using Lucky's real name, the name that carried memories of a broken past.

Lucky's world spun as he rolled away, clutching his face. The pain was a relentless beast, gnawing at his insides, and tears blurred his vision. Stella, desperate to reach him, crawled forward, but Cas interposed. His grip on her arm was sturdy as he pulled her back bitterly.

Sash's taunts continued. 'Oh look, Mr Unlucky is crying like a little baby,' he jeered, sending a powerful kick to Lucky's stomach. He then strode up to Cas with a smirk spread across his face. 'So, bro, what are we gonna do with these girls if they ain't the right ones?'

'Well, they should know where Alexandria is because I saw them leave the house with her,' Cas said, turning to Stella. 'Listen, girl, tell me where yer big sister is.'

Stella looked up at him, tears glistening in her eyes. 'She's lost in dark secrets,' she stammered.

'Stop talkin' indirectly and tell me where she is!' Cas shouted, advancing towards her, the knife in his hand glimmering.

Suddenly, the noise of a car's engine revving sliced through the thick tension. Lucky, who had been sprawled on the ground moments ago, now sat defiantly in his sleek Aston Martin DB11. His bloodied face mirrored unwavering determination. The polished vehicle surged backwards, its tyres screeching against the tarmac.

'Get out of the way,' Sash yelled, pulling Cas by the arm. Their eyes were wide with terror as the car hurtled towards them.

Layla, ever resourceful, reacted swiftly. She seized Stella, her grip unyielding, and flung her onto the hard, unforgiving pavement. Stella gasped, pain radiating through her body, but Layla's actions had saved her from the impending collision.

Meanwhile, Lucky's resolve solidified. He drove straight at Cas and Sash. They ran, their breaths ragged, their fear transforming them into mice fleeing from a relentless cat. Lucky cornered them, his car trapping them against a brick wall.

NEVER UNDERESTIMATE GIRLS!

With a swift leap, he abandoned the safety of the car. His trainers hit the ground, and pain shot through his legs, but adrenaline surged through his veins, urging him forward. He sprinted, though each step sent a jolt of agony through his battered body. The distance between himself and the girls closed rapidly. 'Get out of here!' he cried, his voice raw with urgency and pain. He grabbed Stella by the arm, wincing as he guided her towards Layla's motorbike, which lay on its side.

Layla followed suit, her movements fluid and determined. She bent down, her fingers curling around the handles of the motorbike. With a slight groan, she lifted it upright, her muscles straining momentarily. Relief washed over her as she inspected the bike, realising it had survived the collision with Lucky's car with minimal damage. It was still rideable. Without wasting a moment, she swiftly mounted it.

Stella quickly climbed on behind Layla, her arms wrapping tightly around her waist. Her eyes bore into Lucky's, filled with fear and concern. 'What about you?' she asked, her voice trembling.

'Just get out of here. I'll be fine,' Lucky assured her, but the dread etched on his face betrayed his bravado. He was aware of the impending danger. Sash and Cas wouldn't be inclined to treat him kindly after he had assisted their quarry in escaping.

But Stella wouldn't leave him. Tears slipped from her eyes, and she shook her head. 'I'm not leavin' you,' she declared.

Lucky glanced over his shoulder and saw Cas and Sash running towards them. He had to make a split-second decision. Grabbing Layla's arm, he leaned towards her ear. 'Go,' he whispered urgently. 'Keep Stella safe!'

Layla nodded, determination and confusion in her eyes. She started the motorbike, the engine roaring to life. Stella's cry of disapproval echoed through the air as they sped away, leaving Lucky behind. His heart pounded, torn between compassion and fear. But he stood his ground, watching them disappear into the night.

'Why did you leave him?' Stella sobbed. She turned back, her eyes locking onto Lucky's fearful expression.

Layla tried to reassure her. 'Look, Stella, he's goin' to be fine,' she said, her voice trembling.

But as they reached the top of the street, the air thickened with tension. A sudden, dreadful noise of a gunshot pierced the silence, and Lucky's agonising shriek followed. Stella gasped, feeling the impact of the bullet as if it had torn through her own body, its metallic edge slicing into her soul. The pain surged, intertwining with her memories, forgotten moments, shared laughter, and whispered secrets. The agony intensified, and darkness enveloped her. She collapsed, tumbling off the motorbike. Layla hit the brakes in panic. 'Stella!' she gasped, her voice filled with fear as she leapt off the bike.

Stella clutched her hip, her face twisted in pain. 'I've been shot!' she cried out.

Layla knelt beside her, her touch gentle yet firm. 'Stella,' she whispered. 'Ya haven't been shot. Yer just imaginin' things.' She pressed her hand against Stella's hip, searching for any sign of injury. 'Look, there's no blood,' she said.

Stella's eyes fluttered open, tears streaming down her cheeks. The pain still pulsed through her, inexplicably tied to Lucky's suffering. 'Why does my body share Lucky's pain?' she asked, her voice raw with emotion.

Layla's grip tightened on Stella's hand. 'There's somethin' deeper at play here,' she murmured. 'Somethin' beyond what our eyes can see.' As she helped Stella back onto the motorbike, Cas's bike suddenly appeared behind them.

Layla straddled her motorbike, fingers wrapping around the cool handlebars. The engine roared to life beneath her. She tightened her grip, ready for what lay ahead. She twisted the throttle with a determined glance over her shoulder, and they shot forward, the wind whipping through her hair. Cas's bike trailed closely behind, a shadow

NEVER UNDERESTIMATE GIRLS!

in pursuit. The road stretched out before her, a ribbon of asphalt that promised both freedom and danger.

Layla's heart pounded as they approached a sharp turn onto the main road. She leaned into the curve, body shifting with the precision of a seasoned rider. The tyres gripped the road, and adrenaline surged through her veins. And then, like a beacon of salvation, it appeared: a police car, its blue and red lights flashing, a lifeline in the chaos. Relief washed over Layla. She twisted the throttle, urging her motorbike faster.

Cas, sensing the danger, veered sharply into a side street, disappearing from sight.

Layla's focus remained on the police car ahead. She wove through traffic, the siren's wail echoing in her ears. The motorbike hummed beneath her, the vibrations resonating through her bones. The world blurred as she lined up with the police car, uncertainty and hope running within her. As she gazed through the police car's side window, she didn't know whether to smile or cry.

Michael sat in the passenger seat, his face etched with stress and worry. His eyes darted around, scanning the surroundings. As soon as he caught sight of Layla, a small, weary smile spread across his face. He leaned forward, his voice urgent. 'Officer Luca, park over,' he ordered, and the police car obediently pulled to the side.

Layla parked her motorbike behind the car, the engine's growl fading into silence. Stella, perched on the back, leaned towards her. 'Don't tell anybody about Lucky,' she whispered, her eyes wide with fear.

Layla frowned. 'Why not?' she asked.

'He got shot because of me,' Stella confessed, her voice barely audible. The weight of guilt hung heavy in the air.

Layla nodded slowly, absorbing the truth. She swung her legs over the motorbike and stepped onto the pavement. Her heart raced as she ran to the side of the police car. The door flew open, and before Michael could step out, she threw her arms around him. 'Uncle,' she sobbed, fear and desperation in her voice.

'Layla, we've been lookin' for you non-stop,' he whispered. Tears of relief and joy glistened in his eyes. 'I thought I'd never see ya again.'

'Uncle, ya won't guess what we've been through,' Layla continued, her gaze locking with his. The memories of their desperate escape flooded her mind: the mysterious teenager, the ruthless fight, and the fear that had coiled around their hearts.

Michael's attention shifted to Stella, who remained on the motorbike. 'Where's Alex?' he asked, his voice trembling with fear.

Layla's sobs intensified. 'Uncle,' she choked out. 'She said she'd found her dad and that she's not coming back.'

Michael stared at Layla, his disbelief palpable. 'Layla, you're lying, ain't ya?' he asked.

'Uncle, she's not lying,' Stella interjected, walking towards them. Her face bore the marks of their harrowing journey: bruises, scratches, blood and a raw determination.

'Stella!' Michael gasped, running towards her. His arms enveloped her, and she buried her head into his shoulder. Her tears seeped through his T-shirt, wetting his skin.

'Uncle,' she whispered. 'We need to get Alex back.'

The weight of their shared determination settled upon them, a fragile hope in a world that had tested their bonds to the limit. Layla's tear-streaked face bore the marks of pain, but her resolve remained unwavering. The path ahead would be treacherous, filled with uncertainty and hidden dangers, but she clung to the belief that they would find Alexandria no matter the cost.

'We'll bring her back,' Micheal vowed, his voice carrying the weight of a thousand promises.

Stella, bruised and battered, stepped backwards. Her gaze met Layla's, and in that shared look, they reaffirmed their purpose to bring Alexandria back home.

Chapter 14

One month later

Alexandria stepped into a narrow alleyway, the cobblestone worn smooth by centuries of footsteps. The air was thick with the scent of dampness and decay, and the flickering light bulbs of old lampposts cast eerie shadows on the brick walls. She pulled her coat tighter around herself, the fabric offering little protection against the chill that seeped into her bones. The alley twisted and turned, its walls closing in on her. Each step echoed, bouncing off the ancient stones.

Suddenly, a strange noise resounded from behind her. She glanced over her shoulder, half-expecting to see someone, a stranger, perhaps, or a shadowy figure, but the alley remained empty.

Yet, the feeling persisted, a prickling at the nape of her neck, a sense of being watched. She quickened her pace, her footsteps now urgent, the darkness swallowing her. She could almost hear the whispers of unseen souls, the rustle of unseen fabric.

Was it her imagination? She wondered. Or was there indeed something following her?

As she tripped over a loose rock, grabbing the rough brick wall in order to avoid falling, she heard the unmistakable sound of someone laughing.

The laughter sent shivers down her spine, and she dared not look back. The alley stretched ahead, seemingly endless, and she pushed herself forward, her breaths shallow and ragged.

And then, as she rounded a corner, she glimpsed a fleeting shadow, darker than the surrounding darkness; it vanished into a side alleyway, leaving a trail of fear in its wake. Alexandria's pulse pounded in her temples, and she forced herself to keep moving.

What was it? A ghost? A creature of the night? Or perhaps something more insidious.

JOSEPH JETHRO

The alleyway seemed to twist upon itself, leading her deeper into its heart. The walls pressed in, and she could no longer see the moon. Her footsteps echoed, but now they were joined by another sound, a soft, rhythmic breathing just behind her.

Alexandria didn't dare turn around. She couldn't. Instead, she pressed forward, her mind racing. She had to find the end of this cursed alley. But with each step, the presence drew closer. Panic clawed at her.

'Who's there?' she shouted with desperation, her voice lost in the oppressive darkness.

No answer came, and then a chilling laugh filled the air. She stopped walking and inhaled deeply. Then she finally turned around, and that's when she saw him, Wound, her father, leaning against the brick wall, a cigarette dangling from his lips.

But why was he here? Why was he following her?

'Daddy, what are you doin' here?' she asked. But Wound didn't move, didn't acknowledge her. He stood there, shrouded in shadows, his presence both familiar and unsettling.

Alexandria took a step closer, her curiosity pulling her towards him. She adored his eyes, which seemed to hold secrets and fatherly love. As she walked towards him, his lips curved into a half-smile as if he knew something she didn't.

'Why?' she whispered. 'Why are you followin' me?'

He tilted his head, studying her. His eyes held a depth she couldn't fathom, a sadness, a longing. With a swift movement, he turned his back on her and started to walk down the alleyway, shadows clinging to him.

Alexandria followed. 'Daddy, what are you doing?' she asked in confusion, but he continued walking without acknowledging her. She trailed behind, watching his every footstep. His mysterious movements intrigued her; his feet barely touched the ground, yet he moved swiftly. Alexandria continued to follow as he turned a corner, only to find him gone. Panic gripped her heart. How had he vanished so quickly?

NEVER UNDERESTIMATE GIRLS!

As Alexandria walked down the dimly lit alleyway, a shiver crawled up her spine. She glanced over her shoulder, convinced she heard faint footsteps behind her. But there was nothing, just the empty darkness. Despair threatened to consume her, and then, suddenly, a woman materialised before her.

Her eyes were a mesmerising shade of haunting blue, like the depths of an ancient ocean. They held an unsettling intensity, a gaze that pierced through Alexandria and whispered secrets of forgotten memories. The woman wore a flowing black cloak that seemed to absorb the feeble light, making her appear otherworldly.

'Alexandria,' the woman's voice was soft, yet it echoed through the alley. 'You've been chosen, but will you let the evil demons thrive off your blood, or will you stop them?'

Alexandria's heart raced. Who was this mysterious stranger? And what did she mean by 'chosen'? Fear ran within her veins, but something told her that running away was no longer an option. She took a tentative step towards the woman, her breath catching in her throat.

The woman was shrouded in an eerie aura. Her pale face, like marble touched by moonlight, bore an ethereal beauty that defied mortal norms. The cloak she wore was as black as midnight, its fabric clinging to her form like a second skin. It billowed around her feet, a living darkness that seemed to defy the moon's glow.

'Who are you?' Alexandria asked, her voice barely audible.

The woman responded with a cryptic smile. Her lips held centuries of knowledge; they spoke of ancient bargains and hidden truths. 'They call me Remona Death,' she said. 'I come to the evil hearts and warn them before it's too late.' She then turned away, her cloak trailing behind her as she glided down the dimly lit alley. Her footsteps were soundless, as if she floated inches above the ground. Her brown, wavy hair flowed down her back like a waterfall.

Alexandria followed, drawn by a magnetic force that pulled her towards this enigmatic figure. 'What do you want from me?' she asked, her left hand brushing against the cool metal of her gun concealed beneath her coat. The weapon felt insignificant against the weight of Remona's gaze, yet she kept her hand clenched on its handle.

'I've come to warn you, Alexandria,' Remona's haunting voice filled the air, a melody of sorrow and foreboding. 'Life is taking a deadly turn, and you must choose the right path.'

'How do you know my name?' Alexandria pressed.

'I've been lurking in these alleys for twenty years,' Remona murmured. 'Why wouldn't I know your name?'

'Who exactly are you?' Alexandria asked, her curiosity spilling forth. She slowly slipped her right hand into the woman's; their fingers entwined, and for an enigmatic moment, a strange sense of unity filled the air.

Remona laughed, a sound that carried both sadness and longing, 'I'm a shadow who seeks justice.'

Alexandria's resolve hardened. 'I've been a shadow for many years, too,' she declared. 'But now my dream is gonna come true. I'm finally gonna get revenge on Kenny!'

Remona sighed, releasing Alexandria's hand. Her footsteps quickened, steady and purposeful. 'That's why I've come to you,' she whispered. 'To warn you.'

Alexandria's fingers tightened around her gun. 'What do you mean?' she demanded, her eyes narrowing.

'The truth about your father,' Remona whispered. 'He's using you, Alexandria. Don't fall into his trap.'

Anger flared within Alexandria. 'My father is not using me!' she retorted sharply.

'Well, that's what you think, but let me tell you,' Remona continued, undeterred. 'He's manipulating you to kill Liam. He's jealous of his wealth. And after he's used you, he'll please the demon by offering what she desires, by taking what rightfully belongs to you!'

'Don't chat rubbish. You don't know what you're talkin' about,' Alexandria shouted, 'and don't think you're gonna stop me from killing Kenny. Too many people have tried to stop me, and I'm sick of it!'

'My dear, that's where you're going wrong. Kenny must be dealt with, but Liam, he's an innocent soul,' Remona replied.

'Kenny is using the name Liam to hide his true identity,' Alexandria scoffed.

Remona's eyes bore into Alexandria's, ancient and knowing. 'Your father, the evil monster, seeks something from you,' she murmured, her voice carrying secrets.

In a surge of fury, Alexandria retrieved her gun, its cold metal a chilling reminder of death. 'Don't call my father an evil monster!' she shouted, pulling the trigger of the gun.

Remona deftly sidestepped, but the bullet grazed her shin, and she collapsed, a painful scream escaping her lips.

Alexandria watched in satisfaction as Remona clutched the wound, blood staining her fingers, but then a voice echoed within her, accusing her: What have you done? You were never meant to spill innocent blood!

Guilt gnawed at Alexandria's insides, and she knelt beside Remona. 'I'm sorry,' she whispered.

Remona laughed softly, her blue eyes glossy from unshed tears. 'No need for apologies,' she said, raising to her feet, wincing slightly at the dull ache that shot through her wounded leg. 'You've merely scratched the surface of my existence, my dear sister.'

'Why are you callin' me sister?' Alexandria asked, stepping backwards, confusion spreading across her features.

Remona lowered her head. 'Your father conceals much,' she whispered. 'You must unlock the truth, but tread carefully. The demon thirsts for your blood, just as she once sought mine.'

Suddenly, because of extreme anxiety, pain exploded in Alexandria's head. Her vision blurred, and her legs betrayed her. She fell to her knees, the cold cobblestones pressing against her skin. Confusion and fear clawed at her chest, her instincts urging her to flee, but she was trapped in a web of secrets and unanswered questions. Her voice emerged as a fragile whisper. 'Who is this demon?' she asked weakly. The air seemed to thicken, suffocating her as if the very darkness held its breath, waiting for the answer.

'The demon,' Remona repeated. 'She's the soul who makes the heart crave for more blood. She's the one who's shattered our father's heart.'

Looking up, Alexandria met Remona's gaze. 'Are you truly my sister? How can that be?' Remona turned her back to Alexandria, her form fading into the murky darkness. 'Answer me!' Alexandria shouted, desperation clawing at her insides.

'Tell no one that I'm your sister,' Remona murmured, her voice a mere whisper. 'The world will turn its back on you.'

Alexandria's legs trembled as she tried to stand, but weakness held her captive. 'How are we connected? How are we from the same blood lineage?'

Remona's answer reverberated off the ancient brick walls. 'We share blood from both parents.' And with that revelation, she vanished, leaving Alexandria alone in the dim alley.

'Please, don't go,' she pleaded, her voice swallowed by the night. 'Stay with me! Together, we'll uncover our family's secrets.'

But Remona had already slipped away, leaving behind unanswered questions and a chill that clung to Alexandria's skin.

She collapsed, surrendering to fear itself. Her bones quivered, and each heartbeat pounded like a desperate plea against the silence that enveloped the alley, not a rustle, not a whisper, only the oppressive stillness.

As she slowly lifted herself, dizziness threatened to pull her back down. The ground seemed to cling to her, reluctant to release its grip.

NEVER UNDERESTIMATE GIRLS!

Her breaths came in ragged gasps, and the air tasted of dampness and decay. Shadows danced on the cracked pavement, mocking her vulnerability.

Remona had vanished, but her presence lingered. Would she return? Would she reveal more cryptic revelations? Alexandria's pulse raced, a drumbeat of urgency urging her onwards.

Chapter 15

The wind swept through the alleyway, tugging at Alexandria's hair and sending a chill through her bones. The gust carried whispers, indistinct, like half-forgotten secrets. She ran, heart pounding in sync with her footsteps. Home beckoned, an oasis of familiarity in a world that had turned enigmatic.

Her father's face materialised in her mind, a lifeline. She longed to grasp his hand, to ask him the questions that clawed at her insides. What connection did she have with Remona? What family secrets lay buried in their shared lineage?

The old skyscraper loomed ahead, the place she now called home. As she reached the old building, its rusted revolving doors groaned as she stepped inside. The lobby lay in ruins, its marble floor cracked and littered with debris. The once-grand chandelier hung precariously from the ceiling, casting elongated shadows that danced like spectres.

Alexandria collapsed onto a worn-out sofa, catching her breath. She closed her eyes, seeking solace from the fear that gnawed at her body like a relentless beast. She would find her father, but first, she needed to steady herself.

She sat alone in the dark lobby, a place that seemed to harbour secrets as ancient as the moon itself. The moonlight, a ghostly visitor, seeped through a cracked window, casting an eerie glow upon the walls. The fluorescent tubes, their flickering rhythm erratic, painted unsettling shadows on the cold marble floor.

Then suddenly, a cold hand, unseen and insubstantial, brushed against her shoulder. The touch sent a shiver down her spine. She turned around, expecting to see her father, but the darkness yielded no form - only silence.

Fear coiled around her heart like a cold serpent tightening its grip. She stood up, distress propelling her forwards. The elevator, once a vessel of convenience, now stood silent and immobile, its cables severed. Alexandria had no choice but to climb the narrow staircase, a winding ascent into the heart of darkness.

Each step of the stairs protested under her weight, creaking like ancient bones. Dust motes swirled in the weak moonlight which filtered through the grimy windows. The walls were adorned with faded wallpaper, once vibrant but now a sickly yellow, decorated with patterns of forgotten flowers, their colours muted, their stories lost in time.

As she ascended, the air grew colder, as if the very walls absorbed her body's warmth.

The second floor stretched out before her, an endless corridor of closed doors. Overhead, flickering bulbs cast erratic shadows, revealing glimpses of peeling paint and old wood. The silence was heavy, broken only by low whispers, their origin elusive, their purpose unknown.

She walked down the hallway, and the whispers intensified. They wrapped around her senses, insistent and eerie. Were they secrets murmured by the walls themselves? Or echoes of forgotten lives?

She pressed her palm against the nearest door, its surface icy to the touch. The brass knob resisted, but with a determined twist, it yielded. The room beyond was empty, void of memories. Dust-covered furniture stood like forgotten sentinels, their fabric moth-eaten and sagging. The windows were boarded up, denying entry to both light and prying eyes.

Alexandria's footsteps echoed through the dimly lit hallway, each sound reverberating off the peeling wallpaper and worn-out wooden floorboards. The air smelled of old mysteries, mingling with the faint scent of cigarette smoke. As she walked past other doors, some ajar, she glimpsed abandoned lives, a forgotten teddy bear, its plastic eyes staring blankly, and a cracked mirror reflecting her pale face, distorted and unfamiliar.

But it was the door at the end of the corridor that drew her attention. A hushed conversation could be heard from within, and her father's voice emerged, muffled yet urgent. Who was he talking to? Alexandria's breath caught in her throat as she pressed her ear against the wood, straining to hear. The voices ceased abruptly, leaving only a haunting echo. Had she truly heard her father's voice, or was it her imagination, a desperate trick of her mind?

Her knuckles met the door's surface in a tentative rhythm, but silence greeted her, thick and suffocating. She rested her trembling hands on the brass handle and pushed. What lay beyond? Darkness? Answers? Or more questions, waiting to consume her?

The door creaked open, hinges groaning as if reluctant to reveal their secrets. The room within was dimly lit, curtains drawn against the outside world. The air smelled of cigarette smoke and long-buried enigmas. And there, seated on a wooden chair, was her father. His face was etched with lines of regret, his eyes hollow and haunted. His gaze was fixed on the floor, and he seemed oblivious to Alexandria's presence.

He began muttering words under his breath, and grey smoke started twisting around him like spectral tendrils. 'Can't we do this another way?' he suddenly shouted, causing Alexandria's heart to skip a beat. The room pulsed with tension.

The smoke swirling around him started to transform into something eerie, a phantom of malevolence. Alexandria gasped, desperate to reach her father, but an invisible force held her back. A spine-chilling laugh filled the room, and that's when a woman appeared behind Wound.

She moved towards him, a vision of enigmatic allure. Her forest green dress flowed behind her like a river winding through ancient woods. The fabric whispered secrets of hidden glades and forgotten spells. Delicate silver jewellery adorned her, each piece a tribute to serpentine elegance. Rings coiled around her fingers, their sinuous forms whispering the ancient wisdom of snakes, and elegant bracelets encircled her wrists, their weight a reminder of power and mystery. But it was the necklace that drew Alexandria's attention. The pendant, a serpent's head poised to strike, hung from her neck. The silver scales seemed to shimmer with a life of their own, and the ruby eyes glinted with hidden agendas.

Her knee-high boots were crafted from black leather and adorned with silver buckles. The heels curved subtly, their shape resembling snake fangs. She left an imprint with each step, a mark of her presence, a trail to follow or flee from.

Her eyes were framed with expertly blended smoky eyeliner, lending her a captivating look that drew attention and intrigue. The dark, smudged eyeliner accentuated her gaze. Alluring and menacing, she invited curiosity and caution in equal measure. Her lips were bright red, as if she had used the blood of her enemies to paint them. They were curved in a half-smile, challenging those who dared approach.

Was she a sorceress, an evil queen, or something altogether more dangerous? Alexandria couldn't say, but she sensed that crossing this enigmatic woman's path would alter her fate forever.

The venomous woman rested her hands on Wound's shoulders. He didn't flinch, as if he already knew she was there. 'Wound,' she whispered, her voice a snake's hiss.

The room trembled, and Alexandria wondered if she had entered a nightmare or a twisted fairy tale. Her heart pounded a storm of fear and desperation. The room, cloaked in shadows, seemed to pulse with malice, and Alexandria's heart raced; she used all her force and energy to break the invisible force that held her back, but there was no escape. As she struggled, black smoke twirled around her wrists and ankles, forming chains. The chains slithered together with malevolent intent, each link snapping into place with a chilling clank. Forged from dark, tarnished metal, they exuded an aura of death. As they twisted and writhed like serpents, their jagged edges glinted ominously.

'Serpentina, please, is there no other way?' Wound implored; his voice was as fragile as flower petals. His gaze remained fixed on the floor as if seeking solace in the worn wooden planks. But the woman behind him, the enigma named Serpentina, was unyielding.

She laughed, the sound slithering through the air like a serpent. Her hands, adorned by gloves, which were crafted from the supple skin of exotic snakes, sank into Wound's jet-black hair. She twisted a lock of his hair between her fingers, then pulled it aggressively, forcing Wound to turn his head in her direction. Her eyes, polished green emeralds, gazed deeply into his, a predator assessing its prey. 'No, Wound,' she hissed. 'There's no other way.'

Wound's defiance flared. He lifted his gaze, hatred flashing in his ice-blue eyes. 'You have to give me another choice!' he said desperately.

Serpentina circled him, graceful as a hunting panther. Her movements held a lethal elegance, each step a promise of danger. 'No more choices,' she hissed. 'You always fail me.' Her words hung in the air, strong and fearless. 'This time, you must accomplish the task, or else I will take what I first desired.'

Wound's hand vanished into his trouser pocket, retrieving a gleaming pocket knife, a desperate gambit. He stood up and charged towards her, eyes aflame. But Serpentina merely turned her back, dismissing him like an insignificant insect. 'How many times have you attempted this act?' she whispered, clicking her fingers. The noise echoed throughout the room, and then a snake suddenly appeared before Wound.

Alexandria had never seen such a snake, for it had a python's body and a serpent's fangs; it slithered towards Wound and wrapped itself around his legs. He couldn't move any further and looked down at his legs, dread and fear engraving deep lines into his face.

Serpentina laughed, and the snake hissed loudly; it slithered up Wound's body and coiled around his chest. Serpentina watched, amusement dancing in her wicked eyes. She clapped her hands together, causing the snake to squeeze Wound. He crumpled, gasping for air, chest constricting.

NEVER UNDERESTIMATE GIRLS!

Alexandria screamed, her legs urging her forward, but the unseen barrier pushed her back again. She watched in horror as Serpentina walked towards Wound and yanked the knife from his hand, thrusting it into his left arm. Pain shot through his body, yet he remained motionless, a puppet in the hands of a malevolent puppeteer.

The room seemed to tilt, reality wavering. Serpentina slowly removed the knife, her eyes glinting with amusement. She seized Wound's wounded arm, and he shrieked in pain. The wooden chair creaked as she forced him to sit, her grip unyielding.

'Wound,' she murmured, her voice a double-edged blade. 'How many times do I have to warn you?' Her laughter was a haunting melody that echoed throughout the room. 'Choices, my dear, have consequences.'

The air thickened with menace, and Alexandria's body trembled. Her father's fate hung in the balance, and she was powerless to intervene. She strained against the invisible bonds that held her back, but her efforts were useless.

She had stumbled upon this clandestine meeting between her father and Serpentina, and her heart felt heavy with fear. And then a question drifted into her mind. What was the task? What dark pact had they forged?

Wound managed to lift his head. 'Serpentina,' he stammered, his voice filled with pain. 'Please, cure it, I beg you.'

Serpentina tilted her head, considering him. Her hands traced patterns in the air. 'Cure it?' she hissed, her smile revealing teeth like sharp snake fangs. 'Very well.'

In a swift movement, she leaned down, her lips brushing against the wound on Wound's arm, and then she sank her teeth deep into his skin. Pain flared, but he didn't pull away. Instead, he watched her with a mix of terror and fascination.

And then, something unusual happened. The wound, once raw and bleeding, began to knit itself together. The edges sealed, leaving behind a faint scar. Wound exhaled, a wave of relief washing over his features.

Serpentina withdrew, her eyes gleaming. 'There,' she said. 'Cured. Are you happy now?'

Alexandria couldn't tear her gaze away from the sorceress. What had she done? Was this healing another layer of her malevolence? And why did Wound willingly submit to her?

As if sensing her thoughts, Serpentina turned towards Alexandria. Her eyes, slit like serpent's, bore into her soul. 'Curious, aren't you?' she purred. 'Your father sought power, bargained with pain. But there's more to unlock,' she stated. The room seemed to close in, the air thickening with evilness.

Wound, still weak, sank further into the chair. His gaze remained fixed on the floor as if lost in a trance. Alexandria couldn't understand why he was acting as though she were invisible. Was he under some dark enchantment? Or perhaps he had glimpsed something beyond the veil of reality, something that had shattered his mind.

Alexandria gulped deeply as Serpentina glided towards her. The woman's movements were sinuous, her steps deliberate. Her gown clung to her like a second skin, and her midnight black hair cascaded down her back in enigmatic waves. The room seemed to shrink, the walls closing in on Alexandria. She tried to back away, but her legs refused to obey. Fear and curiosity battled within her, a tempest of emotions threatening to consume her sanity.

Serpentina's laughter rang out, a chilling sound that scraped against Alexandria's nerves. 'Do you want to know your father's little secret?' she hissed, her voice a venomous whisper. She ungloved her right hand, revealing long red nails curved like talons. She extended a finger, the nail glinting in the dim light.

Alexandria's lips moved against her own command. 'Yeah,' she whispered, her voice barely audible. The word tasted bitter, like regret.

NEVER UNDERESTIMATE GIRLS!

Serpentina's nail descended, digging into Alexandria's chest. Pain shot through her body, a searing agony that threatened to split her mind. She gasped, her vision blurring. Serpentina's nail traced a path down her chest, leaving a crimson trail in its wake. Each second felt like an eternity, the pain intensifying with every millimetre.

'Dad!' shrieked Alexandria, her voice trembling. But Wound stared blankly at her, his glossy blue eyes devoid of recognition. It was as if he'd never seen or encountered her before. His indifference cut deeper than any physical wound.

'The secret lies within,' Serpentina hissed, her nail digging further into Alexandria's skin. She let out an ear-splitting laugh, a sound that seemed to pierce Alexandria's very soul. The room spun, and she collapsed, her body crumpling like a discarded doll. She clawed at the floor, desperate for solace, but her strength soon waned. Darkness closed in, just about to swallow her consciousness.

Through the haze, Alexandria's gaze locked onto Wound's face. His features remained impassive, unmoved by her suffering. 'Dad!' she gasped, her voice a mere whisper. But there was no recognition, no warmth in his eyes, only an abyss of emptiness.

As the room faded into oblivion, Serpentina's laughter echoed, haunting Alexandria even in unconsciousness. The secret remained elusive, buried beneath layers of pain and betrayal. Alexandria wondered if she would ever unlock it or become a forgotten ghost in this twisted dance of shadows and secrets.

Serpentina knelt near Alexandria's helpless body, her eyes glinting with malice. Her lips curved into a sinister smile, revealing razor-sharp teeth. 'Let your heart enjoy what little time it's got left,' she whispered sharply, 'Or do you want me to cure the curse?' Her laughter pierced the air, ear-splitting and mocking. 'I hope you don't want me to cure it because even if you beg me, I won't yield to a foolish girl like you!'

Alexandria's senses blurred as if she had stepped into another realm. The air smelled of iron and decay, and she glimpsed narrow staircases leading to unknown depths. Endless corridors stretched before her, their walls adorned with faded tapestries and ancient symbols. The colours shifted from vibrant to listless, as if reality itself did not exist.

Then suddenly, a sharp tug on her hair snapped her back to consciousness. She screamed, her eyes flying open. Moonlight filtered through a window, casting eerie patterns on the floor. The room she was in felt both familiar and foreign like a forgotten memory clawing its way to the surface. Her heart throbbed, and she struggled to catch her breath.

A soft voice cut through the panic, 'Sweetheart, wake up. You're having a nightmare.'

Alexandria gazed at the silhouette by her bedside, recognition flickering in her eyes. The warm and familiar voice belonged to her father. He was sitting on the edge of her bed, smiling fondly, yet Alexandria detected a hint of distress and pain beneath that happy expression. She reached out, her fingers trembling, and grasped his hand. 'Dad,' she whispered. 'Who was that woman? What curse was she talkin' about?'

Wound stared down at her as if he'd glimpsed a ghost. 'Which woman?' he stammered.

'That woman,' Alexandria insisted. 'The one who stabbed you.'

Wound stared at her, his eyes holding hundreds of untold secrets. His lips moved, but no words came out.

Tears slipped from Alexandria's eyes. 'Why didn't you do anythin' when she was hurtin' me?' she sobbed.

'My sweetheart,' he said softly, leaning towards her. 'I think you had a nightmare.'

'No, I didn't,' Alexandria protested. 'Dad, tell me the truth.'

'Are you saying I'm lying?' Wound asked, raising an eyebrow.

'It all feels so real,' Alexandria whispered. She suddenly grabbed Wound's left arm, searching for any signs of a stab mark, but found nothing. Yet she was determined that what she saw wasn't a dream. 'I don't understand,' she confessed. 'I don't remember fallin' asleep.'

'I found you asleep downstairs in the lobby. You were freezing, so I carried you to your bedroom,' Wound whispered gently.

'I was in the lobby,' Alexandria repeated, suddenly remembering Remona, the mysterious woman she had met in the alleyway. 'Listen, have I got a...' her voice trailed off as she remembered Remona's words: *Tell no one that I'm your sister. The world will turn its back on you.* She exhaled deeply, then said, 'Have I got a...have you got another daughter?'

A regretful sigh escaped Wound's mouth. 'You should get some sleep,' he replied, kissing her forehead. 'You're asking me questions for which I have no answers.'

Alexandria gazed up at her father, her eyes questioning and intense. A small smile spread across his face, and he gently covered her eyes with his hand. 'Go to sleep,' he whispered.

'I'm not a baby,' Alexandria murmured, pushing his hand away.

His smile faded into a sigh. 'Only if I was there to share the happiness of your infancy.'

'If you didn't abandon me, then maybe you would have shared the happiness of my childhood,' Alexandria replied, tears tracing paths down her cheeks.

'I never abandoned you,' Wound whispered. 'Your mother took you away from me. She didn't trust me with you.'

'Why did you and mother break up?' Alexandria asked curiously, slowly wiping her tears away.

Wound hesitated, then replied, 'We disliked each other.'

'If you didn't like my mother,' Alexandria began slowly, 'then why are you helpin' me hunt down her murderer?'

He paused, choosing his words carefully. 'Sweetheart, some things are grown-up matters. You won't understand.'

'You can never give me a straightforward answer, can you?' Alexandria sighed.

'No, I can't,' Wound whispered, grabbing her hand and squeezing it softly.

Alexandria watched as his eyes drifted to the ceiling. He began muttering words she couldn't make sense of. Then he looked back down at her and lowered his body so that his head could rest on her shoulder. 'Your mother,' he whispered, 'I remember seeing her for the last time. I remember the fear in her eyes.' He slowly lifted his head. 'I regret all I've done.'

'What do you regret?' Alexandria asked curiously.

'I have let the darkness take my heart, and now I regret everything I've done. I will also regret many things in the future, but I have no choice, for I have put this burden on my soul and cannot remove it,' he replied mournfully. Every word that left his lips seemed to pulse with suppressed darkness as if the demons themselves thrived off his distressful statement. He abruptly stood up, intending to leave her room. 'Good night,' he said as he walked towards the door.

'But, Dad, you didn't answer me,' Alexandria said, sitting upright.

Wound stopped walking and glanced over his shoulder. 'Andria, what now?' he asked.

'Do I have another sister?' she asked.

'Sometimes it's better not to ask questions that will not benefit you,' Wound whispered, stepping out of her room and shutting the door behind him.

Alexandria stayed silent as the door creaked shut, then let out a low sigh. She stared at the moon outside her window, a gnawing feeling growing within her. Her father was hiding something, a truth darker than any nightmare she'd ever known. Remona's cryptic words lingered in her mind: *'We share blood from both parents.'*

NEVER UNDERESTIMATE GIRLS!

Chapter 16

Stella wandered through the dimly lit streets of London. An icy gust of wind wrapped itself around her, prompting her to pull her hood over her tear-streaked face. Stopping beneath a lamppost, she watched as vehicles sped along the main road, their headlights casting fleeting shadows. The cold seeped into her bones, and she shivered, tucking her hands deep into her pockets.

Earlier that day, as she strolled down the hallway of their house, she had overheard Micheal's voice drifting from the living room. 'The police just gave me a bell,' he had said with a heavy sigh. 'They wanna have a word with us.'

Jacob, who was sprawled on the sofa with his eyes closed in distress, sat up abruptly. 'Is it about Alex?' he asked, his voice carrying a flicker of hope.

'Yeah,' Michael replied in a weary voice. He sank into the sofa opposite Jacob and began to massage his forehead with his thumbs. 'No good news, fam.'

'They haven't found her, have they?' Jacob asked, his sigh filled with sorrow.

'No, they haven't,' Michael confirmed.

'So, what the heck do they want from us!' Jacob shouted, grabbing his head in frustration.

'Calmly, fam,' Micheal replied slowly, though he felt the same.

'Don't bloody tell me to calm down,' Jacob retorted. 'What kind of people are in charge of Alex's case? They seem like a bunch of lazy idiots who can't do anything bloody right!'

Micheal looked down at the soft carpet. 'You used to tell your daughters not to speak like that,' he murmured.

Jacob let out a heavy sigh, burying his face into his hands. 'So, what do they want from us?' he asked again.

NEVER UNDERESTIMATE GIRLS!

'Like I said, they wanna have a word with us, and they'll be comin' in half an hour,' Micheal replied.

Jacob leaned back against the armrest, his gaze distant. 'Ever since Alex went missing, I knew this would happen,' he whispered. 'I knew she wasn't going to return.'

Stella, who had been silently listening, slowly walked into the living room, footsteps deliberate. She sat beside Jacob and took his hand. 'Don't lose hope, Dad,' she whispered with a reassuring smile.

Jacob ran his fingers through her hair, feeling the soft, smooth curls slip through his fingers like silk. He forced a smile, trying to mask the turmoil inside. 'It's hard not to lose hope,' he replied.

Gazing into his glossy green eyes, Stella leaned against his shoulder. 'Alex would never lose hope, so neither will I,' she declared, her voice brimming with determination.

'Alex taught you well,' Micheal replied with a smile. 'We won't lose hope.'

Returning his smile, Stella stood up, ready to leave the room. But just as she reached the door, she heard Jacob's negative remark. 'Michael, there is no hope,' he said. 'She's not coming, and we need to accept that.' The weight of his words lingered in the air, cutting through Stella's heart like a knife.

As she stood by the main road, watching the vehicles rush by, hot tears welled up in her hazel-grey eyes, shimmering with unspoken pain. Slowly, they gathered at the corners, hesitating momentarily before spilling over. One by one, the tears began their journey down her cheeks, leaving glistening trails in their wake. They trickled down, warm and unrelenting, tracing the contours of her face until they reached her trembling lips.

Suddenly, a sharp bark pierced the air behind her, breaking the silence. Startled, Stella turned around to see a small dog, its tail wagging furiously as it continued to bark. Standing next to the dog was a young boy with jet-black hair and dark brown eyes that seemed to sparkle with curiosity. He held the leash tightly, trying to calm his excited pet.

'Stop it, Pompom,' he said sternly. The dog looked up at him, ears flattening against its head. It let out a low whimper and tucked its tail between its legs. 'Didn't mean to upset you, my little mongrel,' the boy laughed, patting the dog on its fluffy head. The dog responded with a loud bark and began to circle the boy happily.

The boy looked up at Stella and smiled. 'Sorry,' he apologised. 'Pompom gets overexcited when she sees new people.'

Stella glanced down at the happy little dog. 'No problem,' she sighed, relieved that the boy hadn't noticed her tears.

'Bye,' the boy said, turning towards his dog. 'Come on, Pompom, we need to get home. It's getting late,' he said, walking away with his dog trailing behind him.

Stella watched as they vanished into a side street. She felt relieved to be alone again, and then more tears escaped her eyes as she recalled when the police had come to their house.

She had been lying on her bed, gazing at an old photo of the beautiful meadow where she and her sisters used to play as little girls, when the police had knocked on the front door. She strained to hear as Michael opened the door, her heart pounding with a mix of hope and dread. She had no idea if the news would be good or bad, but a sinking feeling told her that it was going to be terrible. She could hear Michael's voice from the downstairs hallway, soon joined by the softer, more measured voice of a police officer. The voices grew fainter as Michael led the officer into the sitting room.

Unable to bear the silence any longer, Stella sprang off her bed, determined to hear what the officer had to say. She ran down the stairs and down the hallway until she reached the sitting room door, which was slightly open.

She leaned against the wall, her heart racing as she peered into the room. Jacob and Micheal sat side by side on a sofa, their expressions grim and tense. Opposite them, an officer sat with his fingers pressed together, a look of concern etched on his face.

'So, you're tryna tell us that you haven't even got a clue where Alex might be?' Micheal asked, his voice low and strained.

'I'm sorry, sir, but yes, we can't find her,' the officer confirmed, his tone heavy with remorse. 'We've been trying to track *Calon*, but he too has not been found.'

Stella's thoughts sped uncontrollably as the officer continued to speak. Who was Calon? She'd never heard of the name before and wondered what he had to do with Alexandria. Her eyes abruptly fell on Jacob's face, noticing how he continually pressed his lips together in an awkward manner. His hands, resting on his lap, were also trembling.

'Do any of you know anything about Calon?' the officer asked, his gaze shifting between the two men. 'Any kind of information could help us track him down.'

Micheal exhaled heavily, shaking his head sorrowfully. 'I destroyed ties with him ever since he divorced my sister,' he replied. 'Which now I think was a mistake.'

The officer sighed and turned to face Jacob, whose eyes revealed a deep sense of regret. 'And you?' he asked gently.

'Officer, I have no information about him. I've never seen him,' Jacob replied, his voice trembling with emotion. 'But my wife used to talk about him a lot.'

'And what did she used to say about him?' the officer inquired, leaning forward slightly.

'She used to say that...that...' Jacob's voice trailed off, his eyes welling up with tears. He tried to hold back the sobs, but his shoulders shook with the effort. The officer and Micheal gazed at him, their eyes filled with empathy. 'She used to say to me,' Jacob continued, his words breaking. 'That Calon wanted to kill Alex!'

Still hiding behind the door, Stella gasped loudly at this horrifying revelation. Micheal shot a glance towards the room door but then looked back at Jacob. 'Yeah, she did used to say that,' he whispered. 'And she told me to keep Alex safe, but I bloody failed! Damn it, what type of uncle am I!'

The officer looked at both men, his expression grave. 'Things are just getting worse,' he sighed.

'That's if Calon hasn't already murdered her,' Jacob choked out, his voice filled with despair. 'It's been a month, and you still haven't found her.'

Stella moved slowly through the hallway, her mind reeling from the devastating news she had just heard. She needed time to process it all. As she ascended the staircase, each step felt heavier than the last. She glanced up to see Layla leaning over the upstairs bannister, her eyes filled with hope.

'Any good news?' she asked.

Stella exhaled deeply, shrugging her shoulders. 'Not really,' she replied, her voice barely above a whisper.

Layla's curiosity spilt forth. 'What do ya mean?'

'I don't know,' Stella said, stepping onto the upstairs hallway, her thoughts still a tangled mess.

'What do ya mean by ya don't know?' Layla pressed. 'That doesn't even make sense.'

'Well, that's the thing,' Stella said in a low voice, her frustration evident. 'Nothing's makin' any sense to me.' She walked into her bedroom, with Layla following closely behind, determined to get some answers.

'Have you ever heard Dad or Uncle mention the name Calon?' Stella asked, gazing out of her bedroom window, deeply in thought.

'Calon,' Layla repeated thoughtfully. 'No, I haven't heard them mention this name before, but to be honest with ya, I have heard that name somewhere,' she admitted. 'Anyway, what's that name got to do with anythin'?'

NEVER UNDERESTIMATE GIRLS!

Stella turned to face Layla, her expression serious. 'Because the officer downstairs was talkin' about a guy called Calon to Uncle and Dad, and they seemed to know who he was,' she replied.

'What did the officer say about him, and what has he got to do with Alex?' Layla asked, sitting on the edge of Stella's bed.

'That's what I'm tryna figure out,' Stella said.

'Why don't we just ask Dad once the officer goes?' Layla suggested, her determination unwavering.

'And I think that'll be now,' Stella said as she heard the front door close downstairs.

They both dashed downstairs, their hearts pounding with urgency. They found their uncle and dad in the front room.

Jacob sat on the couch, his face buried in his hands, while Michael stood by the window, arms crossed tightly across his chest.

'Dad, I need to ask you somethin',' Stella said, her voice trembling as she looked at Jacob. He glanced up at her, his eyes red and wet from crying.

Michael, sensing the build-up of tension, spoke up. 'Stella, this is no time for questions,' he said sternly.

Layla, unable to hide her worry, sat beside Jacob. 'What's wrong, Dad?' she asked, her eyes wide with concern.

'Nothing, darling,' Jacob replied, his voice barely a whisper.

'Dad, ya never cry,' Layla pressed, her voice filled with anxiety. 'What's wrong?'

Jacob's trembling hand reached for Layla's. 'Nothing,' he whispered again, his voice breaking.

Stella, unable to contain her curiosity any longer, blurted out, 'Dad, who's Calon?'

Michael and Jacob exchanged a quick, uneasy glance. 'Nobody,' Michael finally said, his voice firm but unconvincing.

'Uncle, that's a beautiful answer,' Stella retorted sarcastically. 'I heard you and Dad talkin' about a guy called Calon with that officer who just left.'

'Look, you don't need to worry about who Calon is,' Micheal replied adamantly.

'I think they should know the truth,' Jacob said. 'Why should we keep it a secret from them?'

Micheal raised an eyebrow. 'Fam, why?' he asked.

'We didn't tell Alex and look what's happened. I don't want any more mistakes,' Jacob replied sorrowfully. 'So, I think we should tell them.'

'Ok, if you say so,' Micheal sighed.

The room fell into an uneasy silence as Stella and Layla waited for the next word. Jacob glanced at Micheal, and in turn, Micheal shrugged his shoulders. 'It's your idea, so you tell them,' he whispered.

'I can't,' Jacob replied, his voice low and strained. 'You tell them.'

Micheal exhaled deeply, then turned to face Stella and Layla. 'Let me explain it in a straightforward manner,' he began. 'Calon, the guy you wanna know about is, well, he's Alex's biological dad.'

'Wow, such a big revelation,' Layla sighed, leaning against Jacob's shoulder and letting out a fake yawn.

Stella, who was leaning against a wall, her eyes wide with curiosity, said, 'This doesn't make sense at all. You lot were talkin' about...somethin' like Calon murdering...'

Jacob's voice quivered as he spoke. 'Yes, Stella, you got it right. Calon wants to kill Alex...' his voice trailed off. 'And we believe that she's already...dead.'

'What!' Layla gasped, her mind reeling with confusion. 'You can't be serious. Why would a father wanna kill his daughter?' Tears whelmed up in her eyes. 'This can't be right.'

Micheal shook his head, holding back tears. 'It's true, Layla,' he replied, his voice barely audible.

NEVER UNDERESTIMATE GIRLS!

'So, you're tryna tell me that Alex isn't coming back?' Layla asked, tears streaming out of her eyes.

'*Yeah...*' Jacob whispered, tears running down his cheeks.

'There's still a chance the police might just find her,' Micheal said, but in his heart, he knew the truth; Alexandria had vanished, leaving an aching void.

'It's been a month since she's disappeared,' Jacob replied, his grip on Layla's hand tightening.

Stella's desperate plea filled the room. 'But why would Calon wanna kill her? Why, Dad? Tell me!'

Jacob's response carried the weight of uncertainty. 'I don't know,' he said.

The reality of this painful conversation pressed down on Stella. She wiped her tears away, but fresh ones replaced them. She couldn't wrap her head around what Jacob had told her. 'Why?' she muttered to herself.

She crossed the main road and entered a desolate street. A navy blue sports car was parked on the curb, smoke curling from its windows. Stella glimpsed two young men occupying the front seats as she walked past the car. One of the men glanced at her and leered. 'Pretty girls like you shouldn't be out at this hour,' he mocked, drawing deeply from his cigarette. The ember glowed brightly as he took a long, deliberate drag, the smoke curling around his fingers. He held the cigarette tightly between his fingers, savouring the moment before exhaling a thick cloud of smoke that lingered in the air.

Ignoring him, Stella continued walking down the street until she reached a lamppost. It stood alone at the edge of the pavement, its iron frame rusted and worn. The light it cast was weak and flickering, barely piercing the thick veil of darkness that enveloped the night. A cold wind whispered through the empty street, causing the lamppost to creak and sway slightly as if it were alive and shivering in the chill. The lamppost's glass cover was cracked, allowing the light to escape in jagged beams resembling skeletal fingers reaching out into the night. It stood as a solitary sentinel, a silent witness to the secrets and shadows that lurked just beyond its feeble glow.

Stella's breath got caught in her throat; this was where she'd first glimpsed Lucky a month ago. The memory flooded her eyes with tears, and she fled down the seemingly endless street, her heart pounding against her ribs. Desperate for escape, she darted into a narrow alleyway.

As she ran, the alleyway split before her, branching into two distinct paths. To her right lay an uncharted passage, its secrets veiled in darkness. The leftward route, however, promised familiarity, leading homeward.

As Stella stepped into the shadowy alley on her left, she stopped dead in her tracks, defying her conscious will. She turned, her gaze irresistibly drawn to the other path she'd never explored. A strange, magnetic force tugged at her, urging her forward. Despite her original intent, she found herself walking down the unfamiliar alley.

Her fingertips brushed against the rough stone wall, tracing its ancient texture as she moved deeper into the shadows. The air grew colder, and the alley seemed to whisper secrets, pulling her further away from the safety of home.

As she walked past a graffiti-covered wall, she suddenly stopped and stared at the patterns. The graffiti was a mix of colours, with vibrant reds, electric blues, and neon greens swirling together in chaotic harmony. Something seemed familiar about how the letters curved and twisted unexpectedly, forming intricate shapes and symbols. She concentrated on the letters and patterns and soon realised they formed the name Alexandria.

'Alex!' she cried out, hastily removing her backpack. Rummaging through it, she retrieved an old piece of paper she had kept safe for many years. Unfolding the paper, she pressed it against the stone wall. There was no difference between the sketch on the paper and the graffiti painted on the wall. Every line and colour were the same, from the bold strokes of the letters to the delicate details of the background.

The edges of the letters were still wet, glistening in the dim light, indicating that the graffiti had been painted not that long ago. A glimpse of hope materialised within Stella's heart. Alexandria was still alive!

Hurriedly, she shoved the piece of paper into her pocket, swung her backpack onto her shoulders, and sprinted up the narrow alleyway. The adrenaline coursing through her veins was fuelled by the exhilarating news she carried.

But as she approached the end of the alley, her excitement and happiness quickly faded. Two men stood on the pathway, their hushed voices weaving a web of intrigue. Dread tightened its grip on Stella's heart; she recognised them. They were the same pair from the navy blue car. Their presence transformed her sprint into a cautious stride.

The man who had spoken to her earlier slyly grinned at her and leaned against the brick wall. 'You look nervous, girl,' he teased, his voice a low rumble. His complexion was a rich, earthy shade, resembling the colour of cocoa beans, and his grey eyes sparkled with defiance, daring her to react. 'I've never seen a girl with eyes like yours,' he added, catching her off guard.

Stella felt a horrible prickling sensation at the bottom of her neck. 'What?' she blurted out, her shyness momentarily forgotten.

The man's companion chuckled, breaking the tension. 'That's Zane,' he said, nodding towards the first man. 'Full of shit, that one.'

Zane, undeterred by his companion's comment, stepped closer to Stella. Dread flickered across her features, but she couldn't look away. His penetrating gaze made her painfully aware of her loneliness and defencelessness. He held a folded slip of paper in his hands. He pressed it into her trembling palm. 'Open it,' he murmured.

'I don't know you!' Stella's voice wavered as she dropped the paper. Panic surged within her. What had she stumbled into? She spun on her heels, fleeing up the alley. Glancing over her shoulder, she glimpsed the two men laughing. 'Shit heads,' she muttered, clenching her fists. She felt like a frightened puppy fleeing from a menacing werewolf. 'Only if Layla and Alex were with me,' she deliberated, 'they would have shown those weirdos how to laugh at somebody.' The thought triggered memories of the good old days when she would walk with her two sisters. She felt safe and spirited back then, but now she felt helpless and vulnerable.

She ran homeward; adrenaline flowed through her veins, fuelled by her desperate longing for better days to return.

As she neared her house, she slowed her pace and jumped over the side wall instead of bothering with the main gate. She landed on the soft, manicured grass with a soft thud. She stood up, eyes fixed on the house they'd recently moved into. A heavy sigh escaped her lips; the sight of their old home, now a distant memory, tugged at her heart. But it was Alexandria, her beloved sister, whom she missed the most. After Alexandria's disappearance, they'd been forced to abandon their former residence, which was deemed unsafe by Micheal.

Silently, she made her way to the back of the house, slipping through an opened window with practised ease. She couldn't risk waking Jacob; he'd be furious if he discovered she'd slipped out of the house at such a late hour.

The hallway which she jumped into led her to the grand staircase. She ascended, eager to share the news she had gathered with Layla. Knowing that Alexandria was still alive, even if not entirely safe, eased the ache in her heart. She soon forgot about the two awkward men.

She dashed to Layla's room and knocked on her door urgently. 'Who is it?' Layla's weary voice emerged from within.

'It's me, Stella. I need to tell you somethin',' Stella replied, her fingers tightening on the door handle.

'Come in,' before the words entirely left Layla's lips, Stella pushed the door open and stepped into the room. Layla lay in bed with the sheets pulled over her face. Stella ran up to her and pulled the sheets away. 'What are ya doin'?' Layla cried sleepily. Tears still clung to her eyes. 'Why do ya look so happy? Don't ya care...' her voice broke.

Stella sat on the edge of Layla's bed and sighed, 'I do care, sister, but I've got good news to share.'

'What!' Layla shouted. 'I don't wanna hear from ya. Yer a heartless girl.' She pulled her bed sheet over her face and began to sob softly. 'What Dad told us before, it's makin' me feel sick. Why would a father wanna kill his own daughter?'

Stella's gaze softened. 'Layla, it made me feel sick too, but I've got proof that Alex is still alive.'

Layla suddenly sat up, staring into Stella's eyes. 'What! Did ya just say ya've got proof that Alex is still alive?'

Stella slowly nodded her head. 'Yep, I was out just a few moments ago and...'

'What the hell were ya doin' out?' Layla screamed, her voice filled with panic and fear. 'Don't ya remember what Dad said?'

Stella clamped her hand over Layla's mouth. 'Quiet! Dad will wake up, and then I won't be able to share the good news.' They suddenly heard footsteps in the hallway. Stella's heart pounded. 'Don't say anythin' to Dad,' she whispered. 'Or I'm toast.'

The room door creaked open, and Jacob walked in. 'Layla, I heard you scream. Everything okay?' he asked, half-asleep. 'Stella, what are you doing here?'

'I was just tryna console Layla,' Stella stammered nervously.

Jacob approached the bed, embracing his daughters in his arms. 'I know what I told you. It's a lot for little girls like you,' he said. 'But I had to tell you the truth because Alex isn't returning.'

Stella fought back a smile. She knew the truth, but she had no intention of revealing it to her father. She gently took his hand. 'Dad, we understand,' she whispered.

JOSEPH JETHRO

Jacob looked at her, surprised by her calm demeanour. 'You're a brave girl,' he murmured, kissing her forehead. 'Now, I think you both should get some sleep. It's very late.'

Stella hesitated, her heart fluttering with hope. 'Dad,' she began, her voice tentative, 'could I stay with Layla for a bit longer?'

Jacob sighed, his expression weary. 'Very well,' he conceded, standing up. 'But only for a little bit.'

As he left the room, Stella let out a sigh of relief. 'That was a close one,' she whispered.

Layla, known for her persistence, grabbed Stella's arm. 'Listen,' she urged. 'Quickly tell me about the good news.'

Stella's smile danced on her lips. 'When I was out, I walked into an alleyway, and guess what I saw?' she teased.

Layla leaned forward, curiosity overwhelming her. 'Come on,' she pleaded. 'Tell me.'

'Ok, Ok,' Stella said. 'I saw some graffiti on a wall.'

Layla's disappointment was evident in her voice. 'Is that all?'

Stella's eyes sparkled. 'Yes, but it wasn't just any graffiti,' she declared. 'It was Alex's.'

Layla sank back. 'Miss Detective,' she scoffed, 'I'm gonna beat ya up. How can ya be sure it was Alex's graffiti?'

Stella swiftly slipped her hand into her pocket, retrieving a piece of paper. She unfolded it, revealing the familiar markings.

'Take a look at this,' she said, offering it to Layla.

Layla accepted the paper with a heavy sigh, scrutinising the graffiti drawn on it. 'And?' she prompted.

'There was no difference,' Stella replied, her voice triumphant, 'between this graffiti, which Alex drew for me when we were little girls, and the one that was painted on the wall.'

'So,' Layla mused, 'yer tellin' me sis is lurkin' around.'

Stella's excitement bubbled over. 'Yes!' she exclaimed. 'She's out there.'

NEVER UNDERESTIMATE GIRLS!

'But,' Layla countered, 'what Dad told us about Calon and what yer sayin' just doesn't add up, Stella.'

'It doesn't matter,' Stella insisted. 'At least we know she's alive.'

Layla's doubt persisted. 'The police have searched every corner of London. How come they haven't found her?'

Stella's eyes flashed with frustration. 'Because the police never do anythin' right,' she retorted. 'Remember that day when we saw that guy take Alex into the buildin'?'

Layla nodded. 'Yeah, I do.'

'And,' Stella continued, 'when the police searched the buildin', she wasn't there.'

Layla's brow furrowed. 'And what's yer point?'

'My point,' Stella declared, 'is that if Dad and Uncle let us help find her, we would have found her by now.'

'So,' Layla said slowly, 'yer tryna tell me that we should go and try to find her ourselves?'

Stella grinned. 'What else?' The hope in her heart burned brighter than ever.

Layla's voice wavered with uncertainty. 'I'm not sure about this, Stella,' she replied, her eyes searching her sister's face. 'It's gonna be dangerous.'

Stella's determination blazed in her eyes. 'I'm gonna look for Alex,' she confessed, her voice firm. 'And nobody's gonna stop me.'

Layla's concern deepened. 'Stella, I agree with ya,' she said, her brow furrowing. 'We should try to find Alex. But how? That's the question. We don't have a clue where she is.'

'I know how we're gonna find her,' Stella whispered.

'Ya do?' Layla asked eagerly, hope flickering in her voice.

'Yeah,' Stella smiled. 'Yesterday, when I went out with Uncle Michael, Officer Scoot caught sight of us and started talkin' to Uncle about...'

Layla leaned closer. 'Then what happened?' she insisted, excitement bubbling.

'He said that the police suspect Kenny's men to be at Blue Glass Skyscraper tomorrow,' Stella revealed. 'And that means if we can get there tomorrow, we might be able to find clues about where Alex is!'

Layla gazed at Stella in confusion. 'What's Kenny got to do with findin' sis?' she asked.

'Layla, use your brain,' Stella sighed. 'We all know Alex wants to kill Kenny, don't we?' Layla slowly nodded her head. 'So, if Kenny's gonna be at Blue Glass Skyscraper, Alex is ought to be there.'

'You've got a good point,' Layla confessed.

Stella held Layla's gaze, her voice urgent. 'Are you in?'

Layla hesitated, then hugged Stella tightly. 'I know tryna find Alex is gonna be perilous and probably life-threatenin',' she whispered, 'but yeah, I'm with ya.'

Chapter 17

Alexandria wandered through the crumbling remains of the old skyscraper, her footsteps echoing off the decaying walls. The air was thick with dust, and shafts of sunlight sliced through the broken windows, casting long shadows on the cracked floor. Each step she took felt like a descent into the past, a journey back to a time when this desolate place thrived with purpose.

Last night's haunting memory clung to her mind. Her father had dismissed it as a nightmare, but its vividness felt too real. What was he hiding from her? And why hadn't she seen him today? Where was he?

The thought made her wince. She gazed down at the cracked marble, and her reflection stared back. 'Why is my life so twisted?' she asked herself.

'Because that's who you are!' a voice screamed within her. 'You're the light in your dark linage. Find the truth. Prove you're not cursed like your father!'

'My dad isn't cursed!' Alexandria retorted, a solitary tear escaping her eye.

'How do you know?' the voice whispered. 'He barely speaks to you.'

'He always talks to me,' she scoffed, wiping her tear away, but the truth weighed heavily on her heart.

As she approached a bend in the skyscraper's corridor, gentle whispers rode the cold draft and into her ears. Her breath caught in her throat. What awaited her?

Remona, the enigmatic woman who had claimed to be her sister, loomed large in her thoughts. Her dark and mysterious eyes seemed to pierce through Alexandria's very soul. What secrets did she hold? What truths lay hidden in her family's history?

As Alexandria imagined turning the bend, she saw him: her father. He looked very distressed, the lines on his face eternally etched by the weight of responsibility. Beside him stood the malevolent woman, Serpentina, who had whispered cryptic secrets and veiled threats.

The old skyscraper held memories, both known and unknown. It was a place of revelation and reckoning. The past clawed at the present, demanding answers. Alexandria's heart raced, torn between Remona's cryptic warnings and the malevolent woman's ominous words. She stood at the crossroads, her family's secrets converging like fractured light, threatening to shatter her sensitive understanding of who she was and what she carried within.

Suddenly, Alexandria jolted out of her imagination. She hesitated, caught between curiosity and fear, longing and dread. After drawing in a deep and steady breath, she walked around the bend. A dark hallway stretched out before her, its walls adorned with faded wallpaper that peeled away in places, revealing the crumbling plaster beneath. The dim light from a flickering bulb cast elongated shadows on the worn-out marble, and the air hung heavy, carrying the musty scent of decay.

Her footsteps echoed, each click of her heels resonating through the silence. The hallway seemed to stretch infinitely, its twists and turns defying logic. Cobwebs clung to the corners, their delicate threads swaying as if stirred by unseen breaths. The old skyscraper was full of secrets, and this hallway kept them well-protected.

As she walked, the temperature dropped, and goosebumps prickled her skin. The walls seemed to close in, pressing against her, whispering forgotten tales.

Then came a shrill laugh. It sliced through the stillness, a discordant note that sent a chill down her spine. She spun around, her heart pounding, but the hallway remained empty. The laugh lingered, echoing off the walls, mocking her vulnerability.

'Why are you acting insane?' a voice whispered in her mind.

Alexandria's frustration bubbled. She opened her mouth, but her scream got caught in her throat as two figures materialised at the far end of the hallway. Fear clawed at her chest, urging her to flee.

NEVER UNDERESTIMATE GIRLS!

Without thinking, she ran, her footsteps pounding against the worn-out marble. The figures followed her, their presence a weight on her back; she dared not look back. Their intentions remained a mystery. Only one thing was clear: the old skyscraper held more than memories; it harboured something ancient and hungry.

'Andria!' the voice was familiar, yet Alexandria didn't stop running. As she neared a bend, she twisted her head to glance over her shoulder, her breaths ragged from the adrenaline-filled run. Her left foot slipped on a piece of cracked marble, and she tried desperately to regain balance, but her efforts were futile. She stumbled forward, her head colliding with the corner of the wall. Pain exploded through her skull and down her neck.

She would have faced a perilous fall if two arms hadn't caught her just in time. Her vision blurred, and the world swirled in a haze.

'Are you all right?' a gentle voice whispered. The stranger's face appeared and disappeared, leaving her disoriented. She strained her eyes, ignoring the throbbing ache in her head. Slowly, her vision cleared, and she recognised the person who was cradling her like a young child.

'Ethan!' she gasped, feeling a mix of embarrassment and relief.

He smiled, his well-polished teeth glistening in the dim light. A month ago, Alexandria's father had appointed Ethan as her training instructor, marking the beginning of an intense and transformative journey.

Their eyes met, and something unspoken passed between them. His right arm, supporting her head, vibrated uneasily. They held each other's gaze for a few seconds, and the pain that had once consumed her seemed to vanish. His dark black eyes held secrets, drawing her in.

But then she tore her gaze away and attempted to extricate herself from his unyielding arms. The pain in her head resurfaced, causing her body to sag, tears slipping from her eyes.

'You're all right,' Ethan whispered, his presence both comforting and unsettling.

A sudden, sharp voice sliced through the air like a blade. 'I wonder why you were running like you'd seen a devil?'

Alexandria turned her head slowly, following the sound. Her eyes fell upon her father. He wore a long black robe, an unfamiliar garment for him. The fabric draped down his body in sinuous waves, flowing like dark ink freshly spilt from an ancient pot. He wore a dark expression on his ghost-white face, and his indigo eyes bore into hers, glinting with malice.

Ethan, holding Alexandria protectively, had expected a different reaction. Perhaps her father would embrace her and offer solace. But Wound remained rigid, towering over them both, his gaze furious.

'Dad, I didn't realise it was you,' Alexandria stammered, her voice strained. 'You look so wicked,' she added bluntly.

Ethan couldn't resist grinning, 'Yeah, your dad looks really *wicked*, girl.'

'I don't think she meant that type of wicked,' Wound growled, his gaze piercing Alexandria's weakened eyes. 'Did you?' His laughter held a dangerous edge. 'Tell me, which type of wicked do you call me?'

Fear coiled around Alexandria's heart, rendering her speechless; she turned her face away from Wound and buried it in Ethan's chest, tears streaming down her face. 'My head hurts,' she sobbed.

Wound's patience wore thin. 'I asked you something!' he snapped. He seized her face, yanking it towards him. 'Which type of wicked do you call me?' Alexandria stared at him but didn't answer. He slapped her viciously across the face, his eyes blazing with fury. She let out a shriek of pain and began to cry uncontrollably.

'Easy, boss,' Ethan gasped, tightening his grip on Alexandria, ready to protect her from whatever malevolence her father had in store.

'Answer me, Andria!' Wound shouted; his voice sliced through the tension, leaving no room for evasion.

NEVER UNDERESTIMATE GIRLS!

Alexandria's breath hitched, and she stammered, 'You're evil!'

Wound felt the exhilaration of triumph flowing through his veins, a heady rush that made the world blur at the edges. His laughter, a twisted melody, filled the air. The hallway seemed to shrink, closing in on him as if it shared his malevolent glee. 'It's nice to know you think that way about me,' he whispered, his tone oozing with deceptive charm. 'For soon, you'll see the true darkness that resides within my heart.'

Alexandria met Wound's sharp gaze; her blue eyes, like flawless diamonds, held stories and secrets that only he could read. Her vulnerable eyes held the pain of a lifetime, longing, desperation and fractured love. 'Don't look into my eyes,' he roared, but Alexandria wouldn't divert her gaze; she wanted answers. His fingers, like vipers, coiled around her delicate neck. The air thickened, suffocating her, as he tightened his grip. Her eyes widened, pupils dilating in terror. Desperation etched lines on her face as she clawed at his hands, seeking release from this macabre dance.

Ethan, confused, felt a surge of panic. If he tried to pry Wound's hands away, he risked dropping Alexandria. Desperation fuelled his decision. He raised his foot, intending to kick Wound away, but before he could strike, Wound released Alexandria.

The smirk on Wound's face was unsettling. He locked eyes with Ethan, who quickly lowered his foot, feigning innocence. It was a dangerous game, and Ethan hoped he'd played it well.

'I wanted you to review tomorrow's drill with Andria, the one involving her mission to eliminate Kenny,' Wound declared, his gaze unwavering. 'But she needs to rest for now.' He studied Alexandria's tear-streaked face. 'Take care of her and keep her out of my way!'

Ethan slowly nodded his head, concealing his confusion. 'Of course,' he replied, masking his true feelings.

As Wound turned away, his black robe billowing like smoke, Ethan wondered what secrets lay hidden beneath that dark exterior. The hallway swallowed Wound's retreating figure, leaving Ethan alone with Alexandria's fragile form and a sense of impending danger.

Ethan's gaze wandered into the empty darkness, lost in contemplation. His eyes shifted downwards, landing on Alexandria, who remained cradled in his arms. Her face, pale and vulnerable, looked up at him, seeking solace amidst the chaos.

Ethan's lips curved into a gentle smile, a warmth that reached deep into Alexandria's heart. 'You'll be safe with me,' he whispered, the promise carrying more weight than mere words. His unwavering gaze held hers, a silent vow woven between them.

Alexandria's voice trembled as she choked out her reply. 'I'll remember that,' she managed, her fingers clutching the fabric of his shirt.

Ethan's smile softened further. 'Always remember,' he affirmed, his thumb brushing against her cheek.

The pain in Alexandria's head throbbed, an unwelcome companion. Her lungs fought for air, each breath a struggle. 'I need to lie down,' she murmured, her eyelids heavy.

Ethan surveyed the hallway and assessed their surroundings. 'Shall I take you to your room?' he offered, concern curving lines on his forehead.

Alexandria's nod was a fragile surrender. Her eyes fluttered shut, the pull of exhaustion tugging at her like invisible hands. She found herself too weak to resist. She surrendered to the darkness with a deep breath, trusting Ethan's promise to watch over her and protect her from the shadows that threatened to consume her.

Chapter 18

The world blurred as Alexandria drifted into a half-conscious state. Time lost its grip, and she floated on the edge of dreams. She felt something cold and soothing press softly against her forehead in that fragile space between wakefulness and slumber. Her eyes snapped open, and reality rushed back. She found herself staring at Ethan. He sat on the edge of her bed, his presence both comforting and unsettling. He held an ice pack in his hand, which he had gently placed on her head. The pain that had once gnawed at her skull was now reduced to a mere throb. 'Thanks,' she whispered, her voice barely audible.

Ethan's smile was warm. 'Feelin' better now?' he asked.

'Yeah,' Alexandria sighed, sitting upright. The world tilted, but she steadied herself and surveyed her bedroom; the open window allowed a playful breeze to dance through the room, making the curtains flutter. She shivered, suddenly aware of the chill in the air.

'Here, hold this,' Ethan said, passing her the ice pack. She took it from his hand, grateful for the relief it brought. She placed it back on her head and watched as he stood up, crossing the room to the window. The wind tousled his jet-black hair, and he breathed in the fresh air. His smile was fleeting as if he held secrets he couldn't share. 'The weather today is beautiful. But if you'd like the window shut, I can close it,' he said.

'No,' Alexandria replied, smiling. 'Leave it open.'

Ethan settled on the window ledge, staring out at the world beyond. Alexandria's gaze remained fixed on him. An enigmatic aura surrounded him, pulsing with secrets and unspoken thoughts. The wind played with his black hair, causing it to fall over his eyes. He brushed it back with his fingers, then met her gaze. His eyes held a question, a vulnerability. But before he could speak, he glanced down at his lap, fidgeting with his fingers, an awkward hesitation, as if he desperately wanted to say something but held it back.

JOSEPH JETHRO

Alexandria leaned back into the comfort of her pillow, her gaze drifting upward to the ceiling. Her thoughts flowed freely, weaving memories and dreams together. A soft smile curved her lips as she stole a glance at Ethan, who was tapping the windowpane with gentle fingers. The rhythmic sound echoed in Alexandria's ears, evoking a sense of nostalgia, a distant memory from her innocent past.

She remembered twirling and dancing as a young child, her mother's laughter accompanying each joyful step.

One sun-drenched spring day, as they wandered through the local park, birds flitted from tree to tree, their cheerful chirps blending with Alexandria's laughter. Her mother playfully ruffled her hair, and Jacob, grinning, swung Alexandria into the air. 'Again!' she cried.

'One more time then,' Jacob laughed happily and swung her skyward again.

'Alex, come with me!' Stella's voice interrupted Alexandria's cheerful laughter. She ran towards her and grabbed her hand.

Jacob and Sera smiled as they watched their two daughters run down the path.

Alexandria ran alongside her little sister, curiosity bubbling. Stella led her towards a cluster of trees, mischief dancing in her eyes. 'Layla has a surprise for you,' she giggled, pointing towards the wooded area.

Anticipation fluttered in Alexandria's chest as she pushed through the trees, with Stella following close behind. 'Wow!' she gasped as they entered a sunlit clearing among the trees. A blossom tree stood proudly in the middle, and little pink flowers fell from its branches like snowflakes. 'Where's Layla?' she asked, looking around.

Before Stella could answer, Layla burst forth from a heap of leaves and blossoms. Her laughter filled the air as she scooped up handfuls of petals, tossing them at Alexandria and Stella. The three sisters giggled, caught in a moment of shared sisterhood.

NEVER UNDERESTIMATE GIRLS!

Yet their joy was interrupted by a sudden, rhythmic drumming noise. Confusion furrowed their brows. 'What's that noise?' Layla asked.

Alexandria scanned the surroundings, her azure eyes following the sound. Then, with unbridled excitement, she pointed towards a tall pine tree. 'Look there! Can you see that bird? It's the one makin' the noise!'

Stella's delighted exclamation pierced the air. 'What type of bird is that? It's so cute!' Her enthusiasm was affectionate, and Alexandria couldn't help but smile.

Jacob materialised behind them, his presence as sudden as a summer breeze. Scooping Stella off the ground, he tossed her into the air, her bouncy hair dancing in all directions. Stella's shriek of joy drifted through the clearing as Jacob gently caught her and put her back down. Then, with tenderness, he combed her hair back with his fingers. 'It's a woodpecker, dear,' he whispered.

'A woodpecker,' Layla repeated, her eyes tracing the bird's movements. 'I like it. It's beautiful.'

Alexandria's gaze remained fixed on Jacob. His smile held warmth, but her sharp stare seemed to pierce through him, causing him to frown. 'Baby, what's wrong?' he asked, his voice gentle.

Her cheeks flushed crimson. 'I'm not a baby!' she retorted, crossing her arms defiantly.

Jacob chuckled. 'You'll always be my baby.' He reached out to playfully tug her hair, but as his fingers caught her hair, she screamed, 'Get your hands off me, Jacob!'

'You're supposed to call me Dad, not Jacob,' he said gently.

'I'm not gonna call you dad,' Alexandria retorted. 'Cause you're not my dad!'

Bewilderment flickered across Jacob's face as she turned away, sprinting through the trees. She ran, her breath coming in ragged gasps, until she found her mother, Sera, sitting on a bench, lost in thought.

'Mummy!' Alexandria screamed, tears glimmering in her eyes.

'What's wrong, sweety?' Sera asked, startled.

Alexandria flung herself into her mother's arms, her sobs escaping freely. 'What happened?' Sera asked Jacob, who had followed her.

Jacob sat beside them, concern spreading across his features. 'What's wrong with you, *baby...Alex*?' he softly said.

'Don't talk to me!' Alexandria shouted.

'Sweety!' Sera gasped. 'Tell me what happened?'

Tears traced paths down Alexandria's cheeks. 'Where's my daddy?' Her voice trembled with longing.

Sera and Jacob exchanged glances, their unspoken communication heavy with shared history. Sera pulled Alexandria close and whispered, 'Let's find Layla and Stella, shall we?'

'Answer me, Mummy,' Alexandria sobbed.

Sera sighed, a long, heavy exhale that seemed to carry the world's weight. She gazed up at the blue sky, her lips moving, murmuring something Alexandria strained to hear but couldn't quite make out. Alexandria stood there, caught between anticipation and trepidation. Her heart pounded, threatening to burst through her ribcage.

At such a tender age, she had yearned to know where her father was. And now, after years of longing, she had finally found him. Yet, he wasn't the type of father she had envisioned. He held more secrets from her than her stepfather, Jacob, and engaged in inexplicable actions that defied all fatherhood norms.

'You seem lost in thought,' Ethan's voice broke through Alexandria's fragile moment, and she snapped back to reality.

She held her tears back as she stared blankly at Ethan, her emotions swirling. Should she cry in front of him?

Tears slipped from her eyes, defying her attempts to control them. She covered her face with trembling hands and sobbed softly, the weight of her discoveries and disappointments overwhelming her.

NEVER UNDERESTIMATE GIRLS!

Ethan, concerned, rose and approached her. He sat before her. 'What's up, girl?' he asked gently, his features softening with empathy.

'Why is my life so...why is my dad so...why can't anythin' go right?' Alexandria's voice broke as she poured out her frustration.

Ethan leaned towards her, placing his hands gently on her shoulders. 'Tomorrow will go according to plan,' he whispered. 'Especially with me around.' His attempt at reassurance felt inadequate in the face of her turmoil.

But Alexandria wasn't talking about tomorrow; she needed answers about today. 'Why was my dad tryna strangle me?' she blurted out, her gaze locked onto Ethan's eyes, seeking clarity.

Ethan's confusion mirrored her own. 'I don't really know,' he stuttered, making a thinking face. 'Perhaps it's a gangster's twisted way of saying...I love you, my dear daughter.'

'What!' Alexandria snapped. 'How on earth is that a declaration of love?' She flung her legs over the edge of her bed in frustration and rested her elbows on her knees. 'That doesn't make sense,' she muttered.

Ethan let out a sigh and sat down next to her. 'I agree, it baffles me too,' he admitted. 'But it can't mean anything else.' A sheepish smile played on his lips, softening the intensity of their conversation. 'Because just before we saw you running down the hallway and banging your head into the wall, we were...' His voice trailed off as he placed his hand on Alexandria's arm, staring directly into her eyes.

'You were what?' she asked, moving his hand away from her arm.

'We were talking about you,' Ethan said, 'and Wound was praising you, expressing how much he loves you.' His weirdness intensified, and Alexandria's discomfort grew. 'Then I was about to share my big dream for the future when we saw you...' he paused, and Alexandria sensed he'd revealed something he shouldn't have. He quickly changed the subject, adopting a more confident tone. 'May I ask why you were running down the hallway like that?'

Ignoring his question, Alexandria leaned towards him. 'So, what's your big dream?' she asked, curiosity overcoming her emotional turmoil.

Ethan's face turned ten shades paler than usual, and his cheeks flushed crimson. Alexandria nearly burst into laughter at the sight, but she managed to control herself. She watched as Ethan squirmed, feeling uncomfortable.

'You'll find out after tomorrow's mission,' he replied, his smile wobbly and alluring. It was the most endearing expression Alexandria had ever seen. She bit her molars to stifle her laughter.

Suppressing her laughter, Alexandria's thoughts took her into the future. Tomorrow held secrets, and Ethan's dream remained tantalisingly elusive. Yet amidst the uncertainty, she sensed a fragile bond connecting them in this strange, unpredictable world.

She stood up, and Ethan's gaze followed her. The sun's rays seeped through the window, casting beams of light across the floor, and she crossed it with purposeful steps, her movements fluid and confident. Leaning against the cool wall, she fixed her eyes on Ethan. His expression remained nervous, and his eyes seemed to reveal intense emotion.

'So, my dad must really trust you since he's sendin' you with me on my mission to kill Kenny,' she said, pulling her phone out of her pocket. Her fingers danced across the screen as she waited for him to answer.

Ethan shifted nervously, choosing his words carefully. 'It's not entirely about trust,' he replied, his voice measured. 'I'm new here, you know.'

Alexandria raised an eyebrow, glancing at him and then back at her phone. 'New?' she repeated. 'But you were here before I arrived a month ago.'

'True,' Ethan conceded, 'but I only got to know your dad a week before your arrival. So, relatively speaking, I'm still the new guy.'

NEVER UNDERESTIMATE GIRLS!

'If you're new, then why has my dad made you into my instructor and...' Before Alexandria could press further, Ethan's tone changed, and he spoke with a hint of pride.

'My qualifications extend beyond mere newness,' he declared. 'My flexibility is astounding, my agility unmatched, and my coordination flawless. And let's not forget my absolute coolness,' he continued boasting about himself, but Alexandria was no longer listening to him.

Her finger hovered over Layla's phone number, memories of promises made and broken tugging at her conscience. Stella's name caught her eye, a reminder of loyalty forsaken. She had vowed to be there for Stella, but now she didn't even know where her stepsisters were. The sisterhood they once shared now felt like a distant dream. Regret gnawed at her insides. She dared not call them; the weight of her betrayal was too heavy. Ethan's voice drifted into her ears as she powered off her phone, and she looked up sharply.

'My ability to charm my way out of any situation is legendary,' he laughed. 'And my photographic memory? It's invaluable for memorising blueprints and secret codes. As for danger, my intuition is sharper than a razor blade. I sense danger before it even registers.'

Alexandria's sigh drifted through the room, a soft sound that hung in the air like a fading note of a melancholic melody. 'Wow,' she said, her voice heavy with both exasperation and sarcasm. 'You shouldn't boast so much.'

Ethan stared at her, his bravado faltering like an abandoned fizz drink. His mouth went dry, and his throat tightened. 'I...I'm not boasting,' he stammered. 'Just telling you how awesome I am.'

'Well, I don't need to know!' Alexandria snapped, her patience waning. 'Don't tell me about it, you shithead!' Her gaze bore into Ethan, who looked like he might pass out or maybe pass away right on the spot. She suddenly regretted her outburst and stammered out an apology. 'I'm sorry,' she sighed, her anger dissipating.

She glanced down at the floor, the weight of her words settling heavily in her mind. 'I'm sorry,' she repeated.

The room hung heavy with tension. Alexandria's gaze remained fixed on the worn wooden floor, her lashes casting delicate shadows on her cheeks. She willed herself not to look up, afraid of what she might find in Ethan's eyes. She knew she had wounded him with her sharp and unforgiving words, and at that moment, the weight of her pride was unbearable. Alexandria was no heartless creature. She didn't want to see Ethan hurt or upset. Not now, not ever. If she pushed him away, severed the fragile thread that bound them, he might refuse to aid her in tomorrow's dangerous mission. And that, she feared, would be the end of her world.

Finally, the silence cracked like thin ice. Ethan's voice, anxious and hesitant, broke through. 'So, so are...' he stammered. 'Are we still friends?' he managed to choke out.

Her head snapped up, relief washing her anxiety away. 'We're not friends,' she declared softly, her lips curving into a bittersweet smile. 'We never were.'

Ethan's eyes widened, surprise and confusion overcoming him. 'What?'

'I wasn't finished,' Alexandria laughed. 'As I was saying, we were never friends. We are teacher and student, bound by duty, not camaraderie. Let's keep it that way.'

Ethan's smile was both delightful and hopeful. 'Until tomorrow's mission,' he murmured.

'Yes,' Alexandria muttered; she crossed the room to her drawer and opened one of the compartments. She retrieved a black box and sat on the floor. With deft fingers, she undid the crimson ribbon that held the box closed. The hinges creaked as she lifted the lid, revealing the gleam of polished silver, a lethal beauty nestled within.

NEVER UNDERESTIMATE GIRLS!

Ethan watched, curiosity dancing in his eyes. 'I hope you're not planning to use that on me,' he joked, rising from the bed and closing the distance between them.

Her smirk was like a blade's edge. 'One more step, and I just might,' she smiled, the gun cool and deadly in her hand. Its weight whispered danger, a promise of finality.

Ethan laughed nervously, retreating to the safety of the bed. 'So, what are you doing with that thing?' he asked, eyes flickering between her and the weapon.

Alexandria's laughter filled the room, a chilling sound that seemed to cling to the walls. 'Dad gave this to me the first day I met him,' she said, her voice filled with vengeance. 'And it's gonna have the pleasure of bangin' a hole through Kenny's cursed head,' she spat out the words, her eyes flashing with anger.

Ethan leaned against the cold stone wall, his expression serious. 'I'm here to help you on this mission,' he said, his voice low. 'But honestly, I don't know what's going on. Why are you so determined to send him six feet down?'

Alexandria's face flushed under her makeup. 'That bloody jerk,' she said, her voice trembling, 'he's the one who killed my mother!' She fought back tears, her grip tightening on the gun.

Ethan gasped, 'He killed your mum!'

'Yeah,' Alexandria whispered, wiping away a tear. 'Kenny, Kenny,' she muttered, her voice filled with loathing. 'He's the evil shithead who ruined my family.'

Ethan's brow furrowed. 'I'm sorry,' he said softly, 'but I don't actually know how you feel. I've never seen my mum.'

'How come?' Alexandria asked, swinging the pistol in the air and catching it effortlessly.

'Because she left my dad and abandoned me and my brother when I was only two,' Ethan replied. The sadness in his eyes was evident.

'Why would someone do that?' Alexandria asked.

'I don't know,' Ethan confessed. 'I don't know anything about my mother. I only know her name, which is Kenzie.'

'Kenzie,' Alexandria repeated. 'Rhymes with Kenny.'

Ethan seized the opportunity to divert his thoughts from his own pain. 'So why do you call the guy Kenny?' he asked. 'Everyone else has been telling me his name is *Liam*...Liam Maxwell.'

Alexandria placed the gun back in its box and closed the lid. 'He uses the name Liam as a cover-up,' she explained. 'So, the police can't catch him. But his true identity is Kenny.'

Ethan frowned. 'Nobody ever told me that,' he said. 'Even your dad didn't mention it. But since Kenny reminds me of my mother's name, I won't be calling him that. I think I'll stick to Liam.'

'No,' Alexandria retorted. 'You're gonna call him Kenny. By his cursed name.'

'I don't wanna,' Ethan replied, shrugging his shoulders.

'You better call him Kenny!' Alexandria's tone was sharp.

'Fine,' Ethan said, grinning. 'I won't call him Liam, but I won't call him Kenny either. Let's go with...*Target*.'

'*Target*?' Alexandria exclaimed. 'Why would you call him that?'

Ethan chuckled. 'Because he's the one we're targeting. Once he's dead, we'll call him...*Dead*.' He glanced at Alexandria, who was now smiling. 'Get the joke?' Alexandria gave a slight nod. 'Good. Now that your head isn't hurting anymore, let's go over tomorrow's mission.'

Alexandria's sigh drifted throughout the room. 'We've gone over that drill thirty times over,' she said. 'It's makin' me go loopy.'

Ethan nodded in acknowledgement. 'Yes, but that doesn't mean we're not gonna go over the drill.'

'Ethan, go do something better,' she urged. 'Chill out with your mates. I don't feel like doing the drill, so there's no point in arguing.'

'Ok, but don't tell your dad that we didn't go over it. He'll get pissed off,' Ethan chuckled, walking over to the door. He swung it open and stepped out into the hallway. 'Do you wanna come with me?' he suddenly asked, glancing at Alexandria.

'No way,' she replied firmly, crossing the room to the door. 'Bye, see ya tomorrow morning,' she said, slamming the door in his face, leaving him to stare at the old, varnished wood.

As he walked down the corridor, he couldn't help but shake his head. 'Strange girl,' he mused, a smile playing on his lips.

Meanwhile, Alexandria slumped onto her bed, her gaze fixed on the ceiling. Anger and tension bubbled within her veins. She grappled with her father's actions, but each attempt felt like adding zero to zero, an equation that yielded nothing. The weight of it all settled heavily upon her, leaving her adrift in a sea of emotions and unanswered questions.

And then a searing pain shot through her chest, causing her to wince. She glanced down, her breath catching in her throat. The sight that met her eyes left her bewildered. An intricate scar adorned her chest. It seemed to pulse with ancient secrets, and the pain radiating from it held a strange familiarity. She blinked twice, doubting her senses, but the scar remained, a testament to her peculiar encounter with Serpentina. Her eyes widened in shock. 'I thought it was a dream,' she whispered aloud.

Chapter 19

The helicopter sliced through the air, its powerful rotor blades creating a wind storm. Ethan clung to the edge of the helicopter's open door, adrenaline surging through his veins. 'How much time do we have left, Captain?' he shouted over the deafening roar.

'Seven minutes,' Captain Skyhawk replied, his eyes fixed on the mission ahead. 'It's time you get on the skids, Ethan.'

Ethan's lips curved into a half smile. 'Wish me luck,' he said, his voice barely audible against the chopper's clamour.

'But why, Ethan? Why do this?' Skyhawk's gaze bore into him. 'What you told me last night, was it true?'

Ethan pushed back a lock of unruly hair. 'After this mission, I'll have Andria under wraps,' he laughed, determination flashing in his eyes.

Skyhawk's expression darkened. 'You're ignorant regarding this mission's true nature,' he said.

Ethan turned to face him. 'What are you banging on about?' he spat.

'Have you ever heard of the demon?' Skyhawk inquired.

'Are you talking about that woman called Serpentina?' Ethan scoffed. 'The one who haunts everyone's nightmares?'

'Yes,' Skyhawk confirmed, his voice filled with frustration. 'She's the puppeteer behind this operation, pulling Wound's strings.'

Ethan rolled his eyes. 'Serpentina's just a myth, Captain. A tale whispered in London's shadowed alleys.'

'She's no myth,' Skyhawk retorted. 'Believe me, Ethan.'

'Retire, Captain,' Ethan sneered. 'All this flying has addled your mind. You're acting like you've encountered her,' he scoffed.

Skyhawk's jaw tightened. 'Watch your insolence, lad. She instructed me to help out with this mission. I despise the bloodshed,

NEVER UNDERESTIMATE GIRLS!

but I can't escape from her powerful grasp. Ethan, beware and be very careful, or she'll influence you and destroy your mind.'

Ethan glanced out of the window, dismissing Skyhawk's warning. 'Your eyes and ears must be playing tricks on you,' he muttered. 'Serpentina? She's just a figment of imagination.'

Skyhawk's deep sigh hung in the air. 'Get on the skids, but Ethan,' he warned. 'After completing this mission, it's best not to raise your hopes too high for the future you desire because it's not going to happen.'

'We'll see about that,' Ethan jeered. The helicopter blades sliced through the air, creating a rhythmic pulse that reverberated through his chest. Clutching the door frame, he prepared to step out into the unknown.

The skids, thin metal supports protruding from beneath the helicopter, awaited him, poised over the gaping chasm below. Ethan's gloved fingers clutched the frame, knuckles pale with tension. The wind clawed at him, threatening to snatch him away.

Drawing in a determined breath, he swung one leg out, boots scraping against the cold metal. The rush of air stole his breath as he stepped fully onto the skid. The world tilted, and he adjusted himself, finding his balance. The helicopter's downdraft threatened to push him off, but he held firm.

Below, the city sprawled, a mix of lights and shadows. Ethan glanced back at Skyhawk, who gave a curt nod. The chopper hovered, waiting for him to release the safety harness. His heart pounded as he unclipped the buckle.

'Ten seconds, Ethan. Get ready,' Skyhawk shouted.

Blue Glass Skyscraper loomed below, its glass facade shimmering, reflecting the sun's harsh glare. Ethan adjusted his stance, determination fuelling his every move.

JOSEPH JETHRO

The mission lay before him, and to please Andria, he wouldn't let anything come in his way. He calculated the leap; the rooftop seemed impossibly distant, a shimmering oasis in an urban desert.

'Go!' Skyhawk commanded.

Ethan leaned forward, boots gripping the metal. The abyss yawned beneath him, but he focused on the mission. He jumped off the skid, plummeting into uncertainty. The wind swallowed his scream, and then he was falling, freefalling towards the rooftop.

The parachute deployed, jerking him upwards. The city rushed towards him, and he prayed he'd land unseen. The stakes were high, and Ethan knew he had only one chance to prove himself. As the rooftop rushed closer, he clenched his jaw, ready to face whatever awaited him. The cityscape spun, and he fought to maintain his concentration.

The rooftop, a concrete expanse dotted with ventilation shafts and satellite dishes, materialised. Ethan's boots hit hard, knees bending to absorb the impact. He rolled, momentum carrying him forward. Concrete scraped against his palms as he regained his footing. As he stood, chest heaving, adrenaline still roaring, Skyhawk gave him a thumbs-up, and the helicopter ascended, disappearing into the sky.

Ethan scanned the rooftop, senses alert. Shadows clung to corners, and the glass door leading inside beckoned. The mission awaited a delicate balance of stealth and speed. As he sprinted towards the glass door, he pressed his earpiece. 'Andria, I'm on the roof. Get ready for action,' he laughed.

'That's epic. I can't wait. Stay safe,' Alexandria replied calmly despite the nervousness clawing at her insides. She stood beside the safety railing of the River Thames, her fingers gripping the cold metal. The murky waters of the river flowed below, reflecting the blue London sky. With a deep breath, she turned away from the water, her gaze drawn upward to the sleek glass skyscrapers that pierced the skyline.

NEVER UNDERESTIMATE GIRLS!

The wind, like a mischievous accomplice, tousled her hair as she ascended the grand staircase leading to Blue Glass Skyscraper. Its entrance beckoned, its glass doors reflecting the bustling cityscape.

As she stepped through the grand revolving doors, she entered an outstanding lobby. Her gait was deliberate, each step measured and purposeful. She moved with the grace of a seasoned professional, her black heels clicking against the marble floor. Her attire spoke volumes: a tailored charcoal-grey skirt, crisply pressed, and a grey jacket, which she wore over a silk blouse. Her face was adorned with soft makeup; light pink eye shadow highlighted her eyelids, and her lips were beautified with baby pink lipstick, giving her a youthful, almost doll-like appearance.

She blended flawlessly with the throng of business people who streamed in and out of the building. Her demeanour was unassuming, her eyes scanning the lobby for any signs of surveillance. No one would suspect that beneath her composed exterior lay a clandestine purpose, a mission that required her to infiltrate the heart of corporate intrigue.

Yet two young security guards, Owen and Jack, scrutinised her every move. Their eyes tracked her as she glided through the lobby. Owen, with his slicked-back hair, dismissed her as just another face in the crowd. But Jack, always suspicious, couldn't shake the feeling that something was wrong.

'Hey, Owen,' Jack nudged his companion, 'doesn't that girl look a bit...suspicious? Look at the way her eyes dart from right to left.'

Owen chuckled. 'Oh, Jack, everyone seems suspicious to you. Maybe she's just lost.'

'But she can't be a businesswoman,' Jack insisted. 'She looks too young. What's her game, I wonder?'

'Maybe she wandered into the wrong building,' Owen suggested. 'Why don't you ask her?'

'Yeah, I better,' Jack muttered, his gaze still fixed on Alexandria. He crossed the lobby and called out, 'Hey, you!'

JOSEPH JETHRO

Alexandria's heart throbbed. She pretended not to hear him and turned her face away. 'Stay calm,' she reminded herself. Jack's footsteps approached, and she prepared herself for the inevitable barrage of questions.

'Are you lost?' Jack asked, his tone probing.

'I'm new here,' Alexandria stammered, her mouth dry. 'I've lost my way.'

'Where are you heading?' Jack pressed.

'The seventh floor,' she replied. 'That's where I need to be.'

'The seventh floor,' Jack repeated slowly. 'And what's your business there?'

Just then, Ethan's voice crackled through Alexandria's hidden earpiece. 'I'm in the security room. I've got *Target* on camera, third floor. You need to hurry.'

Jack raised an eyebrow. 'Well?'

Alexandria turned away from him causally, whispering, 'Ethan, I've hit a snag. You'll need to intervene.'

'Got it,' Ethan replied calmly.

Jack's eyes bore into Alexandria, suspicion growing. 'Where's your...' he began, but before he could finish, a man swooped in, grabbing Alexandria's arm and pulling her towards him. 'Oh, sweetie, I've been looking for you everywhere!'

'James Starling,' Jack gasped. 'What a pleasure to see you.'

James released Alexandria, who stood there, paralysed. He shook hands with Jack. 'Good to see you, my old friend,' he laughed. 'How have things been going?'

'All the same,' Jack replied, his gaze settling on Alexandria, who seemed poised to run. 'So, who is she?' he asked, nodding towards her.

James smiled, gripping her arm again and causally leaning towards her. 'Will you stay in one place?' he hissed in her ear. 'She's my...she's my wife,' he smiled, gazing into Jack's eyes.

'Wife!' Alexandria and Jack exclaimed simultaneously.

NEVER UNDERESTIMATE GIRLS!

James blushed, squeezing her arm. He hoped she'd get the drift and play along. 'Jack, I can't believe you can't recognise her. You were at the wedding,' he stammered.

Alexandria stared at James in bewilderment. 'What the flip...'

'Andria, I can see you through the cameras,' Ethan's voice came through her hidden earpiece. 'Please play along.'

Not knowing how else to respond, Alexandria forced a smile and held James's hand.

Jack observed them, then slowly nodded. 'Your wife, very well.'

James glanced at his watch. 'I'd best be going. Lots to do.'

'Sure, have a good day,' Jack smiled, returning to Owen, who was leaning against a wall, absorbed in his phone.

'Hey, Owen,' Jack called out.

Owen looked up. 'Yeah, mate?'

'That *girl...w*oman really doesn't look like James's wife,' Jack whispered. 'I'm pretty sure his wife is much older and not so...strange.'

Owen sighed, 'Why would he say she's his wife if she's not? Are you thick or something?'

'No, I'm not,' Jack retorted. 'Just look at them.' He gestured towards James and Alexandria, who were walking up the lobby together.

Owen frowned. James was holding Alexandria's arm tightly, and she kept trying to pull away. 'Mind your own business,' Owen muttered. 'They're probably going through a shaky patch. That's a norm in a marriage.'

Jack stared at Owen, disbelief etched on his face. 'I can't believe you're acting like this,' he muttered. As he watched James and Alexandria, apprehension gnawed at him. Something didn't add up.

JOSEPH JETHRO

Chapter 20

With a mischievous glint in his eyes, James led Alexandria towards the gleaming doors of an elevator. His laughter echoed through the marble-floored hallway, a playful challenge. 'You really don't know how to play along, do you?' he teased.

Alexandria's response was swift and sharp. She wrenched her arm free from James's grasp, her irritation showing up in her voice. 'Get off my arm, you flippin' fool,' she snapped. 'I don't even know who you are.'

James smiled, his voice a low murmur. 'I'm your dad's man,' he confessed, a sly smile dancing on his lips. He gripped her shoulders, turning her to face him. 'Shall I tell you something?'

'I don't wanna hear it,' Alexandria spat, her fist flying through the air. She aimed for James's face, but he deftly sidestepped her attack.

His smile widened. 'Wow, you're just like your dad,' he remarked, very impressed.

'Good,' she retorted, stepping into the elevator. 'Now get lost.'

As the doors closed, James couldn't resist one last jab. 'Hey,' he called, 'you wouldn't have gotten this far if it wasn't for my good acting, girl!'

Inside the elevator, Alexandria sighed, her frustration evident. 'Ethan!' she scolded, pressing her earpiece, her voice sharp. 'What type of plan was that? Why the heck did you tell that guy to act like he was my husband?'

Ethan's response came through her earpiece, his voice heavy with displeasure. 'Hey, there was no other way,' he retorted. 'And besides, I didn't tell James to act like you were his wife. I told him to act like you were his assistant.'

Alexandria rolled her eyes, her annoyance palpable. 'Liar,' she muttered under her breath.

Ethan's laughter bubbled up. 'Listen,' he said. 'Why would I make James act like your husband, girl?' he paused dramatically. 'I'm the one that wants to be...' his voice trailed off, leaving Alexandria intrigued.

'What?' she asked, her forehead creasing with curiosity.

Ethan hesitated, then said, 'Never mind,' he chuckled. 'You'll find out after this mission.'

Alexandria's smile widened. 'I think I already know,' she teased.

Ethan's voice softened. 'No, you don't,' he replied.

'Yes, I do,' she giggled. 'You want me to be your partner.' The words slipped out, hanging in the air, and she waited for his reaction.

An uneasy silence settled between them, leaving Ethan momentarily speechless. 'Oh,' he finally managed to say, his voice filled with surprise.

'So,' she pressed, her heart racing, 'am I right?'

'What type of partner are you referring to?' Ethan asked.

'What type of question is that?' Alexandria laughed. 'You should know which type of partner I'm referring to.'

'I actually don't know?' Ethan confessed. 'You can use the word partner for a variety of different things.'

'Well, I'm talking about the...' Alexandria paused, choosing her words carefully. 'You know the mission type of partner. I think it's cool me and you doing missions together,' she smiled.

'Well, it is,' Ethan laughed, his voice filled with amusement. 'Me and you, we're the best team in London.'

'Do you think so?' Alexandria asked, her voice thoughtful.

'Of course,' Ethan smiled. 'And today is the day to prove ourselves. So, prepare yourself. You're nearing the third floor.'

Alexandria felt a surge of anxiety. 'I'm feelin' really nervous,' she admitted.

'Don't worry,' Ethan reassured, his words hanging in the air like a promise. 'You won't be alone.'

Alexandria took a deep breath. 'I'm trustin' you,' she whispered.

NEVER UNDERESTIMATE GIRLS!

'Trust me with an open heart, Andria,' Ethan murmured.

The elevator abruptly came to a halt, and the doors parted, revealing a magnificent hallway. Alexandria emerged from the elevator, the glossy marble floor echoing with the rhythmic click of her heels. Her eyes widened in awe at the opulence around her. The air carried the sweet scent of jasmine and lavender, enveloping her senses, and tall windows filled the hallway with rays of sunlight.

The floor opened at the heart of this grand space, revealing the level below. Leaning against the golden bannister that encircled the immaculate opening, Alexandria gazed upwards. She realised that every floor, up to the eighth, where a stunning chandelier hung, had open spaces.

She looked around at her surroundings. The hallway stretched before her, empty and noiseless. Only the distant hum of an air condenser disturbed the serene quietness. Alexandria breathed in the cool air that flowed through the open windows.

'Andria, don't get distracted. You're on a mission,' Ethan's sudden warning came through her earpiece, shattering the peaceful atmosphere.

She sighed, remembering the reason why she was in this grand building. 'Where's *Target*?' she asked, the weight of her mission heavy on her shoulders.

'I'm tracking him down,' Ethan replied, the noise of his fingers dancing across a keyboard echoing in her ears. 'He'll be entering your hallway in approximately half a minute.'

Alexandria's eyes lifted to a clock hanging on the wall, its hands ticking relentlessly. Her pulse quickened, and her heart tightened. The man she'd been hunting for what seemed like a lifetime would soon be before her, but then a negative thought crossed her mind. What if she was doing the wrong thing?

The time continued to tick, and Alexandria's anxiety grew. Remona, the woman she'd met in the dark alleyway, materialised in her mind, her words reverberating: *'Kenny must be dealt with, but Liam, he's an innocent soul.'*

'What? What did that statement mean?' Alexandria wondered aloud, her fingers tracing the delicate patterns of the golden bannister.

She remembered sitting by a flowing river with her two little sisters. 'We'll apprehend Kenny,' Layla had whispered, in a determined voice.

'Yeah,' Alexandria had agreed, twisting her mother's gun in her hands.

'But remember,' Stella had said, gripping Alexandria's arm. 'We're only gonna apprehend Kenny.'

'What are you tryna tell me?' Alexandria had asked.

'We mustn't harm him,' Stella had replied, her voice soft yet commanding.

'Why not?' Alexandria had exclaimed. 'He deserves to be six feet down!'

'I know,' Layla had sighed. 'But I agree with Stella. We'll catch him and hand him over to the police, nothin' more.'

Alexandria gazed at the clear blue sky. 'Yeah, I guess that's the right thing to do.'

The sudden echo of footsteps reverberated through the hallway, causing Alexandria's heart to skip a beat. Her sisters' conversation faded into a distant haze as she spun around, her gaze locking onto a man who moved with deliberate steps. Dark secrets clung to him like shadows, poised to unravel at the slightest misstep. His fingers, encircling the silver handle of a sleek black briefcase, betrayed tension. But when his eyes met Alexandria's, he offered a charming smile. 'What are you doing up here, little girl?' he asked, his voice holding a kindness that clashed with the intensity in his eyes.

'Little girl!' Alexandria muttered.

The man raised an eyebrow, studying her. 'My apologies if my words offended you,' he said. 'But I must admit, you appear quite young, about fifteen, I'm guessing.'

NEVER UNDERESTIMATE GIRLS!

Alexandria sighed. 'I'm not interested in what you've got to say!' she retorted bitterly.

His smile widened. 'Ah, I see,' he said. 'I'll leave you to it, then.' With a graceful pivot, he walked away, disappearing into the waiting elevator.

As Alexandria watched the elevator descend, she shivered. It was unsettling how he had scrutinised her, like a predator assessing its prey.

'*Target's* rounding the bend,' the opulent walls seemed to close in on Alexandria as Ethan's urgent update reached her ears.

Her eyes scanned the hallway frantically, her panic escalating. 'Which bend?' she demanded. 'There are about fifty of them in this cursed hallway!'

'He'll be on your right-hand side,' Ethan replied, his voice unwavering.

Following his directions, Alexandria turned to her right. At the far end of the hallway stood the man they had code-named 'Target.'

'Shit!' she gasped. Unprepared, her heart hammered against her rib cage like a caged bird, and a sudden pang of fear and uncertainty washed over her.

Target moved forward, flanked by three other men. Each exuded danger, their slicked-back hair and purposeful strides sending a clear message. They all wore impeccably tailored suits, except for the youngest among them. His dark blue jeans and snug black T-shirt clung to him like ivy, accentuating his lean frame. His steps were light and bouncy, as if he was dancing to a rhythm only he could hear. He wore a silver chain around his neck with pride. His piercing eyes seemed to reach Alexandria's soul, and his smirk caused her throat to tighten painfully.

She stood frozen as if entangled in an invisible net. 'Andria, make your move,' Ethan commanded, but she stood motionless, her hand not reaching for her weapon. 'Andria, is something wrong?' he asked worriedly.

Alexandria's mouth opened and closed, but no sound emerged, her confusion rendering her speechless as she stared at the four men advancing. 'Yo, check the chick. Think I've got her paralysed,' she heard the young man sneer, but she paid no attention to him; her blue eyes were locked on *Target*. He wore slick, black-tinted shades that masked his actual features. Something didn't add up. This man walked with the carefree joy of a family man, a stark contrast to the menacing stride Alexandria would have expected from a ruthless murderer. He swiftly removed his shades, revealing his cool grey eyes. He glanced at Alexandria, and she stared back, her eyes wide with bewilderment. 'No, this can't be right,' she murmured.

'What's not right, Andria? Why aren't you following the plan?' Ethan shouted. '*Target's* practically five meters away, and you've turned into a statue!'

'He's not the right guy,' Alexandria whispered, her eyes glued to *Target's*. 'Kenny's got ice blue eyes, not grey!'

Suddenly, Ethan gasped; the tension in the air was palpable. 'Andria, get out of there!' he shouted. 'It's an *ambu...*' His words trailed off, replaced by the sickening sound of metal slicing through flesh. This was followed by an ear-splitting shriek that echoed in the air and then a chilling, oppressive silence.

'Ethan, Ethan!' Alexandria called, her voice trembling with panic. 'Do you copy me!'

'Yo, who's Ethan? I reckon he ain't gonna be able to help ya on your mission.' The words hung heavy in the air, dripping with mockery. She sharply looked up to see the young man striding towards her. Their eyes met, his sneer a silent provocation.

As he closed the distance, Alexandria's mind raced. Who was this man? How did he know Ethan?

Ethan's last desperate words lingered in her mind: 'Andria, get out of there!'

NEVER UNDERESTIMATE GIRLS!

She turned to leave, but the man's hand shot out, gripping her wrist and pulling her towards him. His touch was warm and soft, sending a shiver down her spine. The sensation was both familiar and electrifying. Had she met this man before? She gazed into his eyes, finding them as hard and unyielding as steel. Yet, beneath the tough exterior, she glimpsed a flicker of vulnerability.

Abruptly, he released her hand, and they stood there, locked in a tense standoff, each assessing the other. But then the fragile silence shattered like glass as one of the other men accompanying *Target* approached, jeering, 'Oi, Bravado, you're always saying your brothers get sidetracked. Check yourself out!'

Bravado tore his gaze away from Alexandria and smirked. 'Dune, the words not 'sidetracked', it's 'considering', thick skull!' he mocked.

'And what are you considering?' Dune asked, rolling his eyes.

'Finkin' whether this girl's worth a shot,' Bravado replied, his gaze lingering on Alexandria.

Alexandria felt her body tense up as Bravado and Dune burst into mocking laughter. 'What?' she asked, her voice low.

'I don't think ya want me to show ya, do ya?' Bravado taunted. Before Alexandria could reply, his fist crashed into her face, the rings on his fingers smashing into her jawbone. The sudden impact sent her flying backwards, her vision blurring as she fell to the floor. The world around her turned into a haze as she lay on the cold, hard marble floor. Memories began to intermingle with the present, pulling her back to the first day she met her father. He had promised her that he would help her take vengeance on Kenny, the man who had taken her mother's life. Following his instructions had led her to this man with cheerful eyes and a joyful walk, whom Alexandria was certain was not Kenny. But who was this young man - Bravado - who had just punched her square in the face? How did he know Ethan? What had happened to Ethan? The thought made her feel sick and distressed.

'Bravado!' An authoritative voice cut through the air like a blade, causing Alexandria to glance upwards, her vision slowly clearing.

Target approached her, his footsteps echoing off the marble floor. He outstretched his hand, a polite gesture. 'I'm sorry,' he said, his voice calm yet firm. 'My lil' bro's a bit of a firecracker.'

Alexandria stared up at him, her eyes tracing the lines of his face, and that's when she concluded. This man was definitely not Kenny; no gangster would offer anyone his hand. Despite this realisation, she refused his help and staggered to her feet, the pain in her jawbone igniting a nerve within her. She glared at Bravado, who was leaning against the golden bannister, amusement dancing in his eyes. Alexandria's fury was palpable as she brushed past *Target* and marched up to Bravado, fists clenched. 'Apologies, or you'll face the consequences,' she spat out.

'Apologise?' Bravado scoffed.

'Yes,' Alexandria replied sharply.

Bravado exploded into laughter. 'I'm really gonna apologise to a girl?' he jeered.

'Too many men have said that to me,' Alexandria laughed, her voice dripping with confidence. With a swift move, her leg flew through the air, aiming a crescent kick at his face. But with breathtaking agility, Bravado sidestepped and blocked the incoming kick with his forearm.

'You wanna play dirty, do ya?' he laughed, his eyes gleaming with mischief. 'Then why not, babe? I don't mind,' he taunted, his voice low and mocking.

With lightning-quick speed, he sprung forward, delivering a swift roundhouse kick. Alexandria effortlessly blocked the attack with her forearm, her movement precise and controlled. She countered with a series of rapid punches, her fists moving like lightning. Bravado dodged and weaved, his movements fluid and graceful, each step a calculated dance. He retaliated with a spinning back kick, aiming for her midsection, but she twisted her body just in time, the kick grazing her ribs.

'What the heck!' *Target* shouted, his voice barely audible over the storm of punches and kicks.

The fight intensified, a blur of kicks, punches, and acrobatic flips. Alexandria executed a flawless flying knee strike, but Bravado anticipated her move, catching her leg mid-air and using her momentum to flip her onto the ground. She landed with a thud but quickly rolled to her feet, a determined glint in her eyes.

They paused momentarily, both breathing heavily, their bodies glistening with sweat. And that's when Dune stepped in. He stood in between them and glared at Bravado. 'What the hell are you doing, dude!' he shouted. 'You know why we're here!'

Bravado wiped the sweat from his forehead. 'I know,' he panted. 'But you know this is the...'

'Stop this nonsense,' *Target* shouted, his voice filled with fury.

'When have you seen a man from the Issaba family fighting with a girl?' scoffed the fourth man who had been quietly standing beside *Target*. The name 'Issaba' lingered in Alexandria's thoughts. Why did that name seem all too familiar?

Bravado glared at the man who had made the comment. 'Shut up, Jon!' he shouted.

Alexandria, never the one to back down, took this moment as an advantage. She adjusted her stance and lunged at Bravado. Dune tried to stop her, but she executed a front-snap kick, hitting him in the stomach with tremendous force, causing him to stagger backwards, his back slamming into the bannister behind him. Pain and surprise contorted his features.

Alexandria then launched a series of high kicks, each one more powerful than the last. Bravado, not expecting the sudden attack, staggered backwards as a kick connected with his lip, blood flowing freely. He quickly recovered from the shot and started to block and parry Alexandria's incoming kicks, his arms moving in a blur of defensive manoeuvres.

Bravado pretended to throw a low kick, drawing Alexandria's eyes downwards, and then sprang up with a powerful uppercut. The punch connected with the lower portion of her face, sending her staggering back. She regained her balance, a fierce smile spreading across her face, and charged forward with renewed energy.

Bravado's breath came in ragged gasps, his stamina waning with each passing second. He knew he couldn't fight much longer, but his pride wouldn't allow him to be defeated by a girl. As Alexandria aimed a spinning hook kick to his ribs, he retrieved a gleaming pocketknife from the depths of his trouser pocket.

Before Alexandria could react, he lunged forward, and the knife sliced through the flesh on her arm. She shrieked in agonising pain, the world blurring as she staggered backwards, blood gushing from the wound. Her knees buckled, and she fell to the ground, clutching her arm, tears streaming down her cheeks. In that excruciating moment, she heard a man swear, and someone scream.

Through her blurred vision, she glimpsed *Target*, his face contorted with horror at the sight of her blood. He seemed to be melting, his confidence shattering. Then came the revelation that would change her life forever.

'Bravado, what the hell! You're bloody in deep shit now,' Jon bellowed, rushing towards Alexandria and kneeling beside her. 'Are you alright?' he asked gently, his voice a stark contrast to the chaos around them.

'We're on a mission. Look at what you've done!' Dune yelled at Bravado, his voice filled with fury. 'What's got into you?'

'Don't you understand? *She's the girl*,' Bravado yelled back, his voice dripping with bitterness.

'What!' all three men shouted simultaneously.

NEVER UNDERESTIMATE GIRLS!

'She's Alexandria, the devil, the one that wanted to kill you, Liam!' Bravado yelled, staring at *Target*, his eyes wild and angry.

As *Target* glanced at Alexandria, his face turned pale. 'I can't handle this blood,' he stammered.

'You should be enjoyin' it,' Bravado spat. 'Wound's daughter,' he said sadistically. 'I love seein' her suffer!'

'She can't be that bitch,' *Target* stammered, his voice trembling with disbelief. He clutched his head in distress, his eyes wide as he watched Alexandria's blood trickle from her wounded arm. She winced in pain, letting out a low scream as Jon squeezed her wound in an attempt to stop the bleeding, but his efforts were futile. Alexandria's blood continued to seep from the gash, pooling and spreading across the cold, white marble floor, the rich, dark red liquid a stark contrast to the pristine surface.

'Bro, she is Alexandria Celeste,' Bravado confirmed, his laughter cold.

Sensing the danger, Alexandria's eyes locked on *Target* and Dune, who exchanged urgent glances. She suddenly felt her blood start to boil as she remembered Ethan's unfinished warning: 'It's an ambu...'

'It's an ambush,' she murmured, her voice barely above a whisper. With a sudden burst of strength, she violently swung her fist into Jon's face, using her good arm. The impact was brutal, sending him reeling backwards, his eyes wide with bewilderment. Blood trickled from the corner of his lip, a stark red against his pale skin.

Alexandria staggered to her feet, flipping her gun out of her hidden waist holster. 'Kenny, it's about time you die!' she screamed, pointing the gun directly at *Target*.

'Don't you dare!' Dune shouted, pulling a hidden gun from beneath his jacket.

In this tense moment, Alexandria locked eyes with *Target*. This man was no ordinary man. He had to be Kenny. If he weren't, then how did he and his men know her name, and how did they know she was going to try and kill him? It all added up, and Alexandria was ready to pull the trigger.

NEVER UNDERESTIMATE GIRLS!

Chapter 21

'We've got this far,' giggled Stella, her voice echoing off the stone staircase as she ascended towards the grand entrance of Blue Glass Skyscraper. The building towered above them, its reflective blue facade shimmering in the afternoon sun, casting a kaleidoscope of colours on the pavement below.

'Yeah,' Layla sighed, her shoulders slumping. 'But I doubt Alex is gonna be here.'

'Layla, you're so negative,' Stella said with a playful smile. 'Why can't you at least have some hope?'

'Stella, even if Alex is here for some weird reason, how are we gonna find her? This building is massive,' Layla replied, her eyes widening as she took in the sheer size of the skyscraper. The structure seemed to stretch endlessly into the sky, its glass exterior reflecting the clouds and the bustling city below.

'Simple,' Stella replied with a confident grin. 'We go in and ask if anybody's seen an eighteen-year-old girl with sharp blue eyes,' she said, pausing outside the skyscraper's entrance. The revolving doors spun continuously as people hurried in and out, each occupied in their own world.

'But so many people come in and out of this buildin',' Layla mused, watching a woman in a sleek business suit stride past her and into the building.

'This is a business skyscraper. Not many teenage girls go in it, I hope,' Stella said, her smile fading slightly as she considered the challenge ahead. 'Anyway, come on, let's get crackin'.'

Stella and Layla exchanged determined glances before stepping through the revolving doors of Blue Glass Skyscraper. The cool, conditioned air of the grand lobby embraced them, a stark contrast to the bustling city outside. The lobby was a marvel of modern architecture, with high ceilings and walls lined with sleek, reflective

NEVER UNDERESTIMATE GIRLS!

blue glass. The floor was made of polished marble, gleaming under the soft lighting.

As they walked further, their footsteps echoed softly in the vast space. The lobby buzzed softly with the sounds of business, with professionals hurrying to and fro. Stella's eyes darted around, taking in the elegant décor.

'There,' Layla whispered, nudging Stella and nodding towards a security guard standing near the reception desk. The guard, Owen, was dressed in a crisp uniform. His eyes scanned the lobby with practiced vigilance while his fingers combed through his hair.

Stella and Layla approached him, their hearts pounding with a mix of hope and anxiety.

'Excuse me,' Stella began, her voice steady despite the nervous flutter in her chest. 'We're lookin' for someone. Have you seen a teenage girl?'

Owen glanced at them, frowning his brow as he considered the question. 'A teenage girl, you say?' he repeated, his voice soft and measured.

'Yes,' Layla said, her voice filled with urgency. 'She's about eighteen, with striking blue eyes. It's crucial that we find her.'

Owen scratched his chin thoughtfully. 'Not many teenagers come through here,' he said slowly.

Suddenly, hurried footsteps echoed from behind them. Stella turned around to see Jack, another security guard, approaching them. 'What do these lasses want?' he asked Owen, nodding towards Layla and Stella.

'They're looking for an eighteen-year-old teenage girl with striking blue eyes,' Owen replied, shrugging his shoulders. 'I haven't seen a girl come in here, have you?'

'Of course,' Jack said. 'She's a strange teenager, innit?'

'Yeah, sought of,' Layla replied.

'I saw her alright, a few minutes ago,' Jack confirmed.

Stella's eyes widened with hope. 'Really? Can you tell us where she went?'

Jack nodded. 'She was heading towards the elevators. If you hurry, you might still catch her.'

'Thank you so much!' Stella said, grabbing Layla's hand and pulling her towards the elevators at the far end of the lobby.

'Oi, where you going?' Jack suddenly called.

Layla and Stella both turned around. 'We're goin' to find her,' Stella replied.

To the girls' dismay, Jack shook his head sternly. 'I'm not going to let you go wandering around this building. It's for business, not for little girls...'

'But,' Layla began.

'I wasn't finished,' Jack said. 'I'll come with you if you so desperately want to find her. I want to find her myself anyway. She was acting quite odd when she came in here.'

'Thanks,' Layla smiled.

'One question, before I take you two on a goose chase, why do you want to find her?' Jack asked.

Stella and Layla exchanged a glance. 'We need her,' Stella replied nervously.

'It's personal,' Layla suddenly said.

'I can guess that girl is your big sister,' Jack smiled. 'You two are quite strange, just like her,' he laughed with a playful roll of his eyes. 'So, do you know the number of the office she is in?'

Layla stared at Stella in dismay. Then she turned back to face Jack. 'Not really,' she replied.

'How do you suppose we're going to find her then?' Jack asked. 'This building has about thirty floors. You're not planning on searching all of them, are you?'

'Oh god,' Stella groaned. 'This is harder than I thought.'

NEVER UNDERESTIMATE GIRLS!

Jack gazed at the two girls' disappointed faces and suddenly said, 'She might be on the seventh floor. She happened to tell me that she was going to be there.'

'Oh, good, let's go and find her,' Stella said.

Smiling softly, Jack guided Layla and Stella to the elevators. They walked through the bustling lobby, their footsteps echoing softly against the marble floor. Jack pressed the call button as they reached the elevator, and the doors slid open with a gentle chime.

Layla and Stella stepped inside, their eyes glancing around the sleek, mirrored interior. Jack followed, pressing the button for the seventh floor. The doors closed smoothly, and the elevator began its ascent, the soft hum of the machinery filling the small space.

'You spoke to our big sister, didn't you?' Stella asked, leaning against the elevator's cold wall.

Before Jack could reply, Layla's heavy sigh cut through the air. 'Stella, you're saying *big sister,* but we don't even know if the girl this man saw was her. Just imagine it wasn't her.'

'Layla, you're so disheartening,' Stella muttered, pushing her hands into her pockets.

'You're funny, Stella,' Layla said.

'What do you mean?' Stella asked.

'I just realised yer not actin' shy like normally,' Layla replied.

'I'm so worried about Alex,' Stella whispered, gazing at the floor.

'It's none of my business, but why do you two seem so distressed? Is there something more to this than you're telling me?' asked Jack.

'No,' sighed Layla.

The machinery's hum gradually softened as the elevator neared the seventh floor. The gentle upward motion slowed as the elevator prepared to stop. With a soft ding, the elevator came to a smooth halt. The doors glided open effortlessly, unveiling their destination.

Jack stepped out first, and Layla and Stella followed, their eyes intently scanning their surroundings. A grand hallway stretched out before them, its walls adorned with numerous doors. Each door was uniquely marked, hinting at the different offices and rooms they led to. Plush carpets muffled their footsteps as they walked up the hallway, and the faint scent of polished wood and fresh flowers filled the air.

In the heart of the hallway, the floor gave way to a grand opening, bordered by a chic, modern railing. The opening provided a clear view of the floors below, where similar hallways branched out, creating a labyrinth of interconnected spaces.

The atmosphere was one of quiet efficiency, with the occasional murmur of conversations and the soft click of doors opening and closing. It was a place where business thrived, each door leading to a different world of activity and purpose.

Stella's eyes darted from door to door, furrowing her brow, lost in thought. She moved with purpose, peeking into each room through the small windows on the doors, hoping to catch a glimpse of Alexandria. The hallway seemed endless, each door a potential hiding place. She paused occasionally, listening for any familiar sounds that might indicate Alexandria's presence.

Layla followed closely behind, her steps slower and more deliberate. She watched intently as Stella searched with determination, her own hope gradually waning. After several minutes of hopeless searching, Layla stopped walking, leaned against a wall, and sighed deeply.

'I don't think Alexandria is here,' she said softly, her voice filled with disappointment.

Stella turned to face her, a look of sorrow crossing her face. 'I was dumb to think she'd be here,' she whispered.

Layla's eyes darted around the hallway. 'So, what are we gonna do now?' she asked, her voice heavy with anxiety.

'You always act like I'm the big sister,' she replied, her frustration evident. 'Can't you think of somethin'?'

'No, I can't,' Layla admitted, her shoulders slumping.

NEVER UNDERESTIMATE GIRLS!

A stern voice behind them suddenly cut through the tension like a knife, 'Are you lost?' The sharpness of the words made Layla spin around to find a man approaching. His presence seemed to fill the hallway with dread, and his expression was etched with disapproval.

'No,' Layla stammered, her voice barely audible. 'We're just lookin' for someone.'

The man's gaze bore into them. 'Who are you with?' he demanded, his tone brooking no nonsense.

Before Layla could respond, Jack materialised behind the man. 'They're with me,' he said in a steady voice.

The man turned around, his confusion evident. 'Jack, aren't you supposed to be on duty?' he asked scornfully.

'I am on duty,' Jack replied. 'Looking for a girl, if you can believe it.'

'No, I can't,' the man snapped. 'You're supposed to be on the ground floor, not up here.'

'I know but...' Jack began.

'No 'buts",' the man interrupted. 'You're supposed to be on the ground floor, so I don't want you up here.'

Jack controlled his frustration and gave a polite nod. 'Yes, sir,' he responded. He glanced at Layla and Stella. 'Come on,' he instructed, signalling them to follow. 'Let's head out.'

'And who are these girls?' the man demanded, pointing towards Layla and Stella.

'They're looking for their sister,' Jack replied, turning to Stella. 'What's her name?'

'Alexandria,' Stella replied.

'Alexandria,' the man repeated, his voice filled with surprise. 'No such person comes to this place with that name. Jack, take these girls out of here. This is no playground.' With that, he strode up the hallway and disappeared around a bend.

'I don't understand how you handled that guy's attitude,' whispered Layla.

Jack glanced at her, his expression weary. 'When you work for someone, you've got to accept their attitude or risk getting fired,' he said softly.

'You work for that guy?' Layla asked.

'He's in control of this building's safety,' Jack explained, his voice low. 'Say anything wrong to him, and you're out. It's happened to plenty of guys who thought they could go against him. So, we should get going before I get the sack. I'm sorry we couldn't find your sister.'

Layla and Stella exchanged a sorrowful glance, their hopes dwindling. They had no choice but to trail behind Jack as he walked back down the hallway towards the elevators.

'You know what?' Stella whispered, nudging Layla.

'What?' Layla asked, glancing at Stella, her curiosity piqued.

'That guy we just bumped into,' Stella replied, her voice a low whisper. 'It seems to me as if he didn't want us to find Alex.'

Layla raised an eyebrow. 'Stella, that doesn't even make sense,' she said.

'I'm just tellin' you what I think,' Stella exhaled deeply.

'But why? Why would that thought even cross yer mind?' Layla asked, her curiosity mounting.

'Because...' Stella paused, her attention caught by an unusual sound resonating through the hallway. Jack froze, too, his eyes narrowing warily.

The grand hallway seemed to hold its breath as the strange noise reverberated through the air. Conversations abruptly stopped, footsteps ceased, and every eye turned towards the unknown source of the disturbance. The tension was palpable, thickening the atmosphere like an impending storm.

Jack, ever vigilant, stepped away from Layla and Stella, his gaze narrowing. He walked purposefully towards the railing that encircled the opening in the floor. He leaned over, peering downward, his knuckles white as he gripped the railing.

NEVER UNDERESTIMATE GIRLS!

And then it came a shrill, bone-chilling shriek. It echoed off the walls, bouncing from floor to ceiling, slicing through the silence. A chill ran down Jack's spine, making the hairs on the back of his neck stand up. He clenched his jaw, his eyes scanning the levels below.

Layla's eyes grew wide, a mix of curiosity and fear battling within her. 'What was that?' she asked.

'It came from the third floor,' Jack replied. 'I'm going to check it out.'

The tension in the hallway thickened as Stella's gasp sliced through the air like a blade. 'Alex,' she cried, her voice desperate and urgent. Before anyone could blink, she sprinted towards the nearest elevator, followed by Layla, whose expression was a mix of concern and urgency.

Stella's fingers jabbed at the elevator's call button. The metal doors slid open, revealing the dimly lit compartment, but just as she was about to step inside, Jack's hand shot out, gripping her arm with an iron resolve.

'Get off my arm!' Stella snapped, her eyes flashing with determination.

Jack's jaw tightened, his grip unyielding. 'Listen, girl,' he said, his voice low and insistent. 'I'm not letting you go anywhere until you give me an answer. Why did you shout out the name 'Alex'?'

Stella struggled, trying to free herself from his grasp. 'That's Alex,' she gasped. 'On the third floor!'

'What?' Layla asked, her voice trembling. 'I mean, how do you know?'

Stella locked eyes with Layla, her desperation evident. 'Layla,' she pleaded, 'if you ask me another question, I won't speak to you again. That was Alex's shriek. I know it. I can recognise her cry from a mile away.'

Jack released Stella's arm, and she darted into the elevator. 'Are you coming or not?' she asked Layla, who seemed to hesitate slightly outside the lift.

JOSEPH JETHRO

Layla and Jack stepped into the elevator, it's polished metal walls reflecting their anticipation. Stella hit the button for the third floor, and the elevator door slowly slid shut.

'You didn't think I'd let you go alone?' Jack asked as the elevator began its descent. 'I didn't like the sound of that shriek. Somethings up.'

Chapter 22

'We can talk about this,' *Target* stammered, his body trembling as he gazed at Alexandria's finger tightening around the trigger.

'Really?' Alexandria scoffed, her voice dripping with venom. 'After you killed my mother!'

'I swear I never killed your mother,' *Target* pleaded, his eyes wide with fear. 'But I know who did. So can you put that gun down, and we'll talk about it.'

Alexandria's laughter was chilling. 'We'll talk about nothin',' she confessed, her eyes cold and unyielding.

'Oh, yeah, ya bloody will!' Bravado shouted from behind Alexandria, his fists clenched tightly, knuckles white with tension.

Alexandria glanced down at her left arm, watching the blood drip onto the marble floor, a stark reminder of Bravado's earlier attack. A surge of anger ignited within her, fuelling her resolve. Her eyes flicked to Dune, who had his gun pointed straight at her. With lightning speed, too quick for anyone to follow, she spun around and executed a flying front flip. In mid-air, she fired at Bravado. The bullet struck his arm, sending him crashing to the ground in pain. As Dune's bullet whizzed towards her, she performed a breathtaking aerial manoeuvre, dodging the bullet with grace and precision. She landed elegantly, locking eyes with *Target*. 'Bye, honey,' she taunted.

'Really?' Dune smirked, pulling the trigger of his gun once again. The bullet tore through Alexandria's hand, causing her to scream in pain. Her firearm slipped out of her grasp, but not before she pulled the trigger. The bullet sliced through the air, and *Target's* painful scream filled the hallway as the bullet ripped through his ribs. He collapsed onto the floor, blood gushing from the wound.

Bravado's eyes widened in shock and fear. He staggered to his feet, ignoring the pain in his own wounded arm, and ran to his brother's side. 'Bro,' he gasped, kneeling next to his fallen brother. 'Bro,' he stammered, staring at *Target's* motionless face. He pressed a trembling hand against *Target's* wound, blood seeping through his fingers.

'He's still breathing,' Jon whispered, pressing his hand against *Target's* chest.

Bravado's fist crashed into Jon's jaw in a surge of fury. He staggered backwards, his eyes wide with surprise. 'Do you think that's gonna make me feel better!' Bravado shouted, his voice sharp. 'Call the bloody ambulance!'

As Jon pulled his phone out of his pocket to call the ambulance, Bravado turned around to face Dune, who had his gun pointed at Alexandria. 'Put your hands up and bloody kick your gun away,' Dune commanded.

Alexandria's heart raced as Dune's stern command echoed through the hallway. She knew better than to defy him. With a mixture of fear and defiance, she raised her hands above her head, her wounded hand trembling tremendously.

'Now kick your gun away,' Dune ordered.

Alexandria glanced down at her fallen gun and kicked it away, but she was no mere pawn. Her nerves screamed for a reaction, and she couldn't resist. A cheeky grin tugged at the corners of her lips. With a swift, rebellious motion, she extended her middle finger, its defiance aimed squarely at Dune. It was a silent challenge, a small act of rebellion in the face of authority.

'You cheeky bitch,' Bravado shouted at Alexandria. 'Dune, go to my bro. I've got some business to finish.'

Dune hesitated. 'Bravo...'

'Shut your mouth and head over to my bro,' Bravado yelled. 'Before you get a punch.'

Dune slowly nodded his head, his eyes lingering on Alexandria. After glancing at her one last time, he turned away and walked towards Jon, who was sitting beside *Target*. 'How is he?' he whispered.

NEVER UNDERESTIMATE GIRLS!

'He's in a critical state,' Jon stammered, his voice trembling. 'He needs to be taken to the hospital immediately!'

Bravado strode towards Alexandria, his shoulders moving in a rhythmic motion. 'Yer gonna pay for harmin' ma brother!' he yelled.

'Oh! Poor baby, what ya gonna do, bite me?' Alexandria scoffed, sarcasm dripping from her words.

Bravado lunged at her, executing a powerful reverse sidekick. His foot slammed against her rib cage, sending her flying backwards, her back colliding painfully with the bannister, and she gasped for air. 'How did that feel?' Bravado yelled, grabbing her by the shoulders and yanking her to her feet. 'Tell me!'

Alexandria stared at his face; the pain in her body was unbearable, but her sassiness soon overcame her. 'It felt good,' she replied with a smirk.

'Oh, did it?' Bravado laughed. With a sudden surge of power, he gave her a violent uppercut; the impact jarred Alexandria's bones, momentarily stunning her.

Determined to protect herself, Alexandria raised her already injured arms and tried to block his incoming punches, yet Bravado's punches had turned into an unstoppable force despite his wounded arm. Each strike slipped past her defences with brutal precision, his fists connecting with her torso and sending jolts of pain searing through her body. She screamed with pain, but Bravado was relentless.

Grabbing her head, he slammed her face against his knee continuously, each blow more devastating than the last. Blood splattered, and Alexandria's strength waned. With a final, contemptuous shove, he flung her to the ground, leaving her gasping for breath.

She lay on the floor, blood gushing out of her nose and mouth. Her breathing quickened as she heard Bravado's footsteps approaching. As his trainer smashed into her face, she tried to scream, but blood filled her mouth. 'You thought it'd be easy tryna kill ma bro?' he sneered. 'Well, I'll make sure you wish you were never born!'

'Leave me alone,' Alexandria stammered, blood escaping from the corners of her mouth. Her voice trembled, a mix of defiance and desperation. 'Your brother deserved it!'

Bravado's eyes narrowed with fury as he delivered a brutal kick to her ribs. She gasped, her body curling instinctively to protect itself. Pain radiated through her chest, sharp and unrelenting, each breath a struggle.

As Alexandria's vision blurred, the world around her dissolved into a suffocating darkness. She could no longer see the dimly lit hallway or the menacing figure looming over her. All that remained was the overwhelming blackness pressing in on her from all sides. Her mind swirled with a chaotic blend of fear and agony, each heartbeat echoing the torment she had just endured.

Alexandria felt utterly alone, her strength waning as the darkness threatened to consume her entirely. The taste of blood in her mouth was a bitter reminder of her vulnerability, and the cold, unyielding floor beneath her offered no solace. Pain and fear coursed through her veins, creating a mixture of despair that threatened to drown her. She lay there, motionless, time slipping away in an indistinguishable haze of seconds, minutes and hours. Her only thought was of her mother's face, a beacon of comfort in the sea of pain. She clung to the memory of her warm smile and kind eyes, trying to draw strength from it. *I tried Mother! I tried to get revenge.* She thought.

Then, a faint but familiar voice pierced the darkness from outside the murky haze. It called her name, a lifeline in the gloomy haze she was in. Slowly, her mind began to clear, the fog of pain and fear lifting just enough for her to focus on the sound. The voice grew louder and more insistent, and with it came a glimmer of hope.

Alexandria's breathing steadied, and she forced herself to listen, to hold on to that voice. The darkness still surrounded her, but now it felt

NEVER UNDERESTIMATE GIRLS!

less suffocating, less absolute. Her mother's face remained in her mind, a source of strength as she fought to stay conscious, to survive.

And then, the voice grew louder, more frantic, pulling her back to consciousness. Her eyelids fluttered open, her vision slowly coming back into focus. The air buzzed with the echo of hurried footsteps and urgent voices, a stark contrast to the oppressive silence she had just escaped. As her senses sharpened, Alexandria realised that the emergency forces had arrived. Paramedics and police officers moved swiftly around her, their faces tense with urgency. The atmosphere crackled with the intensity of the chaos that had unfolded within this hallway moments ago.

Two paramedics rushed towards her. They quickly assessed her condition by checking her pulse, breathing, and level of consciousness. One paramedic applied direct pressure to the gunshot wound on her hand, using sterile dressings to control the bleeding, while the other paramedic immobilised her wounded arm with a bandage, reducing her pain and preventing further injury.

As the paramedics tended to her wounds, Alexandria's vision remained hazy like a watercolour painting left out in the rain. Shapes blurred and merged, and the world seemed to spin around her. Each noise, the paramedics' urgent whispers, the clatter of metal instruments, and the distant echo of footsteps, was amplified, assaulting her senses, causing her head to throb in rhythm with her heartbeat. As she tilted her head to the right, she caught sight of two officers engaged in an urgent conversation with Jon, Dune and Jack, the always suspicious security guard. Their voices overlapped, a jumble of urgency and determination.

Alexandria recognised the two officers instantly: Luca, a man she harboured deep resentment towards, and Benjamin, who she knew too well after a startling incident when she nearly got rammed down by a train.

As she continued to stare at the officers, she glanced at two paramedics rushing *Target* out of the hallway. Their urgent whispers reached her ears. 'He's still breathing! He might make it!'

I hope he doesn't live to see another day. Alexandria thought bitterly to herself.

A strange noise abruptly filled her ears; she swivelled her head to the left, where Bravado sat slumped against a wall, his sobs grating on Alexandria's nerves. His torn shirt revealed a gash on his arm, blood seeping through the makeshift bandages. The paramedic attending to him worked with grim determination, his latex-gloved hands moving swiftly. Bravado's tears glistened, tracing paths down his cheeks.

Alexandria was stunned by the transformation of his features. Once marked by ruthless pride, his face now bore a humility she hadn't anticipated. The sharp edges that had once defined his features had softened, and lines etched by battles and burdens now told a different story. His eyes, once cold and unyielding, held a vulnerability, a quiet acknowledgement of his mortality. Gone was the pride that had fuelled his every move; in its place was a calm resolve and a newfound connection to the world around him. It was as if the weight of his past sins had etched a new map upon his skin, one that spoke of redemption, not recklessness. Alexandria stared at him in bewilderment; the transformation was mind-boggling.

And then her gaze fell upon three more officers: Arnold, the gruff sergeant with a permanent scowl; Harry, the detective who always seemed one step ahead; and Luna, the police officer who could read minds better than anyone.

Amidst the chaos and pain, the same voice which had pulled Alexandria out of unconsciousness resonated once more. Her gaze fell upon two familiar faces: Stella and Layla. They ran towards her, eyes wide with worry. Stella knelt beside her, her expression a mix of relief and fear. 'Alex!' she gasped, tears glistening in her eyes.

NEVER UNDERESTIMATE GIRLS!

Seeing them brought a rush of emotions, and Alexandria felt a surge of gratitude and love. 'Stella,' she choked, blood and tears mixing. 'I tried to kill *Target*,' she stammered.

Stella glanced at Alexandria, concerned and confused. 'Alex?' she asked gently.

'I mean Kenny,' Alexandria whispered, correcting herself. 'I tried to kill him?'

Stella burst into tears. 'Kenny,' she sobbed, 'is his name carved into your consciousness?'

Logan, the paramedic attending to Alexandria's wounded hand, glanced at Stella, pity in his eyes. 'She'll be fine,' he reassured.

Layla seized Stella's hand, her touch gentle. 'Stella, don't worry,' she whispered. 'We've found her. She's gonna be fine.'

Alexandria looked at her two sisters. 'You've been lookin' for me?' she asked, recalling the day she had broken ties with them. 'Why?'

'Because we love ya,' Layla murmured. 'Forever.'

Layla's whispered words enveloped Alexandria's battered body, a healing balm for the ache within her. Each syllable became a cherished memory etched into her soul. 'I love you too,' she whispered, her smile faint as blood continued to seep from her mouth.

JOSEPH JETHRO

Chapter 23

Alexandria lay sprawled on the cold, polished marble floor. Her once vibrant clothing was now stained dark red, a testament to the brutal struggle she had endured. The pain in her body was sharp and relentless. Once bright and full of life, her eyes were now half-closed, their azure depths clouded with exhaustion.

Layla knelt beside her, her presence comforting and familiar. She held Alexandria's hand, her touch gentle yet firm. 'We'll be together forever,' she whispered, and Stella nodded her head, the gesture a silent promise.

Alexandria's pain slowly ebbed away, and for a fleeting moment, she felt safe. In that quiet sanctuary, surrounded by love and sisterhood, she closed her eyes. The pain receded, replaced by a profound gratitude. She knew she would heal, not just her body but her spirit too. For as long as her sisters stood by her side, she would endure and rise once more.

As she surrendered to the pull of sleep, the paramedics exchanged urgent glances. 'We need to get this girl to the hospital, Silas,' Logan said to his companion.

Silas, the other paramedic, nodded grimly, his eyes flickering to Alexandria's pale face. 'Of course, Logan. But first, I think I'll send you to the hospital!'

'What?' Logan asked, his eyebrows shooting upwards in surprise.

Silas's next actions were brutal, catching Logan off guard. 'I'm sorry,' he whispered, reaching for a hidden knife which was strapped close to his waist. As he retrieved the blade, its metallic surface caught the dim light, its edge wickedly sharp. 'We need a distraction,' he smirked, lunging at Logan. The blade sliced the air, heading straight for Logan's chest. His movements were swift, fuelled by desperation and adrenaline.

JOSEPH JETHRO

Logan barely had time to react, his instincts kicking in. He twisted away, the blade grazing his shoulder, leaving a searing trail of pain. 'What the heck!' he shouted, adrenaline surging.

Silas spun the knife between his fingers, his sharp gaze locked onto Logan. His lips curved into a jeering smirk as he charged at Logan. Their bodies collided, the blade grazing Logan's flesh.

The sudden outburst hadn't gone unnoticed. Officer Benjamin sprinted towards them, eyes wide with dread. 'Drop the knife!' he shouted, but Silas ignored him, focusing solely on Logan. Benjamin lunged, attempting to tackle Silas from behind.

But Silas whirled around, slashing the knife across Benjamin's chest. The blade sank deep, and he screamed with pain, stumbling back, blood staining the marble floor.

Silas turned back to face Logan, the knife in his hands dripping with blood. He lunged again, aiming for Logan's stomach. But Logan's leg shot up, connecting with Silas's ribs. As Silas staggered backwards, he managed to slice Logan's thigh, blood spraying. The pain was blinding, but Logan fought back, fuelled by fear and rage. The hallway blurred as they grappled, each desperate to survive this unexpected battle of life and death. Blood, adrenaline, and desperation painted the scene, leaving no room for hesitation.

Silas threw the knife viciously at Logan. The blade pierced the side of Logan's body, causing him to let out an ear-splitting scream. He collapsed onto the floor, blood gushing out of the wound. Silas laughed wickedly. 'You trusted me,' he smirked, kneeling beside Logan and removing the knife from his flesh. 'Now, here are the consequences,' he said, raising his knife above Logan's body.

Before he could act, Officer Luca and Officer Arnold, sprang into action. Their movements were swift, honed by years of training and fuelled by adrenaline. Luca tackled Silas from the side, wrapping his arms around his waist, whilst Arnold aimed for Silas's legs, attempting to bring him down.

NEVER UNDERESTIMATE GIRLS!

Silas fought back, his face contorted with determination and desperation. The knife glinted in the dim light as he struggled to maintain his grip. Luca grunted, using his strength to force Silas's arm upwards. Arnold seized the opportunity, his gloved fingers digging into Silas's wrist. With a determined twist, he wrenched the knife from his hand, sending it clattering across the floor.

Yet, Silas's eyes narrowed, and a primal rage ignited within him. He wasn't done fighting. With a sudden surge of strength, he twisted his body, muscles straining against the officers' grip. He clenched his fists and unleashed a flurry of punches and kicks, striking with raw determination. The officers staggered, caught off guard, and Silas broke free, fuelled by sheer willpower.

He pulled two short knives out of his waist belt and flung them at the officers; the blades cut through the air, one hitting Luca in the arm and the other slicing through Arnold's leg. Silas laughed with satisfaction, amusement dancing in his green eyes.

'We need backup right away,' Luca shouted through his walkie-talkie, his voice strained as he pulled the knife out of his arm. 'Paramedic's gone mad!'

Silas picked up his knife from the blood-slicked floor. He advanced towards Logan, the corners of his mouth curving into a cruel smile. 'Hi, mate,' he taunted, the words dripping with disdain. Without hesitation, he plunged the blade into Logan's body, relishing the horrible sensation as it slid through flesh and bone. 'Feel's good, doesn't it?' he asked, withdrawing the knife from Logan's shaking body. His voice held a casual indifference as though discussing the weather. 'I'll take your silence as a yes,' he smirked.

He then turned away from Logan's bleeding body and surveyed the chaotic hallway. His gaze fell on Officer Luna; she was kneeling next to Officer Benjamin, who had been gravely injured. 'Next time, try to stop me,' he chuckled before locking eyes with Detective Harry and security guard Jack, who stood frozen at the far end of the hallway, their eyes wide with bewilderment and terror. 'Keep on staring, you idiots,' he sneered. 'I like the attention.'

His gaze then fell on Officer Luca and Officer Arnold, who were clutching their wounds in agony. 'Wow, you're some crazy officers,' he sarcastically complimented. He then looked at Layla and Stella, who sat petrified beside Alexandria's fragile form. 'Stare at your sister, not me,' he whispered venomously. 'Cause I don't think you're going to see her after today.'

'Silas,' a voice echoed from the shadows, dripping with both familiarity and disdain. 'It's been a long time since I've seen you, you devilish man!' The words carried the weight of grudges and unfinished business. Silas turned around, his eyes narrowing as he faced Dune, who had a gun clenched tightly in his hands.

'Put your hands up, dog,' Dune commanded, his voice strained. 'And drop the knife!'

Silas's laughter erupted, a bone-chilling sound, as he defied the order. In a blur of motion, he hurled the knife at Dune, who sidestepped just in time, avoiding the blade's deadly trajectory. It whizzed past his chest, an inch away from piercing his heart.

'I said put your hands up!' Dune's desperation was palpable. Silas, now unarmed, complied, raising his palms in surrender.

Dune wiped the sweat from his forehead, relief flooding through his veins. But just as he dared to believe that the chaos had ended, Bravado's scream, raw and desperate, shattered the fragile peace. Dune whirled around, heart pounding, to see James Starling - who had helped Alexandria back in the building's lobby where Jack, the security guard, had suspiciously questioned her.

He was gripping Bravado in a tight headlock with a gun pointed directly at his head, a silent threat that hung heavy in the air.

'Let go of him!' Dune shouted.

James's lips curved into a nasty smirk. 'Only after you put your gun down,' he taunted, eyes glinting with malice.

NEVER UNDERESTIMATE GIRLS!

Dune's mind raced, his fingers tightening around his weapon. 'Let him go,' he pleaded. 'Then I'll put my gun down.'

'My way or no way,' James threatened, his voice unyielding. Dune hesitated before lowering his gun. 'Drop it, you piece of shit!' James yelled.

Dune dropped the gun, his body trembling. 'Now release him!' he shouted.

James shook his head. 'First, I take Andria,' he declared.

Wounded and in pain, Officer Arnold made a valiant effort to stand. Blood seeped from his leg, staining the marble floor. 'You're not taking anyone!' he shouted.

'Nobody moves,' James smirked, firing a single shot at Arnold. The bullet tore through his body, and he collapsed, blood pooling around him.

Officer Luna's scream filled the hallway, and James's eyes instantly fell on her. 'I don't like hurting women,' he warned, his voice low and dangerous, 'but if I have to, I will.'

Tears welled up in Luna's eyes, her voice trembling. 'James Starling, why are you doing this?' she sobbed. 'I thought you were a good man?'

'Lady, I don't think you want to get involved,' sighed James. 'Don't open your mouth, or you'll die with one of my bullets.' His attention then shifted back to Dune. 'I take Andria, and you get your *baby*,' he mocked, the word 'baby' dripping with hate and disdain.

Bravado, fuelled by anger, struggled against James's iron grip. 'I'm not a bloody baby!' he shouted defiantly.

'Shut your mouth, or you'll die sooner than you think,' James hissed, his voice as cold as ice.

'I'm not gonna shut up!' Bravado yelled, attempting to smash his elbow into James's ribs. But James swiftly retaliated, slamming his gun into Bravado's face, causing him to scream with agony.

Dune, witnessing the brutality, pleaded desperately. 'Take Alexandria, I don't care!'

'Silas, take her,' James commanded.

Silas's smirk widened. 'Sure,' he said, his gaze lingering on Dune's discarded gun. 'And I'll take this,' he said, snatching the weapon off the floor and firing a single shot at Dune's leg. Dune collapsed to the floor, crying in agony. Silas laughed, relishing the pain. He turned to face James, who shot him a sharp look. 'You should know,' Silas jeered, 'I love seeing blood.'

'The police reinforcements will be here soon!' James shouted.

'Calmly, bro,' Silas whispered. 'Or do you want me to put a bullet through your head?'

'Shut the heck up, and take the girl,' James yelled, his frustration boiling over.

Silas turned around and glanced at Alexandria. 'How am I supposed to take her? I think she's unconscious.'

'Pick her up if you have to,' James yelled, his face turning red with annoyance.

'You're not taking her anywhere,' Stella shouted, her eyes wide with panic. 'I won't let you.'

Silas studied Stella, amusement dancing in his sharp green eyes. 'Girls usually run away from me,' he laughed. 'So, suggest you follow the trend and skip off.'

'Never!' Stella yelled.

Silas's gaze pierced into Stella's soul. 'You leave me no choice,' he said, pulling the trigger of his gun.

Stella screamed as the bullet tore through the side of her leg. Tears filled her eyes, and she collapsed, her blood staining the floor crimson.

'Stella,' Layla gasped, clutching her hand. 'Stella!' she screamed, her voice breaking with fear and anguish.

Silas approached, a smirk playing on his lips. 'You can't say I didn't warn her,' he sneered.

Layla turned to face him, tears streaming down her cheeks. 'Why?' she screamed.

NEVER UNDERESTIMATE GIRLS!

'If she's lucky,' Silas mocked, 'she'll recover. But if you interfere with me again, she won't survive 'cause this time I'll put a bullet through her head.'

Layla's eyes blazed with fury as she locked her gaze on Silas. 'Ya evil bitch!' she yelled.

Silas's palm connected with her cheek, the force of the slap sending shockwaves through her. Layla shrieked, her desperate cry reaching Alexandria's ears.

Alexandria's eyes fluttered open. 'Where am I?' she muttered in a puzzled voice; she tried to sit up, but her body ached, causing her to wince.

Silas extended his hand, a sly smile playing on his lips. 'Come on,' he urged.

Alexandria's eyes bore into his face. 'Who are you?' she asked, gripping his hand. He pulled her up from the floor, and she clung to the golden bannister for support. As her surroundings came into focus, she remembered where she was: the opulent hallway, now marred by chaos.

'Look around,' a voice whispered in her heart. 'Take in the chaos. You caused it all!'

Alexandria stood frozen, her breath catching in her throat as she surveyed the grim scene. The once-pristine marble floor was now stained with blood, starkly contrasting with its former elegance. Lifeless bodies lay sprawled on the floor, while critically injured individuals groaned in pain, their faces etched with fear and shock. A group of people stood frozen, unable to comprehend the horror that had unfolded before them, and Bravado, still trapped in James's tight headlock, looked as if he had seen a ghost.

Alexandria's mind spun wildly, desperately searching for a way out of this nightmare. 'I didn't cause this,' she choked out. 'I only tried to kill Kenny!'

And then her eyes fell on Layla, who was sitting beside Stella's wounded body, tears streaming down her face.

'Stella!' Alexandria screamed. Guilt gnawed at her insides as she saw blood seeping through the gash on Stella's leg, soaking her clothes. Her body trembled as she knelt beside her wounded sister; she placed her bandaged hand on Stella's wound.

Stella screamed, her face contorting in pain.

'Stella,' Alexandria gasped. 'Who did this?'

'That shithead,' Layla shouted, glaring at Silas.

Alexandria's tear-filled gaze locked onto Silas's face. 'You bloody dog, how dare you shoot my sister!' she shouted.

Silas suddenly grabbed Alexandria by the arm, yanking her to her feet. 'This is no time to argue over a stupid girl. We've gotta go,' he declared, his eyes devoid of remorse.

'I'm not goin' with you,' she protested. 'Let go of me!'

But Silas remained unyielding. 'I must take you to your father,' he stated, pulling her further away from Stella and Layla.

'Do you actually think I'm gonna go with a guy who just hurt my sister!' Alexandria shouted. Her fist connected with Silas's jaw, fuelled by adrenaline and grief. He staggered, releasing her arm.

'Get her bloody out of here,' James shouted at Silas, who was clutching his face in pain.

'I'm trying!' Silas yelled, marching up to Alexandria, who was kneeling beside Stella. He grabbed her by the shoulders, his fingers like iron.

'Get your hands off me!' Alexandria shouted.

But Silas was relentless, his grip unyielding. 'I need to get you out of here,' he yelled.

Alexandria spun around, kicking Silas between the legs. Pain ran through his body, and he stumbled backwards, howling in agony.

'The police are going to catch you. You need to get out of here right now, Andria,' James shouted, his grip on Bravado tightening.

'I don't care!' she shouted, staring into Stella's vulnerable eyes.

NEVER UNDERESTIMATE GIRLS!

'I'll end both your sisters' lives if you don't do exactly as I say,' Silas shouted, 'Do you understand me!'

'Why are you so persistent?' yelled Alexandria, gazing at Silas's gun, which was pointing straight at Layla.

'It's your father who's persistent,' James shouted. 'Not us.'

'And don't ask another question, or I will use my gun!' Silas shouted, his eyes blazing with anger. 'Hurry up and make your choice,' he yelled. 'If you return to your father, your sisters get to live, but if you stay here, they die!'

Alexandria stood up, her gaze lingering on Stella and Layla, 'I'll go,' she whispered.

'No!' Layla shouted, suddenly standing up. 'No, Alex, don't return to your father. He's a killing machine!' she grabbed Alexandria's uninjured hand, pulling her backwards. 'Don't go,' she pleaded.

Alexandria glanced at Silas's gun and then looked back at Layla. 'Layla, I'm sorry, but I have to go,' she replied. 'For your sake.'

'I don't care if this idiot kills me,' Layla sobbed. 'But I can't bear seeing you return to that monster who you call dad.'

Tears filled Alexandria's eyes. 'He's not a monster,' she whispered, wrapping her arms around Layla's waist.

'He wants to harm you,' Layla murmured, her breath warm against Alexandria's ear.

'That's enough,' Silas said, yanking Layla out of Alexandria's arms.

Layla's eyes, brimming with tears, met Alexandria's, a silent plea.

'I promise I'll come back,' Alexandria whispered.

'Please, don't go!' Layla pleaded.

Alexandria stared at Layla's tear-streaked face; then she glanced down at Stella's fragile body, blood gushing out of her leg. 'Because of me, Stella got hurt,' she said sadly, her voice barely audible. 'I don't wanna see you get hurt because of me.'

Suddenly, the noise of a gunshot pierced the air. The bullet sliced the side of James's body, and he screamed with pain. As he collapsed onto the floor, blood staining his clothes, he let go of Bravado.

Silas spun around, eyes darting in search of the unseen assailant. His gaze locked onto two figures at the far end of the hallway. Both men held weapons, their fingers poised on the triggers. 'Surrender!' one of the men shouted.

Silas's adrenaline surged. 'Why do you Issaba dogs have to always get involved!' he yelled. He lunged for cover behind a marble pillar as the two gunmen advanced.

'Bravado, get to the elevator. We've got your back!' the first man shouted, firing a bullet at the marble pillar which Silas was seeking cover behind.

As Bravado ran down the hallway, Silas peeked around the pillar, eyes narrowing as he assessed the situation. His heart pounded as he leaned out, pulling the trigger. The bullet narrowly missed Bravado's shoulder.

The second gunman began firing at Silas, each bullet rebounding off the floor and chipping marble. A bullet struck Silas's shoulder, causing his body to jerk backwards. 'Bloody heck!' he screamed.

As a bullet grazed Alexandria's forearm, her instincts kicked in. Ignoring the sharp ache in her arm, she picked Stella up, her movements swift and decisive. The air reverberated with the sound of gunfire, bullets whizzing past them, embedding into the walls and shattering glass. With one hand gripping the ornate golden bannister, she peered down at the second floor, assessing the eleven-foot drop beneath her. Her sharp blue eyes locked onto a luxurious sofa that promised a soft landing. 'Stella, you're gonna have to jump,' she whispered urgently, lifting her younger sister onto the bannister. The continuous crackle of gunfire echoed around them, a constant reminder of the danger they were in.

NEVER UNDERESTIMATE GIRLS!

Stella's fingers clung to the cold metal, her eyes wide with fear as she looked down. 'How?' she stammered, her voice trembling.

'Here,' Alexandria said, her voice steady and reassuring despite the chaos. She grabbed Stella's hand firmly. 'I'm gonna lower you.'

'Ok,' Stella whispered, her voice barely audible.

Alexandria took a deep breath, her grip on Stella's hand tightening. She positioned herself carefully, ensuring her injured arm and hand wouldn't stop her. With her good arm, she slowly began to lower Stella over the edge of the bannister. The sound of bullets ricocheting off marble made her heart race, but she remained focused.

'You're doing great, Stella,' she murmured, her voice calm and encouraging. Inch by inch, she eased her sister down, her muscles straining with the effort. Stella's legs dangled in mid-air, her body trembling with fear.

'Just a little more,' Alexandria said, her eyes never leaving Stella's. She could feel the tension in her sister's grip, the cold metal of the bannister pressing into her. 'I've got you. Trust me.'

Finally, Stella was hanging six feet above the sofa. Alexandria's arm burned with the effort, but she held steady. 'Okay, Stella,' she said softly. 'On the count of three, I want you to let go and aim for the sofa. Ready?'

Stella slowly nodded her head, eyes wide with fear and determination.

'One...two...three!' Alexandria squeezed Stella's hand before letting go.

As Stella's fingers slipped out of Alexandria's, her body began to fall. Her arms flailed slightly, instinctively reaching out for something to hold onto. The air rushed past her, tousling her hair. Her descent seemed to stretch on forever, though it was only a matter of seconds. She landed on the sofa with a soft thud, the cushions absorbing the impact. She bounced slightly, her eyes wide with surprise. Her breath came in quick, shallow gasps, but she was safe.

Alexandria let out a breath of relief. She gazed down at Stella, who was lying on the sofa, processing what had just happened. She gripped the bannister and pulled herself onto it, her wounded body protesting with every movement. 'Layla, follow!' she commanded as she pushed herself off the bannister. The world blurred as she fell. The air rushed past her, and her heart pounded furiously.

As she neared the ground, she braced herself. She landed with controlled grace, knees bending to absorb the impact. She rolled forward, the marble floor cool against her skin. The landing was almost silent, a testament to her rigorous training and unwavering focus. She rose swiftly and looked up at the chaotic hallway. Her eyes locked on Layla, who was staring down at her in bewilderment.

'I can't jump!' Layla shrieked, her trembling hands gripping the golden bannister.

'Jump,' Alexandria called urgently. 'I'll catch you!'

'Aargh!' Layla screamed as a bullet screamed past her head. In that dreadful moment, she resolved that jumping was her only option. She pulled herself up onto the bannister and gazed down at Alexandria. 'I'm trustin' ya,' she said, dangling her legs over the edge of the bannister.

'Just blimey jump!' Alexandria extended her arms, ready to catch Layla.

'*Ok...*' Layla swallowed hard before pushing herself off the bannister. As her fingers slipped off the bannister, gravity seized her. The air rushed past her, and her scream echoed as she plummeted into Alexandria's arms.

The impact jarred Alexandria's bones, and she stumbled forward, clutching Layla tightly. They both hit the marble floor with a sickening thud, and Layla screamed with pain as her body slammed against the hard floor.

'Gosh!' Stella cried. 'Are you two alright? Why didn't you jump onto the sofa?'

NEVER UNDERESTIMATE GIRLS!

'I'm fine,' Alexandria winced, standing up. 'What about you?' she asked, glancing at Layla sprawled on the floor.

'Ma bloody body kills,' Layla sobbed, tears escaping her eyes.

'I'm so sorry,' Alexandria said. 'I tried my best to catch you.'

'Yep, ya tried yer best,' Layla replied, staggering to her feet. She grabbed her back in agony, letting out a low scream. 'I think I've broken a bone,' she complained.

JOSEPH JETHRO

Chapter 24

Officer Noah ran down the police station's grand hallway, each stride fuelled by urgency. His breath came in ragged bursts as he approached the door to Officer Zackery's office. The polished wood felt cool against his hand as he knocked rapidly, the sound echoing down the corridor.

'Enter!' Zackery barked from within.

Noah flung the door open and strode into the room. 'Sir,' he gasped, out of breath.

Zackery rose from his seat, his gaze sharp and questioning. 'Noah, what brings you here in such a rush?' he asked.

'Sir, it's Luca,' Noah replied urgently. 'He's at Blue Glass Skyscraper, and he's spotted Alexandria!'

'What!' Zackery's eyes widened in astonishment. 'Has he caught her?'

'No, Sir,' Noah said in a tense tone. 'Luca has been severely injured!'

Zackery's expression hardened. 'Send my officers down there immediately,' he commanded sternly. 'And let me make myself very clear: I don't want her to slip through their fingers.'

'Understood, Sir,' Noah replied. He nodded briskly before exiting the room, his hurried footsteps echoing off the marble floor.

Within Blue Glass Skyscraper, Alexandria, Layla and Stella huddled together in the corner of the empty hallway, staying well away from any suspicious eyes, their hearts pounding furiously. The cold, unforgiving marble floor pressed against their battered bodies.

Wrapping her weak arms around Stella and Layla, Alexandria gazed upwards at the hallway which they had just escaped from; the loud noise of bullets being released boomed non-stop, and the occasional scream of agony reverberated from above.

She sighed deeply and lifted her injured hand to examine it. The bandages wrapped around the wound were soaked in blood, a stark reminder of the recent chaos. Gritting her teeth, she slowly tried to flex her fingers. Pain shot up her arm like a bolt of lightning, making her eyes water. She closed them tightly, trying to breathe through the agony. 'Ow,' she gasped. Despite the severity of the pain, she managed to move her fingers slightly; relief washed over her as she realised that the bullet hadn't caused maximum damage.

Suddenly, a sharp pain shot through Stella's wounded leg, causing her eyes to water. The fabric of her torn jeans clung to the oozing wound, and she wondered if she would ever experience a pain-free walk again. 'My leg kills,' she sobbed, clutching the wound.

Alexandria turned to face Stella, her eyes filled with empathy. 'Here,' she whispered, taking off her blood-soaked jacket, revealing her tattered shirt beneath. With trembling hands, she wrapped it around Stella's injured leg.

'It hurts!' Stella screamed.

Layla gently squeezed her hand. 'Yer gonna be all right, sis,' she said in a steady and reassuring voice.

Stella gazed at her two big sisters, their love and care wrapping around her like a comforting blanket. 'It feels so good to be together again,' she whispered, gripping Alexandria's hand. 'We thought you were dead, Alex!'

Alexandria's eyes widened in disbelief. 'What?' she asked, grimacing in pain as she adjusted her injured arm.

'It's true,' Layla confessed. 'We all thought ya were dead.'

'Why would you think that?' Alexandria asked, her confusion evident.

'The police searched every corner of London,' Layla said. 'But they couldn't find ya.'

A faint smile tugged at Alexandria's lips despite the ache in her body. 'My dad is very skilled at evading them,' she said.

'Yer dad,' Layla's eyes glistened with tears. 'We thought he killed ya.'

'My dad would never do such a thing,' Alexandria gasped.

NEVER UNDERESTIMATE GIRLS!

Stella leaned towards Alexandria. 'Your dad wants you dead,' she whispered, her voice barely audible. She winced in pain as she shifted her injured leg.

'No, he doesn't,' Alexandria retorted, her voice trembling. 'My dad loves me!'

'Alex, stop tryna make yourself believe that he loves ya,' Layla said, wiping a tear away.

'Don't speak about my dad. You've never met him!' Alexandria suddenly shouted, her tears mixing with the blood on her face.

'Mother took ya away from him because she knew he wanted to harm ya,' Layla whispered.

'If that was true, then don't you think he would have already killed me?' Alexandria challenged.

Layla and Stella exchanged a glance. 'Alex, believe us, please,' Stella pleaded, her voice trembling with pain.

'Never,' Alexandria replied. 'Unless you get me proof.'

'Mother had proof against yer dad,' Layla replied.

'And what's the proof?' Alexandria demanded, her desperation evident.

'She witnessed him menacingly holdin' a knife above yer crib when ya were an infant,' Layla replied grimly. 'And he would've killed ya if she hadn't stopped him.'

'What the heck? Who the hell told you all this rubbish!' Alexandria exclaimed.

'Uncle,' Layla replied.

'You're lyin'!' Alexandria retorted.

'No, Alex, I'm not,' Layla insisted.

Tears streamed down Alexandria's cheeks. 'My dad wouldn't do that?' she sobbed, but then she remembered the way he'd tried to strangle her. 'I'm gonna have to confront him myself!' she shouted.

'No way, we're not gonna let ya go back to him!' Layla said.

'I'm gonna have to go back to him,' Alexandria declared, abruptly standing up. She grimaced in pain as she did so. 'I need to unlock the truth.'

Layla stood up, grabbing Alexandria by the arm, her grip unyielding. 'I don't wanna be separated from ya again,' she said.

'I'm so sorry,' Alexandria replied, hugging Layla tightly.

'Yer dad wants ya dead!' Layla sobbed. 'Don't ya believe me?'

'I believe you, and that's why I'm gonna confront him. I need to know why he wants to take my life,' Alexandria whispered. She knelt beside Stella, kissing her forehead. 'Remember, I'll always love you, my dear sisters,' she murmured. She then stood up and pressed her hidden earpiece. 'Captain Skyhawk, bring the helicopter to the western side of Blue Glass Skyscraper, sconed floor,' she stated in a loud and clear voice.

'No, Alex, don't go,' Stella said, her voice breaking. 'Stay with us, and we'll unlock the truth together.'

Alexandria shook her head. 'Stella, no,' she said, glancing at her wounded leg. 'I don't want you to get hurt anymore. I'm gonna find the answers myself.'

Alexandria's earpiece abruptly started to beep loudly, and she pressed it swiftly. 'I've got the helicopter in position,' Skyhawk's crisp voice reached her ears. 'Second balcony.'

'I'll be there,' Alexandria replied. She gave Layla and Stella a fleeting glance. 'Don't worry,' she whispered. 'I promise I'll come back.'

'Why can't you just stay?' Stella pleaded. 'Let's be a team like we once were.'

'Stella, if I stay, the police are gonna take me to court,' Alexandria sighed. 'Don't you remember what Detective Jakie said? He warned me that if I get involved with any criminal activity, I'm gonna be sent straight to prison, and I think I've crossed the line.'

'But...' Stella stammered.

NEVER UNDERESTIMATE GIRLS!

'Stella, think. Would you want me to be trapped behind bars, or would you rather have me strolling the streets freely?' Alexandria asked. 'And I promise we'll secretly meet up every week after dusk.'

'But Alex your dad...he wants you...' Stella began, only to be cut off by Alexandria's loud snigger.

'Forget about my dad. He won't be able to lay a finger on me,' she smiled, winking her eye. 'Remember, girls can bring empires to their knees. So, one guy with evil intentions won't be a problem for me.'

Suddenly, a door at the far end of the hallway swung open, revealing two police officers: Max and Kai. Their eyes held the intensity of predators closing on their prey.

As soon as they spotted the three girls, Max stepped forward and shouted in a sharp voice, 'Alexandria, surrender!'

Alexandria's smirk sent chills down both officers' spines. Kai's grip tightened on the handle of his gun, holstered at his waist. 'You want me to surrender?' Alexandria asked, her gaze challenging. 'I wonder why.'

'No time for questions, lady,' Max replied sternly. 'Put your hands up!'

With a grin, Alexandria raised her hands. Max and Kai approached cautiously; they knew she was unpredictable.

Kai retrieved a pair of handcuffs and slowly walked behind Alexandria. Yanking her hands behind her back, he secured the handcuffs, the cold metal digging into Alexandria's delicate skin. 'I'll escort her out of here, Max,' Kai said. 'You take care of these girls. That one's taken a blow,' he added grimly, glancing down at Stella's bleeding leg. He grabbed Alexandria's arms. 'Come on, get moving,' he ordered.

Alexandria started walking, then abruptly stopped. She turned around and locked eyes with Layla and Stella. 'Remember,' she whispered, a mysterious smile curving her lips. 'I'll be back without a scratch, don't worry.'

'Ok, that's enough,' Kai said, urging Alexandria to continue walking forward.

JOSEPH JETHRO

As Layla and Stella watched her being escorted down the hallway, they knew that this was probably the best way to keep her away from her father.

Chapter 25

As Kai and Alexandria walked through a door and into another hallway, Alexandria suddenly smirked. 'Let go of my arms,' she murmured, her voice barely audible.

Kai halted, frowning. 'Excuse me?' he asked.

'I said let go of my arms, please,' Alexandria repeated, her eyes glinting with hidden intentions. 'You're hurting me.'

'Girls,' Kai muttered, loosening his grip on her arms. 'Is that better?' he asked gruffly.

'Sure,' Alexandria replied.

'Then hurry up and start walking,' Kai ordered harshly.

'I don't listen to orders,' Alexandria smirked. She spun around, executing a powerful front snap kick. Her foot slammed against Kai's chest, and he staggered backwards, crashing into the wall. Recovering quickly, he lunged at her, but Alexandria was no ordinary girl. She launched a series of breathtaking kicks, each more powerful than the last.

Kai, a blue-belt martial artist, sensed the pressing need to act swiftly. He blocked Alexandria's incoming kicks with his forearms, his body moving swiftly to deflect the blows.

Alexandria, driven by a surge of energy and urgency, kicked Kai in the face; blood sprayed from his lip, but he maintained his composure. Determined, he aimed a kick towards her side, but she swiftly sidestepped, a smirk playing on her lips. 'Good moves, mate,' she taunted. 'But not good enough!'

She instinctively tried to raise her hands to block Kai's incoming kick, but just then, a horrifying realisation struck her - her handcuffs rendered her vulnerable, tipping the scales in Kai's favour; the cold metal bit into her wrists, a cruel reminder of her captivity.

Kai moved with lightning-quick speed. His powerful sidekick connected with her already battered body; she screeched with pain. He smirked and aimed a roundhouse kick at Alexandria's face, but her leg shot upwards, colliding painfully with his.

Kai grunted, his face twisting with pain. 'Bloody heck!' he shouted, punching Alexandria in the face.

'Shithead!' she screamed before delivering a spinning back kick to Kai's ribs.

He screamed with pain but quickly recovered and launched a flawless front snap kick. The heel of his foot struck Alexandria's eye, momentarily blinding her. Blood seeped from her injured eye and streamed down her cheek.

He delivered a swift, brutal kick to her shoulder, sending her sprawling to the floor. He moved with fluid precision, pinning her down. With force, he pressed his knee against her chest, restricting her movements.

But Alexandria wasn't defeated. Her defiant gaze met Kai's determined eyes. She had to escape. With a surge of determination, Alexandria summoned her last reserves of strength. With a swift twist of her hips, she drove her knee into Kai's stomach, leaving him gasping in agony.

His grip faltered as he reflexively grabbed his stomach in pain. Alexandria took this as an advantage and kicked him in the groin. He let out a blood-curdling cry, his grip waning. She wriggled out of his grasp, rolled away, and sprang to her feet, her pulse racing.

Kai staggered to his feet, leaning against a wall for support. 'You're dead, dumb cow!' he screamed, gritting his teeth.

Alexandria laughed. 'See ya, officer,' she jeered, sprinting up the hallway.

'Get back here!' Kai shouted. With a trembling hand, he grabbed his walkie-talkie from his waist belt. 'Max, I need you down here right now!' he yelled.

NEVER UNDERESTIMATE GIRLS!

Alexandria's heart raced wildly as she dashed forward, her breaths coming in sharp, uneven gasps. Her legs threatened to give way from exhaustion, but she pushed herself forward; she had to escape.

She glanced over her shoulder as she heard footsteps approaching. 'Gosh, won't you just give up?' she muttered as she caught sight of Kai running towards her.

With unwavering resolve, he dashed after her, every stride closing the distance between them. Alexandria pushed harder, but her pace waned.

With a final burst of speed, Kai caught up to her; he grabbed her hair, yanking her head backwards. 'Alexandria, it's best you surrender. You can't escape!' he whispered in her ear.

'Let go of me!' Alexandria screamed. 'You piece of shit.' But Kai was relentless, his grip tightening with each passing second. 'If you don't let me go, you'll face the consequences!' Alexandria threatened in a sharp voice.

'Consequences?' Kai scoffed, his voice filled with disdain.

'You've had it!' Alexandria shouted. With fierce determination blazing in her eyes, she suddenly headbutted him backwards in the face with a bone-jarring impact. The force of the headbutt reverberated through his skull, sending shockwaves down his spine, but his grip on her hair remained unyielding.

She then summoned every ounce of her strength and delivered another brutal headbutt. The blow landed squarely on his nose this time, causing a sickening crunch. He let out a muffled cry as his teeth clamped down on his tongue, the metallic taste of blood flooding his mouth.

Blood trickled from his lips, painting a crimson trail down his chin as he staggered backwards, his vision blurring. The relentless assault finally broke his hold, and he released her hair, stumbling away with a dazed expression.

JOSEPH JETHRO

Alexandria spun around, delivering a powerful spinning hook kick to his torso. He flew backwards, landing agonisingly on his back. Alexandria angrily walked up to him. 'Putting handcuffs on me was a mistake!' she smirked, kicking him in the face.

'You're going to regret this!' Kai yelled, clutching his injured face.

'I wouldn't have laid a finger on you if you hadn't tried to stop me,' Alexandria sneered. With a mocking grin, she turned around and sprinted up the hallway.

Her breaths came in ragged gasps as she continued to sprint through the dimly lit hallway. Her heart pounded furiously as she reached the skyscraper's balcony doors. Adrenaline surged through her veins, urging her to open the unyielding doors, but her hands were bound by cold, unforgiving handcuffs, rendering her powerless. She looked rapidly around the hallway, her eyes darting from right to left.

Her eyes finally landed on the sharp corner of a wall. Without hesitation, she walked towards it and leaned against it, her breath catching as she pressed the handcuffs against the unforgiving surface.

Determination fuelled her actions as she raised the cuffs and brought them down forcefully against the sharp corner. Each blow sent shockwaves of pain through her hands, but she persisted. Blood sprayed, and she gritted her teeth, refusing to yield. With a final burst of strength, the handcuffs snapped in half, freeing her.

She let out a sigh of relief and collapsed onto her knees. She looked down at her injured hands; the cold metal rings of the handcuffs were still attached to her wrists, but at least she was free.

She stood up and walked towards the balcony doors, grasping the metal handles with her battered hands. Sliding them open, she stepped onto the balcony, the cold wind tugging at her hair.

She pressed her earpiece and urgently called out, 'Captain Skyhawk! I need you to come to the northern side of Blue Glass Skyscraper immediately. I'm on a balcony!'

'I'm on my way,' Skyhawk replied in a crisp voice.

NEVER UNDERESTIMATE GIRLS!

Alexandria leaned against the metal safety railing of the balcony and gazed down at the bustling river below. The water shimmered in the sunlight, reflecting the surrounding cityscape. Boats glided along its surface, leaving gentle ripples in their wake, while pedestrians strolled along the riverbank, their voices blending with the distant hum of traffic.

And then Alexandria's eyes shot upwards as she heard the unmistakable noise of a helicopter's rotor blades slicing through the air. Her eyes caught sight of Skyhawk's sleek helicopter soaring through the sky. She pulled her phone out of her pocket and turned the flashlight on.

With a sharp eye, Skyhawk saw her and smoothly adjusted the aircraft's course, hovering it just beyond the balcony. He pressed his earpiece and urgently shouted, 'Andria, you must jump!'

With adrenaline coursing through her veins, Alexandria stepped backwards, her eyes fixed on the helicopter. She then ran forward, each stride more determined than the last; reaching the balcony's edge, she launched herself into the open air. The wind roared past her, drowning out her heartbeat. Her uninjured hand latched onto the helicopter's skid with determination, but the metal was covered with dew, and her grip faltered. One finger slipped, then another, until she was left to cling precariously, her strength waning.

Just as despair threatened to consume her, the helicopter tilted. Skyhawk leaned out, muscles straining against the wind. His gloved hand shot towards her, fingers closing around her hand. The force of his pull nearly tore her shoulder from its socket.

With a final surge of effort, Skyhawk hauled her up, and she collapsed onto the helicopter floor, gasping for air.

Their eyes met, a silent acknowledgement of survival. Skyhawk's stern expression softened, and he removed his helmet, revealing a face etched with determination. 'You're lucky I grabbed your hand,' he said, sitting back in his seat.

JOSEPH JETHRO

As the helicopter flew away from Blue Glass Skyscraper, Alexandria stood up from the cold metal floor, her eyes fixed on Skyhawk. 'Captain,' she murmured.

Skyhawk nodded his head in acknowledgement. 'Yeah?'

'Take me to my father immediately. I must have a word with him,' Alexandria said, her voice filled with resolve.

Skyhawk turned his head in her direction, his jaw set. 'Andria,' he whispered. 'I'm sorry.'

Alexandria raised an eyebrow, placing her hand on his shoulder. 'Captain,' she asked in a concerned voice. 'Why are you sorry?'

'I'm sorry, but I can't take you to your father,' Skyhawk replied firmly, his gaze unwavering.

'Why not?' Alexandria demanded.

'Because...' Skyhawk hesitated. 'I won't take you to a liar.'

'Who the hell do you think you're callin' a liar!' Alexandria shouted, her anger flaring.

'I'm calling your bloody dad a liar!' Skyhawk shouted back, chest heaving.

'My dad is not a liar,' Alexandria retorted.

'Look at the pain you've endured because of his damn lies,' Skyhawk yelled, gazing at Alexandria's blood-soaked clothes.

'What are you talkin' about? Explain yourself!' Alexandria's voice started trembling.

'Andria,' Skyhawk's tone softened, 'that man you tried to kill, he wasn't Kenny.'

'What?' Alexandria asked, her disbelief palpable, 'You're a bloody liar!'

'I'm not,' Skyhawk insisted. 'Your dad has been deceiving you all along.'

'Why didn't you tell me sooner?' Alexandria asked.

'Because...,' Skyhawk sighed deeply, 'Serpentina ordered me to keep quiet. But I don't care about her anymore!'

NEVER UNDERESTIMATE GIRLS!

Alexandria was stunned. 'I thought she was...I thought she was just a part of imagination,' she stammered.

'Well, here's the plain truth: she's real,' Skyhawk revealed. 'She controls your father, and she's ordered him to kill you, and he will obey her commands.'

'Well, then take me to him. I need to confront him!' Alexandria screamed, tears streaming down her cheeks.

'I won't lead an innocent girl to her death,' Skyhawk said, standing up from his seat. The helicopter swayed slightly, and Alexandria lost her footing, bumping clumsily into the helicopter's side.

'This isn't a request; it's an order. Take me to him,' Alexandria shouted, straightening her posture.

Skyhawk sighed, opening the door of the helicopter. He gazed out before turning to face Alexandria. 'Andria,' he whispered, gripping her shoulders.

'What?' Alexandria snapped, locking eyes with him.

'The river will provide a safe landing,' he said, pulling her towards the helicopter's doors.

'What!' Alexandria exclaimed, her shock evident.

'You're a girl the world shouldn't underestimate,' Skyhawk murmured, and with that, he pushed her out into the unknown.

As Alexandria plummeted from the helicopter, the wind roared in her ears, drowning out her screams. The world spun around her, and panic gripped her chest.

As she fell, thoughts raced through her mind. *If he wasn't Kenny,* she wondered, *then who is Kenny?* The man she'd attacked, believing him to be her mother's murderer, had been a decoy. A pawn in a deadly game orchestrated by Serpentina, the very woman she'd dismissed until now. Her father's lies had led her here, and Skyhawk's revelation echoed in her mind as she hurtled towards the water.

The river rushed up to meet Alexandria, its surface a blur of churning foam. Her body twisted, limbs flailing as she plummeted downwards into the cold water, sending shock waves throughout her body and stealing her breath away. She lost all sense of direction momentarily, disoriented by the impact.

Then, her instincts kicked in. She fought against the water's pull, arms and legs working desperately. Her lungs screamed for air, and she kicked upwards, breaking the surface. Gasping, she gulped in precious oxygen. As the river tugged at her, dragging her downstream, she glimpsed the helicopter above, blades spinning relentlessly. It vanished into the horizon, leaving her alone to battle against the overpowering pull of the river's current.

The tempestuous river suddenly surged, causing a colossal wave to rise like an enraged giant. It bore down upon Alexandria, a force of nature that defied her strength. The salty water clung to her skin, and her heart raced as she grappled with the raw power of nature. The cerulean abyss swallowed her, pulling her down into its fathomless depths.

Her lungs screamed for oxygen, but the water pressed against her chest, a relentless weight that threatened to crush her ribcage. Sunlight filtered through the turbulent surface, casting fractured beams of light in the murky water. Panic surged within her, a fierce instinct urging her to fight, to claw her way back to the surface.

Yet, the river's embrace was unyielding. It tugged at her limbs, dragging her deeper and deeper until the world above blurred into a distant memory. The cold seeped into her bones, numbing her senses. At that moment, she pondered whether she would ever unlock her father's secrets or if her existence would dissolve into the river's watery embrace.

Author's Note

People often underestimate girls, and sometimes, even girls underestimate themselves. Witnessing how society's comments can make them feel like they can't achieve their dreams or overcome challenges is disheartening. However, it is crucial not to let these negative perceptions define anyone.

Girls are capable of incredible strength and resilience. When faced with adversity, their courage and determination can shine through, proving that they are more than capable of achieving greatness. It is important to remember that no one should let anyone's doubts or criticisms make them feel less than they are.

It is essential to believe in girls' abilities and encourage them to stand tall against any obstacles that come their way. By doing so, doubts are dispelled, and girls are inspired to recognise their potential.

Embracing their power, intelligence, and compassion shows the world that they are unstoppable.

JOSEPH JETHRO

Coming soon!

Never Underestimate Girls
Part two

As Alexandria battles against the relentless current of the river, her muscles burning with the effort to break the surface, a profound thought pierces through her mind: Does she truly want to resurface and face the harsh reality of her father's deceit, or would it be easier to surrender to the river's depths and become a forgotten soul, lost to the world above?

The water is cold and unforgiving, swirling around her with a ferocity that mirrors the turmoil within her heart. Her lungs scream for air, and her mind is clouded with doubt and confusion. Her father's lies have shattered her heart, leaving her adrift in a river of uncertainty. Why would he submit to Serpentina, and why had he lied to her that Liam Maxwell - the man she tried to kill - was Kenny?

As she struggles, memories flood her mind - moments of betrayal, the sting of broken promises, and the weight of unspoken truths.

The river's roar is deafening, but it can not drown out the inner conflict that rages within her.

To resurface means to confront the pain, to demand answers, and to rebuild her shattered world. But the thought of staying submerged, to let the river claim her, offers a twisted sense of peace - a way to escape the hurt and disappointment.

But she had promised her little sisters, Layla and Stella, that she'd return unharmed.

If you enjoyed 'Never Underestimate Girls!', you'll definitely love the upcoming thriller!

NEVER UNDERESTIMATE GIRLS!

Here's a little teaser to keep you on the edge!

Horror Dudes

Chapter 1
The haunting chase

Talon sprinted down the narrow alley, his feet splashing in murky puddles of water. The cold liquid splashed violently around his legs, seeping through the fabric of his trousers and chilling his skin. His breaths came in laboured gasps, each inhale a struggle, each exhale a desperate plea for mercy. He glanced over his shoulder, and there they were - the cloaked figure he was trying to outrun.

The figure moved with the grace of a hunting panther, fluid and sinister. Their black cloak billowed around them, shrouding them in an inky darkness that obscured their features. The blades in their hands gleamed malevolently, reflecting the moon's ghostly glow. Each stride brought them closer to Talon, whose skin had turned pale out of sheer fear.

He ran continuously, never slowing down. His body felt heavy, and his knees threatened to buckle, but he urged himself onwards, determined to escape the cloaked figure who seemed relentless, a predator closing in on its prey, their every movement a promise of doom.

Abandoned buildings lined the dark alleyway, their stone structures crumbling and decaying. Shattered windows and unpleasant weeds adorned their walls, adding to the sense of desolation. As he ran, his eyes darted frantically from one decrepit building to another, desperately seeking an escape route.

The thick stems of overgrown raspberry bushes whipped at his arms, their harsh thorns slashing his skin with every stride. He winced as the unforgiving thorns lashed at his face, leaving crimson welts in their wake. The alley seemed to close in around him, the oppressive darkness pressing down like a suffocating shroud.

Every shadow seemed to writhe with malevolent intent, and the air was thick with the scent of decay and despair. The buildings loomed

NEVER UNDERESTIMATE GIRLS!

over him, silent witnesses to his terror, their broken walls hiding secrets best left undisturbed.

He could feel the cloaked figure's presence drawing nearer, an inescapable force of dread that seemed to steal the very strength of his limbs.

The wind blew furiously, rustling the leaves of tall trees that loomed overhead like ancient sentinels. Their branches swung angrily, fighting against the wind's strength, casting eerie shadows on the ground. Suddenly, the loud sound of wood splinting shattered the silence of the night. A massive tree collapsed, falling in front of him with a deafening thud.

He halted, eyes widening in terror as he gazed at the fallen tree blocking his path. The twisted branches and thick foliage formed an impenetrable barrier. Panic surged through him as he heard the relentless footsteps of the cloaked figure drawing nearer. The sound was a chilling reminder of the danger closing in.

Desperation clawed at him as he tried to scramble over the tree, but its lush branches seemed to conspire against him, tangling around his limbs and defying his every effort. The rough bark scraped his skin, and the sharp twigs tore at his clothes, leaving him feeling trapped and helpless.

The rain battered his hair, each raindrop mirroring his frantic heartbeat. The downpour was persistent, a curtain of water that blurred his vision and soaked him to the bone. As he strained his eyes against the furious storm, he caught sight of a broken door to his left. Panic surged through him, and he bolted towards it, his feet slipping on the wet ground.

He burst through the door and stumbled into an old barn. The floor was covered with aged hay, its musty scent mingling with the sour smell of horse manure. The barn was a relic of the past, its wooden beams creaking under the weight of years. Three walls stood strong and tall, but the fourth had collapsed, leaving a gaping hole that allowed the frosty night wind to howl through the barn.

The wind whipped through the opening, sending dust and bits of hay swirling around him like ghostly apparitions. The barn was pitch black, the only illumination coming from the occasional flash of lightning that pierced the darkness. Shadows danced on the walls, creating eerie shapes that seemed to move with a life of their own.

Glancing at the door from which he'd entered, he quickly started to survey his surroundings, but to his utmost dismay, he was trapped! His eyes scanned the opening in the barn where the wall had collapsed, but it offered no solace, for it was jammed with trees, bushes and weeds, forming an impenetrable barrier.

Suddenly, he heard footsteps from outside the barn. His heart began pounding furiously as his gaze locked onto the barn's door. He started walking backwards, his legs trembling with fear; he knew the cloaked figure was lurking just beyond the broken door.

Lightning flashed, illuminating the barn with a stark, eerie light, and thunder rumbled, adding to his uneasiness. The rain battered hard against the already sagging roof, and the barn's wooden frame creaked eerily as if it knew what horrors awaited him and was urging him to flee.

The oppressive atmosphere pressed down on him; the shadows in the barn seemed to grow darker and more menacing with each passing second. The wind howled through the broken wall, carrying with it the faint, ghostly whispers of the past.

The barn, once a potential refuge, had become a nightmarish trap, and he was running out of time. The relentless storm outside mirrored the turmoil within him, each flash of lightning and crash of thunder highlighting the reality of his dire situation. The barn's wooden frame seemed to groan in sympathy, urging him to find a way out before it was too late.

NEVER UNDERESTIMATE GIRLS!

Suddenly, the cloaked figure appeared outside the broken door. They stood motionless for a moment, their presence exuding an aura of malevolence. Lightning slashed across the sky, illuminating their eerie silhouette. The blades in their hands caught the light, gleaming with a wicked, deadly promise.

The terrified man stumbled backwards as the figure stepped into the barn. 'Blood on ma hands,' the figure hissed, their voice an evil whisper. A bone-chilling laugh escaped their lips, slicing through the tension and sending shivers of fear down Talon's spine. He retreated further, his back colliding with the rough, splintered wood of the wall.

The figure's face was hidden deep within a shadowy hood, revealing only the lower part of their eyes, which glinted with an unnatural, sinister glow. Their lips were stained in a dark, ominous red, suggesting they had recently tasted the blood of their last victim.

'What do you want?' Talon stammered, pressing himself against the wall, yearning for it to swallow him whole and offer refuge from the nightmare unfolding before him.

Chapter 2
Blood Sucker

The figure's lips curved into a sinister smirk as they advanced towards Talon, brandishing both knives threateningly. 'I want yer blood!' they snarled, their voice dripping with malice.

'Please, leave me alone,' Talon begged, his body quaking with overwhelming fear. His voice was barely more than a whisper.

'Fear,' the figure jeered, savouring the word as if it were a delicacy. Their eyes gleamed with sadistic delight, feeding off Talon's palpable dread. Their smirk widened into a nasty grin as they lunged forward, both knives glinting ominously in the dim light.

To be continued...

JOSEPH JETHRO

Don't miss Joseph Jethro's upcoming books!

- Life's Twisted: Love's Harsh
- Eliminated
- Don and Devil
- Triple Caste Gangster Part 2: Love Is Venomous
- Triple Caste Gangster Part 3: Promise me
- Drama Mum
- DID: He's Hunting Himself
- Stock Shock: When Millionaires Go Mad
- The Forest's Heartbeat
- Dangerous Street Boys
- Brotherhood Battle
- Ego Downfall
- I'm Lurking Behind You
- The Gangster's shadow
- The Broken Heart
- The Call for Freedom

Don't miss out!

Visit the website below and you can sign up to receive emails whenever Joseph Jethro publishes a new book. There's no charge and no obligation.

https://books2read.com/r/B-A-TDFLC-WBXDF

BOOKS2READ

Connecting independent readers to independent writers.

Did you love *Never Underestimate Girls!*? Then you should read *Triple Caste Gangster*[1] by Joseph Jethro!

New York City, a sprawling metropolis teeming with life, is ruled by an enigmatic gangster.

His iron grip extends to every street and shadow, and he reigns as the ultimate gangster.

His brutal life is dedicated to dismantling evil, which is why the entirety of America's dark side seeks to bring him down.

His name alone strikes terror into the hearts of criminals. They know that no matter how cunningly they attempt to evade him, he is always lurking behind them, ready to shoot a swift bullet in their back.

But on a day that seemed like any other, the air in one of New York's usual peaceful squares is charged with an unusual tension. As the

---

1. https://books2read.com/u/3LBkg1

2. https://books2read.com/u/3LBkg1

gangster prepares to confront the heart of the problem, he is blindsided by an unexpected encounter with a teenage girl, her eyes holding a story he can't yet decipher.

The famous American gangster clings to the dark shadows, hiding a secret that lies only in the girl's smile!

Her enigmatic grin weaves an unseen thread, drawing him inexorably closer!